⚜ THE ⚜
Faceless Fiend

To Austin —

Have fun with this book — OR ELSE!!

Howard Whitehouse

⚜ THE ⚜
Faceless Fiend

Being the Tale of a
Criminal Mastermind, His Masked Minions
and a Princess with a Butter Knife, Involving
Explosives and a Certain Amount of
Pushing and Shoving

By Howard Whitehouse

With illustrations by Bill Slavin

Kids Can Press

To my father, George Whitehouse, teller of stories to my sister, Anne, and me.
&
To my father-in-law, Lee H. Knight, inventor of a one-man submarine and a machine for inserting sticks into corn dogs (but not mad in the slightest) – H.W.

Thanks again to Tara and Bill for their amazing efforts, to Bill Powell, Edan and Elda Thomas, Joanne Schwartz, the Parliament St. Writers' Group, to Bruce Pettipas for his portrayal of a Victorian balloonist, and to Bob Charette, who invented the Masked Minions (but let me use their name anyway). Especially to Lori, for putting up with me this last quarter century and more.

Text © 2007 Howard Whitehouse
Illustrations © 2007 Bill Slavin

This is a work of fiction and any resemblance of characters to persons living or dead is purely coincidental.

Kids Can Press acknowledges the financial support of the Government of Ontario, through the Ontario Media Development Corporation's Ontario Book Initiative; the Ontario Arts Council; the Canada Council for the Arts; and the Government of Canada, through the BPIDP, for our publishing activity.

Published in Canada by	Published in the U.S. by
Kids Can Press Ltd.	Kids Can Press Ltd.
29 Birch Avenue	2250 Military Road
Toronto, ON M4V 1E2	Tonawanda, NY 14150

www.kidscanpress.com

Edited by Tara Walker
Designed by Marie Bartholomew
Printed and bound in Canada

CM 07 0 9 8 7 6 5 4 3 2 1
CM PA 07 0 9 8 7 6 5 4 3 2 1

Library and Archives Canada Cataloguing in Publication

Whitehouse, Howard

    Faceless fiend: being the tale of a criminal mastermind, his masked minions and a princess with a butter knife, involving explosives and a certain amount of pushing and shoving / by Howard Whitehouse; with illustrations by Bill Slavin.

(The mad misadventures of Emmaline and Rubberbones)
ISBN 978-1-55453-130-1 (bound)
ISBN 978-1-55453-180-6 (pbk.)

I. Slavin, Bill II. Title. III. Series: Whitehouse, Howard. Mad Misadventures of Emmaline and Rubberbones

Kids Can Press is a **CORUS**™ Entertainment company

CONTENTS

DRAMATIS PERSONAE

Emmaline Cayley
A Pioneer of Aviation

Rubberbones
A Bouncing Boy

Aunt Lucy
The Best Sort of Aunt

Lal Singh
A Mysterious and Heroic Butler

Professor Bellbuckle
A Mad Inventor

Princess Purnah
A Royal Personage from a Distant Land

Faceless Fiend

A Criminal Mastermind

Masked Minion

A Horrible Henchman

Mr. Black & Mr. White

Untruthful Underlings

Peachey

A London Lad

Sherlock Holmes

A Famous Detective

Banjo

A Veteran of Rat-fights

CHAPTER 1

A Scientific Education

"Everybody, listen to me! We all need to jump off the roof before teatime! Please get a move on, Emmaline!" shouted the man at the bottom of the ladder. He had an American accent, a shock of wild gray hair and seemed to be some kind of escaped lunatic.

It was a windy, late-autumn morning. Fallen leaves swirled around the naked trees. Men lost their hats and chased them down the street, cursing. Small children were knocked over and cried for their mothers. Women in bulky, old-fashioned skirts stayed inside for decency's sake.

At Mad Mrs. Butterworth's house, three youngsters clambered up onto the roof. Mrs. Butterworth was a widow. Her husband had been an army officer. He had fallen off a camel, fatally, in India, or Afghanistan, or somewhere. Everyone in the village knew that. So everyone expected her to be respectable, sensible and a bit snooty. But Mrs. Butterworth wasn't any of those things. She was short and stout, and collected nettles and leaves and roots to make strange cakes and pies and other things that didn't bear thinking about. She had a tall, silent man in Indian dress as her butler. She had a niece who wanted to fly. She paid a lad from the village twice what an errand boy should earn to do odd jobs around the place. And now she had an American, an inventor, living at the house as well, teaching the niece and the errand boy and another girl—a foreign-looking lass with a wild expression on her face. The lessons all seemed odd, too. It wasn't right. At least, everyone in the village said so.

The three youngsters stood on the sloping tiles of the roof. They all had wings attached to their arms, like bats. The one at the end was flapping them. Below, in the overgrown garden, their tutor blew a whistle. All three figures ran forward and plunged off the edge of the roof. Two of them immediately dropped into the bushes beneath. The one in the middle managed to glide forward as a gust of wind caught under the wings, then slipped into a shallow dive and gently wafted fifty feet onto a patch of wet earth.

The whistle sounded again. There was a burst of gleeful laughter from the garden, several voices tittering and guffawing and generally ha-ha-ha-ing. A small dog ran about, yipping playfully.

If anyone had been watching, it would have just proved what everyone thought.

"And that, my young friends, is why a human being cannot fly like a bird. The arms simply cannot carry enough wing area to attain and continue flight. Furthermore, human muscles are not designed to flap in the avian fashion."

It was the man with wild gray hair speaking. He had a slow, drawling intonation to his voice and tugged on the tip of his small, pointed beard. He carried a bale of straw into the barn as he talked. The youngsters also carried bales; one of them, a tall and rather gawky girl of fourteen, had straw in her mousy brown hair and mud on her knees. Still, it was better to get straw in your hair than to fall on the hard ground. The girl was glad she had suggested putting the bales out as a soft place to land because their tutor had not thought of it.

"Yes, Professor Bellbuckle, we already knew that," she

replied. "It was fun, of course, but it has long been established that the area of wing surface needed to—"

"Ha! Emma-line Cay-lee!" interrupted the girl behind her. "You so serious about things! Jump off roof with wings-a-flappy! Excellent! Not break no legs, neither. What a hooty-hoot! Trikk!"

This girl was shorter, with fierce dark eyes, black hair splayed in all directions (also with a certain amount of straw in it) and an air of wild excitement. Her accent was clearly "foreign," and her use of the English language was, well, different.

"What I mean to say, Purnah, is that there is no scientific value in disproving a theory that everyone already knows to be wrong." The taller girl spoke seriously because these things mattered to her.

"Ha! Porok! You might knows it! I doesn't know it! I considers myself much educated by fine Professor Bellbuckle this day. I be happy to jump off roof every day to get my lessons! And don't call me Purnah, you commoner, you! Is 'Princess Purnah.' Lucky you my friend. In my country, get strangled for rudeness! Glekk!"

Her Majesty made the actions that indicate execution by strangling. She grabbed herself by the throat, wiggled her head about and stuck out her tongue.

"I do wish you wouldn't do that," said Emmaline. "It's very … um … well, don't do it!"

"That were champion, that were!" said the small boy following behind. "Do all princesses pull faces like that?"

"In Chiligrit, stranglings is everyday-goings-on. Also other murderings, and kidnappings and daily thievings of sheep and goats. I miss it very much."

"Time for tea!" called out Aunt Lucy—which is what Emmaline called Mad Mrs. Butterworth, being her niece—

from the kitchen doorway. It was the left-hand kitchen, because the house had two, and you never knew where your next meal was coming from. "I've made a nice cake from dandelions and slugs, but not so many slugs as last time, when you didn't eat it."

Emmaline still didn't feel like eating a cake made with any slugs at all, though Princess Purnah was willing to give it a taste. The small boy dived in and crammed his rosy red cheeks. His name was Robert Burns—after the poet—but he was generally known in the village as Rubberbones. He'd received this nickname for a very simple reason: you couldn't hurt him. You couldn't hurt him by knocking him off a wall, or throwing him down a flight of stairs, or tripping him up on ice, or throwing bricks at him. Ever since he was a little lad the village boys had known that there was something strange about "Rab," as he was also called. He was quite tiny at that time, though he'd grown rather gangly in the past few months, but his indestructible body and ferocious enthusiasm meant that he was a hero in all the playground games and street scuffles. He'd take on grown men at football—big men who worked in the fields and mills—and run around them as they tried to kick his feet away.

And he could fly, which was another story entirely. But right now he was doing something astounding in its own right. He was enjoying Aunt Lucy's cooking.

Emmaline tried not to gag.

Princess Purnah announced that eating slugs was against her religion. She was not exactly firm in following the rules of her faith on a day-to-day basis—and nobody else knew much about the strange old tribal religion of Chiligrit—but she knew about eating slugs. Hlunchee, the God of Eating, had forbidden it. He was dead set against slugs.

"God of Eatings say 'No eat sliming things, is horrid abominations.' He say—he say eat more chocolate!"

Emmaline thought this was probably not true at all. But she wished she could claim that her religion was against eating slugs. The old vicar had never mentioned it at all, and Aunt Lucy clearly took his silence on the matter as a "yes." Apparently it had never occurred to him to throw in a quick "no slugs in the afternoon teacakes" reference in any of his sermons. Pity, really.

The dog, whose name was Stanley, was eager to take Emmaline's leftovers, essentially the whole plate. Stanley belonged to the old vicar, who had left him behind while he was visiting his sister. He—the dog, not the old vicar—was small and brown and active, and had no reservations about Aunt Lucy's cookery.

CHAPTER 2

A Gentle Walk in the Woods

"Watch out, Robert!" shouted the professor. "I do believe she's about to blow!"

Rubberbones was pushing a sort of wheelbarrow. It had been a perfectly ordinary wheelbarrow until three days ago when he and the two girls had installed a steam boiler, which powered gears that operated rods that turned the wheels. This was all part of Professor Bellbuckle's plan to teach engineering, arithmetic, science and gymnastics all in one lesson. It was Rab's turn to steer the thing, which really meant holding on to the handles and making sure it didn't run into a tree stump. Stanley ran around getting in the way, as enthusiastic small dogs are expected to do. Sometimes he barked to encourage the humans in their efforts; he was very considerate in that way.

Emmaline had no idea what the device was actually supposed to do. She had let the creation escape, and it scurried across a flower bed, smoking like a chimney fire, before getting tangled in a rosebush.

Princess Purnah had excitedly leapt on top of the thing. It was boiling hot—that's where the word "boiler" comes in, as you might have guessed, although she had not—and so she leapt off, screaming in Chiligriti. The wheelbarrow got caught in long grass and fizzled dangerously.

Having a mad inventor for your teacher was interesting,

thought Emmaline. Professor Bellbuckle was clearly a mad scientist of the most advanced and extreme type. He had been expelled—that was really the only word Emmaline could think of—from his home in Savannah, Georgia, by his loving family after an event (either an explosion that started a fire or a fire that started an explosion) many years ago. They sent him money to stay away, since he was far too crazy to keep any sort of normal scientific job, and they didn't want him to come back and live in his old bedroom. If it was still there, of course, after the fire, explosion and what have you.

And it was time for another explosion. The wheelbarrow was belching not just black smoke in torrents—that was normal for all of the professor's devices, including kitchen appliances and watches—but there were flames coming out of the wooden frame of the barrow. Stanley shied away to the cover of a laurel bush. Rubberbones continued to push the cart as if nothing were wrong until Lal Singh, Aunt Lucy's Indian butler—appearing from nowhere—hurled himself across the lawn and flung the boy to the ground. The wheelbarrow burst into flames and then, with a tremendous bang, blew up.

"Zapka-powee!" announced Princess Purnah, using a word known only to her savage mountain people. "Zmithereeenz!"

"Gosh!" exclaimed Emmaline as she arose from the ditch she had flung herself into.

"That were fantastic!" cried Rubberbones. "That were grand!"

"Was grand, Robert," said the professor. "The correct phrase is 'That was grand.' I guess it was, pretty much. The Bellbuckle Steam Turbine Barrow, Mark I, I shall call it. The creation of Mark II will begin in the morning."

"Porok! Glekk! Eeee-ratty-ratty!" said the princess as Aunt Lucy bandaged the burns on her arms and knees. "Is nothing. Honorable woundings to bear proudishly. Ekkh!"

Emmaline and Princess Purnah thought that Professor Bellbuckle was the finest teacher ("tutor" is the word for a private teacher, as Emmaline told Rab) they could possibly have. Rab, whose experience of teachers was limited to the grumbly old fellow who had been in charge of the village school, agreed. Until now he had thought teachers were bad-tempered people with a cane in one hand and a scratchy piece of chalk in the other, scraping shapes on a blackboard and speaking sharply to any child who dared speak, move or breathe too loudly. He'd left school when he turned eleven. Emmaline's experience of school was even worse. She and the princess had both been pupils at St. Grimelda's School for Young Ladies, where they had escaped separately on the same day. It was a horrible place, so we'll say no more about it at present. Later, but not now.

"Let's go on a nature walk!" suggested Professor Bellbuckle. He was trying not to look at Lal Singh, who would no doubt clean up the mess once everything had stopped smoking and cooled down. That wasn't really his job, but Emmaline knew that when they came back from this alleged nature walk, the garden would be clear of debris. She looked at Lal Singh quickly and saw no expression at all on his face. That meant something in itself.

She knew what it was. Lal Singh thought that the professor was a dangerous lunatic who should not be put in charge of children, dogs or heavy machinery of any kind. He was probably right. He was right about most things.

———————

Professor Bellbuckle's concept of a "nature walk" was a bit different from the usual excursion that teachers liked to take their classes on—you know, a jaunt in some safe countryside, where there are trees and birds to point at and creepy-crawly things to place in matchboxes and jam jars and abduct from their homes. A Bellbuckle expedition was characterized by adventure. Danger. At the very least, haring off into the brambles without bothering to put on a coat or sensible shoes.

They wandered along a woodland path as Professor Bellbuckle pointed out things. "That's a beech tree."

Rubberbones corrected him. "Nawsir, it's an 'orse-chestnut. You get conkers off 'orse-chestnut trees and put string through 'em and play with yer mates," he explained.

Rubberbones spoke with the local West Yorkshire accent, which is different from how the Queen says things.

The professor was unaware of horse-chestnut trees and the ancient game of "conkers," so he went on: "That is a pheasant. It is a young one headed south for the winter."

Emmaline looked at the bird in question. She wasn't an expert on birds, but she was sure it was a robin. English robins do not head south for the winter. If they did, this one ought to be off as soon as he'd packed his toothbrush. All the other birds had migrated weeks before.

Rubberbones looked at Emmaline and rolled his eyes. But he didn't say anything because it would be rude, and Rab was never rude. Not on purpose, anyway.

The professor was not at his best when it came to the great outdoors. He was more a pioneer of the great indoors. That was where he could invent his experimental creations. The world outside was where they didn't work, often quite loudly. But he was always full of enthusiasm; he put his best foot forward, and that was the main thing.

Right now he was putting his best foot into a filthy puddle of muck. "By criminy!" he exclaimed. "Lost my shoe!"

Rubberbones knew there was a pond farther along where the professor could wash his foot.

A mile into the woods a torrential downpour began, accompanied by black clouds that made it seem like the dead of night, even though it was not much past lunchtime. Lunch itself was a touchy subject. There hadn't been any. The outing had begun in haste, as Professor Bellbuckle retreated from the scene of his exploding steam engine and the stern disapproval of Lal Singh. Nobody had raincoats. Rubberbones had his old tweed cap that his gran made him wear in cold weather. Princess Purnah wore ballet shoes, for reasons nobody understood, except that she had found them in a box in the attic and thought they were "pritteee!"

The professor had one shoe, a layer of muck on one leg and his usual clothes, which consisted of a stained and patched formal suit—the kind you might wear to the opera if you were a music-loving tramp.

The sky had opened and poured forth water like a farmyard pump. Within a minute everyone was drenched.

"By George, that's done it!" said the professor. "My leg's perfectly clean again!"

The group huddled under the spreading branches of an oak tree.

"This fantastic!" shouted Princess Purnah. "Is wonderful! Tok-tok!"

"We could start a fire if we had some kindling," said Emmaline.

"Everything's all wet. It won't light," replied Rubberbones.

"And that's your science lesson for the day," said Professor Bellbuckle. He was anxious to make the whole affair as educational as possible. He brightened up as a thought struck him. "I have my experimental radiophonic device with me! I'll contact the house and let 'em know where we are."

From inside his drenched tailcoat he pulled out a weird-looking device like a fork stuck into a tube with wires sticking out at all angles. There was a wheel underneath that he spun around while poking the wires in different directions. "This should sound a buzzer at the receptor unit, which I recall is in the drawing room at the house, and Miss Lucy or Lal Singh will answer it. Then they'll know we're safe."

A second later they heard a buzzing sound. The professor patted his pockets and pulled out another strange device with a little box, a speaking tube and a buzzer.

"Oh," he said. "I must have picked it up myself this morning. It's not in the drawing room, then."

You could hear the disappointment in his voice.

The device stopped buzzing and fizzled a little.

Princess Purnah took the conversation in a new direction.

"I spy with my litt-ell eye something as is starting with a 'D.'"

"Dark," replied Emmaline promptly.

They lapsed into silence.

When the rain stopped hammering down, Rubberbones declared, "It's all right. We can go 'ome now. It's just a bit wet underfoot."

What he meant was that everyone was just going to have to get drenched again.

"Which way home, then?" said Emmaline. She was being polite, pretending to ask the professor, who was in charge of the expedition; really, she thought that if anyone knew, it would be Rab.

Rubberbones headed off into the woods. Everyone else followed. The lad had been playing among these trees since he could walk. They climbed a fence. They skirted around a hedge. They tramped for ages, following close behind one another in single file, so as not to get left behind. Princess Purnah was at the back, holding onto the professor's soaking wet coattails. She kept saying "Whee-ee!" whenever she slipped on the sopping leaves underfoot. It took a lot to dampen her spirits. Probably this was a great treat to her, what with being wet and starving and lost in the dark. Nobody had been strangled yet, but she could always hope.

"Er … hmm," said Rubberbones when he came to an open space where there was enough light to see one another. "I think it's that way."

He pointed to a dark patch in the trees that might

have been a path. Then again, it might have been a hippopotamus. Stanley moved cautiously toward it. Then he turned around. The rain had taken the familiar smells away. There were none of the usual doggy guideposts for him to sniff and recognize.

Emmaline realized that Rab was lost. She knew that, reasonably, you could only be a little bit lost in a few acres of the Yorkshire dales. It wasn't like the jungles of Borneo. You could be cold and wet and hungry, but as long as you didn't do anything stupid, the sun would come up and you'd follow the path and your family would hug and kiss you, and then yell at you for the rest of the day.

Then somebody did something stupid.

It wasn't Rab, who was climbing a tree to see if he could recognize anything from thirty feet in the air.

It wasn't the professor, who was trying to revive his radiophonic device by making sparks fly while he stood in six inches of water.

It wasn't the princess, who was jumping across a succession of slippery wet boulders while singing an outlandish song (involving goats under the bedclothes) from her homeland.

It wasn't Stanley, who was looking for some fierce forest creature to fight with.

It was Emmaline. She sat down on a fallen tree trunk, which rolled over and away from her. She lost her balance and slipped. She lay on her back. Her left leg didn't work. It moved adequately as far as the knee — a bit below it, in fact — and then not at all. The professor was there right away.

"Hush now, Miss Emmaline. Stop squawling and tell me where it hurts."

Emmaline resented the suggestion that she had been squawling. She wasn't sure what it was, but she had definitely not been doing it. "I can't move my foot."

"That's because you have a cranial fracture of the occluded lesser tibial bone," he announced.

"I what?"

"You have broked your ank-el, Emmaline Cay-lee," said Princess Purnah. "Now we has to shoots you to get you out of our misery."

Among the three of them, they fashioned a splint for Emmaline's foot with two pieces of fallen branch wrapped in the remains of Professor Bellbuckle's coat. Princess Purnah had sliced the garment into strips with a small knife that appeared from her stocking top. Instant bandages! With Emmaline in the middle, the professor and the princess served as props to aid her along the path, her arms on their shoulders. Rab led the way, feeling in front of him for uneven ground. Stanley sniffed ahead, looking for a trail.

"Gosh. Ouch. Thanks. Ouch," said Emmaline. "Ouch."

There was a light ahead. It was moving.

"Hellooowwww!!!" shouted Rubberbones.

"Alloooowweee!" shrieked Princess Purnah, mostly in Emmaline's ear.

"Hello-o-oh!" came the reply.

The light grew closer, and the figures behind it became clear. There was a tall man with a lamp, a medical kit, a picnic hamper and a walking stick; next to him walked a short plump woman carrying six umbrellas.

"Hello, children! Hello, Professor Bellbuckle!" said Aunt Lucy. "How was your nature walk?"

CHAPTER 3

Take Me Out to the Ball Game

The village physician, old Dr. Grout, announced that Emmaline would have to stay in bed with her leg in bandages for at least two weeks and probably a month. He tut-tutted over the deplorable and irresponsible circumstances in which a young lady of genteel upbringing could be injured while lost in the forest on a stormy night, and without a proper chaperone, either. It was the worst sprain he'd seen in forty years.

"Tosh!" said Emmaline when he had gone. "I'm not a china doll. I can run about in the woods if I want to. I can get a bit wet without melting. And if I hurt my leg, it'll mend perfectly well."

"Of course, dear. You'll be hopping about in no time," replied Aunt Lucy. Which was true, although hopping is a terribly risky way of getting down a flight of stairs. So Emmaline was spending most of her time in her bedroom. This was frustrating—she could hear the happy sounds of Princess Purnah threatening Rab with "much beheadings" in the garden outside—but there were interesting things to do in the comfort of her own room. She was doing what any healthy, normal, almost-fifteen-year-old girl would do in the circumstances: she was researching and designing a working flying machine.

The professor had brought her as much of his wildly disorderly library as he could carry. This consisted of books, letters and a battered chest full of old scientific magazines in French, German and some of the minor Slavic languages. He had no idea whether a folder marked "Laughing Gas: Accidental Side-Effects" might contain anything about aeronautics; it might—but it shouldn't. Emmaline spent hours going through the pile, finding various personal letters, laundry lists, threats from lawyers and other things that Professor Bellbuckle had left among his books. There was a letter from Jesse James saying he didn't need help blowing open bank safes. There was an official notice never to come back to the Grand Duchy of Luxembourg, and a list that the professor had made of places he might have left his gold cufflinks in 1876, all of which he had crossed off (including "washstand in cabin on boat to Tahiti" and "Texas—somewhere in"); at the bottom he had scrawled "found in my left brown shoe."

With Emmaline occupied elsewhere, Professor Bellbuckle was teaching Rab and the princess a variety of things that he thought Emmaline already knew but they might not. He had a very vague idea about what children learned in normal schools, and after trying to teach Latin and Greek— which was a failure, completely and utterly, since he could barely remember any of those languages himself—he gave up. Neither Rubberbones nor Princess Purnah could see any reason in learning the languages of dead people when there were so many living ones to talk to. The professor had tried to teach algebra and trigonometry, which he knew quite well, but he could not explain why anyone else would want to learn them. Rab tried hard, since he hero-worshipped the professor, but Purnah simply drew pictures of executions on her slate.

"Can we please play a game, sir?" asked Rubberbones. "My legs is cramped, and me hands, too, from all the writing, like. I need exercise."

"Me as wellish," added Princess Purnah. "I wants to jumping off the roof some mores."

The professor was unwilling to allow any more roof jumping for the moment. He was dolefully aware that fully one-third of his class had been injured while he was supposed to be supervising studies. Simple arithmetic suggested that this might grow to two-thirds easily enough, though mercifully there was no way to hurt young Rab. None that anyone had discovered, yet. Still, no point in taking risks.

"Let's play baseball," he said.

"You what?" said Rubberbones.

"It's what boys play where I come from."

Rab knew the game from his own boyhood. It was called "rounders" and seemed exactly the same as the professor's American sport, although you used your fist against a big ball rather than a bat against a small one. The principle was the same, involving hitting the ball and running around a series of marks on the ground until you could make it back to where you started off.

Princess Purnah only knew about sports where people were savagely injured and maimed for life or, at the very least, used a severed human head instead of a ball. This game seemed dull in comparison, but she wanted to be cooperative.

"I throwings ball, professor hittings. Errand Boy catchings."

Rab decided that the princess was never going to use his proper name. "I'm not a flippin' errand boy!" he hissed. Purnah smiled brightly.

The garden was far too overgrown for any sort of ball game, so they walked out to a patch of meadow across the lane that had a border of gorse bushes and scrubby trees around it.

Professor Bellbuckle had a proper baseball bat, glove and ball. Rab was fascinated by them, as these were strange things never seen in Yorkshire. The professor was standing at a mark beaten in the grass, which he called "home plate." He held the bat upright, like a woodcutter ready to strike. Stanley lurked behind him, waiting for something interesting to happen. Rab crouched some distance off, catcher's glove on his hand. Princess Purnah stood in front of the professor. She had the ball. "I am standing on the pickcher's mountain," she announced.

"Pitcher's mound," corrected Professor Bellbuckle. "You are a 'pitcher,' not a 'picture.' Just throw the ball at me, about head height."

Princess Purnah shouted "Eee-yah!" (a traditional Chiligriti cry) and flung the ball at the professor's head, missing it by inches as he ducked.

"Tarnation, Princess P! You almost took my head clean off!"

Princess Purnah was offended. "Be calling me 'Your Majesty, sir Poffesser. And you telled me to doing that at your headings!"

Rab thought she was right about that last bit. That was what the professor had said.

"All right," growled Professor Bellbuckle. "Try again. Only toward the bat, not my face."

"Eee-yah!" The ball traveled like a thunderbolt toward the professor. He was nearly ready this time. He swung the bat, and the ball struck the wood with a tremendous smack. The ball went up in the air. The professor dropped the bat. He began to run in his bandy-legged fashion. Stanley raced under his legs, and the professor fell over him. The ball came down in a looping drop and Rubberbones caught it.

"Catchings! Trikk! Owwwt!" shouted Princess Purnah.

There was some squabbling as to who should go next. The princess said it should be her, but Rubberbones picked up the bat. The professor wandered out to the middle of the field. Stanley tried to steal the ball from Princess Purnah, but she wasn't allowing that.

"Bad doggy! Go chase Errand Boy when he running!"

Rab stood on the dent in the ground that Professor Bellbuckle had referred to as the "plate." He took up the same stance, as best he could mimic it, that the professor had used, with the bat held up like a Viking hero in a painting he'd seen once. He scowled fiercely, too.

The ball whizzed past his ear at a searing pace. "Strike one!" called out Professor Bellbuckle, who was serving as umpire, coach and player.

"Not fair!" shouted Rubberbones. "She never said that one were coming."

The second ball blistered through the air.

This time the princess helped by announcing her throw with another "Eeeeeee-yahhh!!!" which meant something like "If this huge rock doesn't knock you flat, my little sister has a boulder that will."

Rubberbones swung the bat ferociously. Pure luck made bat and ball connect with an ear-splitting crack. The ball flew over Princess Purnah, over Professor Bellbuckle, over the field and into the bushes fifty yards away. It was a magical moment in Yorkshire baseball.

Until somebody yelled "Aaagh!" which was followed by a sound suspiciously like a body hitting the ground.

———

Emmaline and Aunt Lucy were keeping one another company in Emmaline's room. Aunt Lucy was drawing patterns for some new clothes for Emmaline and Princess Purnah. She always made her own clothes, with very little regard for fashion. She thought that ladies' clothing was designed as a sort of conspiracy by unknown persons to prevent women from doing very much except moving stiffly, breathing carefully and trying not to faint from the tightness of their underwear.

"Corsets! What nonsense!" she said, beginning one of her tirades against the wickedness of female undergarments. "Tight lacings, whalebone supports, all kinds of silly fripperies! All designed to push this part out, hold this part in and bend the natural shape into some freakish contortion intended to—to oppress us and prevent us from leading our lives the way we want! If they stifle us with corsets, we'll never get the vote!"

Emmaline agreed with her aunt in principle. Corsets were ridiculous items. Women's fashion was idiotic. And it was only right for women to be allowed to vote in elections, the same as men. But she didn't really want to talk about those things. She wanted to read about flying machines and people like the French pioneer Alphonse Penaud, who had built a working model in the 1870s using a big rubber band for power but had taken his own life after "disappointments overcame him." She wanted to know about the Russian sea captain Mozhaiski, who had invented a steam flyer in 1884 with a single wing and propellers front and back. His pilot had rolled down a ramp, and the machine had taken the air for perhaps a hundred feet. And there were clippings about the German aviator Otto Lilienthal, who was doing amazing things with gliders. There was even a newspaper item about a "birdman" who was planning to undertake something dangerous, involving flapping wings and possible death, in London sometime soon. Emmaline was certain that men who flap wings were simply finding a way of making themselves look silly as they fell from a great height. The theory was all wrong. She'd seen that only yesterday.

Emmaline looked out of the window to see her friends playing in the field across the lane. She glimpsed something moving in the gorse bushes. Something brown. A dog? A tramp? The last bear in England?

No, it was a man. A man who huddled close to the ground and held something that glinted up to his face. Binoculars. One of those people who watch birds?

"That reminds me," said Aunt Lucy as she cut out a pattern for a skirt that any lady of fashion would have giggled at. "I received a letter regarding dear little Purnah — you know that anything that happens in Chiligrit comes under the India Office of Her Majesty's Government? Apparently they are quite agitated about her — Purnah, not Queen Victoria — running away from that horrid school you both attended. They had no idea where she'd got to, and they seemed to think that lost princesses can't be trusted to look after themselves on the loose."

Princess Purnah was yelling something and jumping up and down while the professor and Stanley lay in a heap in the field.

"So, anyway, they are sending a man from London to visit us on Friday. I have no idea what they'll say. I am going to ask if we can keep her, like Stanley."

"Er, Aunt Lucy. Purnah is a girl. A royal personage, as she tells me seven times each day. Stanley is the vicar's dog."

"Well, exactly. The vicar lets us keep Stanley here even though the vicar is staying with his sister in Frinton. His sister dislikes Stanley, as you know. But Stanley is still the vicar's dog. So, I was thinking, Princess Purnah is the heir to the throne in Chiligrit, but since there is some sort of quarrel about who is in charge there, why don't we look after her until that's all sorted out?"

"Um," said Emmaline. "Why do you mention this now?" Aunt Lucy's mind worked in odd ways.

"Well, it's that man with the binoculars out there behind those bushes, dear. Have you not noticed him, then? He's been watching the house for several days, and he always seems to be looking at Princess Purnah. So I think he's probably a foreign agent."

Emmaline was stunned. A foreign agent!

Then she too heard the "Aaagh!" and the thudding sound. She wondered if the groans that followed were in a foreign accent. They sounded a bit Russian. Or possibly German. She looked out to see Rubberbones racing across the field toward a man who was clutching his head.

She also saw Lal Singh, running at an amazing pace for a dignified butler, cross the lane and leap through the bushes. Reaching the man just after Rab, he took charge of the fellow in a way that suggested he was in no mood for an argument.

"Lal Singh did mention that he wanted a word with the chap when the time was convenient. I expect that would be about now," said Aunt Lucy.

CHAPTER 4

The Secret Agent

The man, as Rubberbones came up to him, was on his knees, clutching his forehead where a giant goose egg was bursting into life. He had a pair of binoculars that he'd dropped in the mud. The baseball lay next to the binoculars, guilty in the eyes of the world.

"Er, sorry about that. Are you all right? Only I din't see you was there," stammered Rubberbones. "I wouldn't have hit yer if I had."

The man groaned and tried to get up. As he did so, Lal Singh took the man prisoner. The huge Sikh bound the man's hands with a rope. Only then did he pull out some bandages to wrap the captive's head.

"Now," Lal Singh pronounced in a no-nonsense, deceive-me-at-your-peril voice. "Explain who it is you are and why you are snooping extensively around the house of Mrs. Butterworth these past several days. Lie to me and I will cut your liver out and feed it to the dog while you are watching!"

Stanley, the dog in question, came over to see about this possible treat. He barked in his most ferocious manner.

The man drooped. Whatever courage he might have brought with him melted at the sight of Stanley's slavering jaws. An Indian giant and a wild dog!

Rubberbones recognized the dog's expression. Stanley was hoping for a peppermint. Or a liquorice allsort. He was not fussy in these matters.

The man squeaked, piteous in his fear. "Don't let him hurt me. I'll tell everything!"

Rab took hold of Stanley, his expression suggesting that he, too, was afraid of the ravening hound. Actually it was because he had stepped on the man's binoculars and thought he might have broken them. So he looked very worried, indeed. "I'll talk!" wheezed the man.

Princess Purnah and Professor Bellbuckle had arrived on the scene. "Oh, goody!" said the princess. "A prisoner! Who is he? What foulish crime has he committed? Can we beatings the soles of his feet, please?"

The professor excused himself. "I'd better fetch Miss Lucy—Mrs. Butterworth—she'll know what to do."

But Lal Singh knew what to do. "Speak truthfully and completely and you will leave here most safely and freely. Otherwise, perhaps not." He smiled in a way that Rubberbones thought was very impressive. Friendly yet frightening. The boy still had no idea why the butler was acting this way, but it was very exciting!

The prisoner confessed immediately. "It was this bloke I met in a pub in Grimethorpe. Two weeks ago or more. He was asking if anyone knew anything about a girl—a dark, foreign-looking girl—about thirteen, as 'ad got lost from school, run away more like, and 'adn't been 'eard of. He didn't want the police involved, just said he'd pay ten pounds to anyone who helped 'im find her. Ten pounds is a terrible lot of money for a lost schoolgirl. I told 'im I traveled about these dales a bit and I'd keep a look out. He said to leave word wi' the landlord of the pub, the Black Bull on the High Street, if I found out anything. So when I gets to Lower Owlthwaite on my rounds—I do a bit of knife sharpening and odd jobs—I hear about this mad old widow who has a niece and another girl and a local lad, all jumping off the roof. So I asks about the girl and they tells me she's not from around 'ere, dark 'air and eyes, talks funny when she come to the shops. Came back from some school with the niece not long ago. So, I contacts the bloke by way of the Black Bull, and 'e meets me and give me these binocker—these glasses, and tells me to keep a close watch on t'house and report if anything 'appens. He gave me ten shillin' to get started."

Lal Singh's eyes narrowed into slits. "This man. Who was he?"

"Don't know 'im. Talked a bit posh. Not Yorkshire. Dressed well. Kept 'is face hidden under a hat. Stayed in a dark corner of the pub."

"Did you tell him where the house is?"

"Oh, er ... no."

Lal Singh reached out and gently placed an arm on his shoulder. "No?"

The man flinched. "Well, yes. He give me the ten shillin', see. Lot of money and promise of more."

Princess Purnah lunged forward. "Oh, the villain! Schizzz! Let me stab him many times so that he bleed most extensively in horrid pain and anguish!" She had the little knife that Rab had seen her use to cut up the professor's coat for Emmaline's bandage. She looked as if she'd used it before.

Lal Singh caught her arm. The knife fell at her feet.

"There will be none of that!" said Aunt Lucy, waddling toward them. "It is not nice to stab our visitors. Even unwelcome visitors. I shall be taking that, thank you!" Rab handed her the blade.

"Now," she continued. "I heard what this man had to say. He is clearly a minion in some fiendish scheme. Are you merely a minion, fellow?"

The man shook his head at the short, plump woman who now held the knife. If he was a "minion," he didn't know it. He'd never heard the word before. He was baffled. Mostly he was terrified.

"I'm sorry, missus! I were just trying to make some

easy money before the winter! I never meant no 'arm to anyone!"

"I'll set this young lady on you if you are lying," said Aunt Lucy in a stern voice. She waved the knife savagely, which made the man cower again in fear. He didn't know she always waved knives around like that when she was cutting up rhubarb or mangel-wurzel for pies.

"No! That's all I know. A bloke in a pub."

"This person. What name did he give?"

"He said to leave a message for a Mr. Brown."

"Aha! Clearly an alias!" cried Aunt Lucy. "Real people are not called 'Mr. Brown'!"

She stopped and thought about this for a moment. "Well, some of them are, but I have no doubt this is not one of them. Lal Singh, do you have any more questions for this man?"

"Yes, Memsahib." He turned to the knife grinder. "What is your name? Your real name—no lies!"

"Edwin Finch, sir."

"And you are to meet Mr. Brown again?"

"I'm to leave another message at the Black Bull."

"Can you read and write?"

"Yes, sir. A bit."

"Then write a message on this paper." Lal Singh produced a pencil and paper, as if by magic. "Write 'Meet me at eight o'clock on Tuesday night. I have news of the girl.' Can you do that?" The man did as he was told. "Now, write a second note apologizing that you cannot be there after all." He did that, too.

"Right. Now be off with you and never be coming back— ever! Do not report this to Mr. Brown, for he will know you have betrayed him to us. Take your ill-gotten ten shillings and be most wretchedly grateful!"

Aunt Lucy used Princess Purnah's knife to cut Edwin Finch's bonds. She did not give the knife back to the girl. This made no difference to Purnah. She had seized the baseball bat from the professor and now brandished it like a club. As Finch stepped away, she launched herself toward him. "I crippling you, bad man! Porok!"

Before anyone could stop her, she was on him, smacking wildly with the baseball bat at his head, his shoulders and, as he turned to flee the attack, his bottom. Purnah landed a solid thwack across his posterior as Finch took off running, and grinned roundly as his cries of "Oh! Oh! Murder!" echoed across the field.

"You much too good peoples," she announced to everyone present. "Letting him go when we can slice his skins off with fruit peeler just for startings! Glekk!"

Aunt Lucy looked a bit pale. "Yes, dear, but this is England. We just use the fruit peeler for apples. Did you have to beat him like that?"

"Oh yes! Chiligriti princess teached early to beat disobedient underlings!" She grinned once more at Rubberbones. "You see what you up against, Errand Boy? You be good when I sez so, yes? Horrrrock!"

The professor took back the bat; Aunt Lucy still did not give back the knife. They all returned to the house.

Emmaline had watched in amazement from the window. It was a hundred feet or more from the meadow, and she could only hear sounds rather than words, even when she flung the window open as wide as she could.

Lal Singh, the perfect butler, had assaulted a complete stranger and tied him up. Aunt Lucy, sweet Aunt Lucy, had threatened the man, with fists raised. Then Princess Purnah had clubbed him with a bat. Even at a distance you could hear the smack across his—well, yes, and you could hear him yelping as he ran away.

That part, at least, was what you'd expect; any day that Purnah did not run amok with weapons was probably unusual in the normal course of her Chiligriti princesshood.

All very … odd. Emmaline began to think, and think deeply. Something strange was going on: there were foreign agents spying on the house, and normally quiet, civilized people were acting as if they needed to defend the family against marauders. Emmaline was stuck in her bedroom, unable to walk, or run, or hit people with baseball bats. There was no doubt about what she had to do.

It was time to build flying machines. Again.

"It turned out he wasn't a foreign agent after all," explained Aunt Lucy. "He was from Grimethorpe. A minion. Possibly a henchman. I thought he might be a spy from the Austrian secret service skulking after dear Professor Bellbuckle, after all that trouble he had with his steam engine blowing up Vienna. But it turns out to be something to do with Princess Purnah. We let him go. I had thought about imprisoning him in the cellar until he divulged all his secrets, but I think he already had, and the cellar is awfully damp."

Ah, yes, thought Emmaline. If you were to take somebody hostage and pry their secrets from them, you'd want them to be comfy. Sometimes she had no idea what was going on in her aunt's mind. The list of sensible people who Emmaline knew consisted of herself, Rubberbones and Lal Singh. And Rubberbones wasn't all that sensible—after all, he regularly risked death and/or dismemberment with no thought about any risks he might be taking. Then again, so far he'd always lived a charmed life. And he could fly. That wasn't sensible at all.

Aunt Lucy was organizing bottles of fresh-caught snails according to size and color. Emmaline had set aside the drawings she had made for a big flying machine that would be powered by one of the professor's steam engines. That was for the future. What she wanted right now was something simple. She wanted to make copies of Rab's old kite. Several months ago, Rubberbones had appeared hovering over the garden attached to an ordinary wood-and-brown-paper kite. The sort of kite that children everywhere make, except that his was big enough to carry a boy above the trees and move about by a sort of wiggling of the arms and legs. He had used that same kite to visit her at night when Emmaline was imprisoned at St. Grimelda's, and had crashed it on the school roof when he was attacked by the school's pterodactyls (that was another story). Emmaline had fixed it up and crashed it into the sea when she escaped. That was that for Rab's kite. So now she wanted to make another one. Another three, in fact.

Chapter 5

In Which Rubberbones Visits a Tavern

"I can't imagine why you'd be wanting three the same, Emmaline," said Professor Bellbuckle. "I make something, see how it works, then I make another with improvements. Or something completely different. Sometimes with rockets, sometimes without."

Emmaline was using crutches that Lal Singh had found and cut down to her size, but at least she could hobble out to the barn. The old barn had been converted to a workshop for building flying machines. The old horse, Ernest, had been moved out and given a bedroom in the house. (Not one of the nicer ones, of course, because those were for people, and a downstairs room, because he was bad with steps.) Since the professor had come, he had stored in the barn all his devices and inventions—both complete and in pieces—along with an assortment of old calendars, broken chairs and telephonic communicators, which were almost like the ones Alexander Graham Bell had invented nearly twenty years before, only powered by gunpowder. Every existing model of the Bellbuckle Telephonic Device was connected to all the others inside this very barn. This was fantastically helpful, since you could call up a person sitting ten feet away, instead of talking a bit louder as you'd have to do otherwise. And you could both get blown up together.

Rubberbones thought the workshop was wonderful. Emmaline thought it was a mess. The professor said it was just like home, which meant it was just like his last house, except that he didn't have to sleep under his desk anymore.

The three flying machines—kites, really—were almost ready. Rubberbones and the professor had done most of the work. Emmaline was able do some sewing of fabric and glueing of wood and paper, but not much else, because of her foot. The princess could not be trusted to do such things, especially when saws and hammers might be involved, so she played with Stanley.

"Ey-oop, Miss Em," said Rubberbones. "It's just like the one I made first off. The one I were flying over the 'ouse with just after you first met me." He was quite nostalgic for that first, simple kite. "But, like the professor says, why three of 'em?"

Emmaline had a theory. "What I believe is that, in a true scientific model for development, you have to use a single initial concept, then make alterations that can be tested precisely against the original version to understand how one single change affects the machine as a whole."

Rubberbones looked at her as if she were speaking Romanian. "You what?" he replied.

"If you change one bit, it affects all the other bits. So you might get one problem sorted out, but mess up something else without realizing it."

"Oh. Why didn't you say that, then? Like when I put a bit of raspberry jam on a piece of bread at me gran's 'ouse, and I spill a bit and she slips on it and yells at me, it's different from when I don't spill the raspberry jam?"

"Exactly right, young Rab," said Professor Bellbuckle, who followed this line of reasoning. "Like when my

Bellbuckle Patent Mole Drill, Mark II, accidentally broke through the wall of that gold mine in South Africa and caused so much trouble to me—unfairly, I might add—well, that was different from all those days that I didn't break into a gold mine."

Emmaline's head was spinning. That wasn't what she meant at all. What she said was what she meant, and neither of her collaborators could understand clear, scientific language. It was very difficult being a pioneer of aeronautics.

Rubberbones was about to go home to his gran's house when Lal Singh tapped him on the shoulder. "Rab-sahib, I am asking you to accompany myself on a most secretive mission on Tuesday night. Please do not be telling anyone about it, unless you wish to create much criticism."

"Promise, Lal Singh! What is it?"

"Do you remember what that scoundrel knife grinder wrote on the note that I forced him to inscribe on pain of horrid mutilation and possible death?"

"Er, something about him meeting that Mr. Brown at a pub in Grimethorpe. But I don't think he'd go. He were dead frightened and— "

"You are misunderstanding whole plan, young fellow. The plan is not for worthless Edwin Finch to go to the Black Bull public house. The plan is to persuade alleged Mr. Brown to appear, so that we can find out about him."

"So we can tie *him* up, too?" Rubberbones liked that idea.

"No tying up at this junction. Perhaps another time. Time for puzzling out what is going on."

Rubberbones thought about this. "That note, then. You want me to take it to Grimethorpe?"

"I have already arranged for that first letter to be delivered. Instead, you will be going to the Black Bull to seek out Mr. Brown and gain particulars of his appearance. You will carry the note saying despicable Finch is not coming."

"You what?" said Rubberbones.

Lal Singh explained what he had in mind. It would be a secret between them.

———————

Emmaline had wanted three kites for a very specific reason, and she was not pleased to see all three wafting about above the garden the next morning. She had explained her plans very badly, but the idea was to have one basic model, try it out, then add some things to an identical model and try that out, then compare them and take it from there. That was what her great-great-uncle, Sir George Cayley, had done with his experiments. That was what real scientists did. It was what prevented you from saying to yourself, "These new wings are fine! I am now flying higher and faster than ever before! And yet I decided to leave off the landing wheels for this version! What was I thinking?" Or, as a number of aeronauts had put it more simply, "Aaaaagghhh!!"

Of course, Professor Bellbuckle's approach was more the "Hey, hey! I have a great idea! Let's try this and see if we are all killed, or not" way of doing things. So he didn't understand Emmaline's reasoning at all and, as a result, all the kites were straining at the end of strings tied to a tree branch.

Rab was attached to one of the kites. He was floating with grace, using his arms and legs to move the kite higher and lower, forward and backward. It was a very natural thing for him to be able to do. It was also contrary to the laws of science. You just can't move your arm and go left thirty feet in the air. It's ridiculous. But that is what he was doing. Emmaline shook her head. She still couldn't believe it, although it was right in front of her eyes.

Princess Purnah was attached to the next one. But where Rab used his body to turn and swoop and sail freely, she was simply trussed into the kite and floating with the wind. "Glekk! Gemmee down! Not likeness whatsoever! Porok!"

Stanley was also tied in place. He scratched at his kite with both sets of paws, wagging his tail and panting with enthusiasm. He bobbled about in the light wind with no effort to control where he went. But, after all, he was a dog. You could only expect so much.

He'll rip that to pieces in a few minutes, thought Emmaline.

She recalled the single time she had flown. The kite had been repaired with materials smuggled into her school. A tailpiece had been made of cardboard and two old hockey sticks. It had worked. Emmaline couldn't steer the contraption, and it simply went forward. But it had flown several hundred yards, dipping slowly until it—well, until it crashed into the sea. But pterodactyls were attacking it at the time, so you could overlook the way it had come down into the water.

Looking up at her friends floating above her, she wanted to fly. Right now. She wanted to throw down her crutches, grab the kite out from under Princess Purnah and soar above the leafless trees.

But, for now, all she could do was watch.

It was eight o'clock on Tuesday evening. Rubberbones was on his way to the Black Bull, his cap pulled low over his eyes. Since his cap was much too big for him, this wasn't difficult.

Lal Singh had explained his plan in more detail on the way to Grimethorpe, five miles over the hills, with Ernest pulling them in the dogcart. They sat on the high seat above the wheels.

"I cannot go into the Black Bull without causing much interest, for I am Sikh, and nobody in Grimethorpe looks like me. I attract much attention. You are a small boy, although a most excellent example of same. One small boy much like another to grown people. You must go into the public house and ask for Mr. Brown. The landlord might be telling you to give him the message to pass along; this you must refuse, saying that you were told to give it only into the hands of Mr. Brown. He will point out that person. What you must do is hand over this note from the wretched Finch man and get a very good look at Mr. Brown. At the same time, operate this device, which Professor Bellbuckle has invented. It is a miniature camera. I am most uncertain that it is working at all, but the professor assures me it makes no sounds or flashings. All the same, I would be most cautious were I to be yourself. Ensure that rapid escapings are possible at all times. I will be with Ernest in the alley behind the Black Bull; should'st you be needing me, here is a most excellent whistle to be blowing."

At the mention of his name, Professor Bellbuckle stuck his head up from the rear of the cart. He'd hidden under a blanket. "Of course my camera works!" he announced, offended. Lal Singh glared at the professor. "I knew you must have intended to ask me along!" explained the inventor. "So I came to provide my invaluable assistance!"

The Black Bull was an ugly building set between two uglier ones in the rough part of Grimethorpe, where rats from better neighborhoods looked down on the local rodent population. The dark alley smelled of rotting cabbages. Rubberbones took his whistle and the camera, which fitted behind a buttonhole in his coat. Then he pushed his way through the pub door.

"Looking for Mr. Brown," he said to the barman.

"Dunno 'im, mate," replied the man. He was wiping glasses with a dirty rag. The Black Bull was not a nice place. Even Rab, who didn't go to nice places, knew that.

"He's supposed to be meeting a bloke 'ere at eight," said Rubberbones. "Only I got a message for 'im."

"Give it 'ere," replied the barman. "I'll pass it on."

"Nawssir. Got to 'and it to 'im meself. I get an extra threepence if I do."

The barman smiled. Threepence was something in the world of small boys. "All right, son. Let me ask Bert."

Bert appeared from the cellar. He was clearly the landlord. He had a red nose, red cheeks, gray side-whiskers and a stomach like a pregnant cow. "You want Mr. Brown, son?"

"Yessir."

"Follow me, then. Only I know that threepence is at stake." He laughed, although not in a very likeable way. Rab followed him down a dark hallway toward a door. "Private room for Mr. Brown. Don't want to sit wi' ordinary customers." He tapped at the door.

"Come!" The voice was deep and educated.

Rab tiptoed in. There was one gas lamp, turned down to create a low, shimmering light. The man sat at a table, his back to the wall, leaning forward so that his hat was tilted down over his brow. His scarf was pulled up over his face, and he kept his coat on despite the coal fire burning in the corner.

"Where is Finch?" he barked.

The landlord shrank back. "Er ... this lad ... got a message." He slipped out of the doorway as the man, "Mr. Brown," turned toward Rubberbones.

"Well?"

Rubberbones pretended to be nervous in the company of this mysterious figure. This was an easy thing to do as Mr. Brown was intimidating, even sitting at a table in an ordinary Yorkshire public house. "Er ... yessir. Got a message here. In me pocket." He reached into the pocket for the letter. Wrong pocket. He tried another. It wasn't there, either.

"Hurry up, boy. I assume this is from Finch?"

"Yessir, I mean, do you mean the knife grinder, sir?"

"You know I do. Stop fidgeting and give me the message."

Rab leaned forward, trying to study Mr. Brown's face as

he rummaged through his pockets. The man's hat and muffler almost met. All he could see were two cold, dark eyes. Rab steeled himself. Sometimes you had to do something rash. Something sudden. Something stupid.

Fortunately, Rubberbones was well accustomed to doing something stupid. Stupidity and he were old friends. As he checked his pockets again, Rab's fingers closed on the letter. He whipped it out in excitement and stumbled forward into the table. Arms flailing, he knocked the hat off Mr. Brown's head with one hand while yanking down his scarf with the other. He jumped back, shouting, "Oops! Sorry!" and reached into his pocket for the rubber bulb that would operate the secret camera. Only then did he look where the man's face should have been.

Mr. Brown glowered at Rubberbones. He was hatless and scarfless. Most of all, he was faceless. This was a man completely without a face, like the "Fiend without a Face" Rab had read about in the penny dreadful papers. Beneath his eye sockets, the man's features had been seared of all detail, leaving a white mass of scar tissue. There was no nose at all, except for nostrils quivering in rage, and no lips, only a gaping hole twisted in anger. Above the eyes was a smooth, bald scalp like a shining skull.

Rubberbones opened his mouth, but could do no more than squeak. He squeezed the bulb. The secret, silent miniature camera whirred loudly and emitted a small flash. A cloud of powder burst above Rab's middle shirtbutton.

"Ruddy 'eck," he thought

Rab turned for the door handle as the horrific figure leapt over the table. "You little scoundrel—" he began.

Rab flung the door open and ran down the hallway. At the end of it he ducked left into the main room, the saloon bar, and came face to face with the landlord. Bert held a tray of empty glasses in his hamlike hands.

"Stop that boy!" shouted Mr. Brown. He was two steps behind Rubberbones. Bert turned to block the way. Rab feinted to his left. The landlord stepped to his right in response. Rab dropped his shoulder to the right and dodged out under the tray. He raised his left elbow and sent the tray flying up into his opponent's face. Bert tried to catch all sixteen glasses at once, lost his balance and grabbed wildly at thin air while glasses shattered on the flagstones below. Mr. Brown cannoned into him. They both fell in a heap as glass splinters flew up in a shower of broken pint pots. Rab turned to look for a moment, pleased at his efforts.

The barman's hand closed on his shoulder. "You aren't going anywhere, sonny."

CHAPTER 6

A Faceless Fiend Is Foiled

Rubberbones shivered. He tried to squirm out of the man's steely grip. The hand only tightened on his shoulder, a sharp finger digging into his collarbone.

"This the boy, boss?"

The Faceless Fiend, as Rab thought of him, stood up. A customer in the corner turned pale and scuttled out without finishing his beer.

Rab's captor clamped a second hand around his waist to stop the boy's wriggling. But Rubberbones was still able to reach into his pocket. He brought the whistle to his lips and blew. The resulting sound was low and had an odd, eastern lilt.

The barman holding him knocked the whistle from Rab's lips. "You'll not bring the bobbies with that toy."

The man without a face laughed. It was a harsh, ugly chortle. The landlord and the barman laughed, too, in a sick, nervous sort of way. All the customers had left, some quietly, others making an undignified bolt for the back door.

Rab's heart sank into his boots. He looked downward, dejected.

So he didn't see the first crash as the big, grimy window blew inward in a shower of broken glass. There was a bright light, a rush of wind and a crash against the far wall. The rush caused all the gas lamps to blow out. Rab knew it was dangerous when gas lamps suddenly go out. There was a good chance of a huge explosion unless someone immediately relit the lamps before the gas built up. When the wallpaper caught fire, as it was doing at that moment ... well, that wasn't a good sign.

The barman holding Rab released his grip and fled screaming. The landlord looked mortified because it was his own place, then dove for a back door. The Faceless Fiend's eyes flashed in anger. He glared as Rab bolted toward the front door—and too far away from him to grab—and strode away.

Rab hauled at the door. As he leaped through, a strong brown hand reached down and pulled him onto the high seat of the dogcart. Ernest wasn't usually frisky, but tonight he was trotting like a two year old. He hadn't moved so fast in years. His timing was excellent because the Black Bull blew up with an impressive boom when the cart was just a few hundred feet away. Rab turned pale and put his hands over his ears.

"Most dangerous work!" pronounced Lal Singh after Rab had told him about unveiling the faceless man. "I am glad you summoned our assistance most promptly."

"What caused the bang?" asked Rubberbones.

"A Bellbuckle Combustible Blaster, Model 1894," announced the professor happily. "I believe that its flight through the inn, which served to extinguish the lights, was instrumental in causing that most gratifying explosion of gas which we just observed."

Lal Singh smiled. "I have observed that the professor, although prone to error in some things, makes most excellent explosive devices. If he uses them at exceedingly short distances, the results are indeed gratifying."

Emmaline was ready to develop the kites in an orderly, scientific fashion. The first kite was a copy of Rab's first creation. The second would be exactly like the one she and Josie Pinner (her one trusted schoolfriend) had built in the games equipment room at St. Grimelda's. This meant adding an extra tailpiece and a big upper wing: the difficulty was getting two hockey sticks of the normal schoolgirl size and type. These had been an important part of the original model. Lower Owlthwaite was always limited when it came to scientific supplies, though you could easily get a pound of cheese or a pair of garden shears. She had bigger plans for the third kite.

"Professor! Would it be possible to build an engine small enough to power one of the kites?" asked Emmaline. "The next step will be to develop a full-fledged mechanical flying machine."

The professor was pottering around the old barn, apparently planning to experiment with more gas explosions. It didn't seem to occur to him that this would destroy his own workshop and perhaps himself. "Oh, sure. You could fix the kite to any of my steam engines."

"Well, yes, but would it fly?"

The professor seemed surprised. "Oh, you mean power it into the air?"

"Yes. Otherwise we'd just be dragging it about on the ground, wouldn't we?" Emmaline bit her tongue. That was a rather snippy thing to say. It was because of the bandages on her foot and not being able to do anything. Especially after Rab had told her about his adventure in Grimethorpe last night. It all sounded terribly exciting! And she, stuck at home, in bed with a book at eight o'clock.

Princess Purnah burst into the barn, bringing cake and snails for tea. She was in a good mood. She'd heard Rab's tale as well and wished that she had been there, at least for the explosion. She was singing a song, a cheery Chiligriti folk tune whose title translated into English as "I have cut the wood for your tomb."

It was Thursday morning, and the local paper was full of the news that the Black Bull had been completely destroyed in a gas explosion. Nobody had been hurt. The landlord claimed he had heroically saved the barman from the raging inferno. The barman declared he had rescued the landlord. But the news from Professor Bellbuckle was even more interesting.

"It took me most of last night to get a good negative and make a print and then magnify it to a useful size, but ... well, look at this!"

Everyone at the breakfast table came round to look. The photograph Rab had taken was blurred, and the light was less than ideal. It was not, say, the picture you'd want to put on a passport or a Christmas greeting. But if you were a Faceless Fiend, you probably didn't send out a lot of Christmas cards.

The photograph revealed the peeled skull, the sinister glint to the dark eyes and, most of all, the horrific deformity of the lower face, where nose, cheeks and lips had been seared away to leave a scarred mass of nothing.

"Goodness!" exclaimed Aunt Lucy. "What a shame for his poor mother!"

"Was he born like that?" asked Emmaline, shivering at the sight.

"I don't think so," replied the professor. "There are people who are born, tragically, with deformities—some as horrible as this man. But I suspect that these are the marks left by burns, or an explosion of some kind. This fella could have looked like anybody, and then, one day, he's changed."

Emmaline stared at the photograph. Who was this terrifying man and, more important, why was he so interested in Princess Purnah?

CHAPTER 7

The Men from the Ministry

They were all still gathered around the table when there was a knock at the front door. Lal Singh went to answer it.

After a few moments he returned. "Memsahib, it is two gentlemen who are saying they come from the India Office in London. I am showing them into the front parlor."

Aunt Lucy looked up from her plate. "That will be about the princess, no doubt. Purnah, my dear, why don't you come and meet them."

"Proutt! Boggirdem-bote," growled the princess.

Lal Singh raised a hand. "It might be better if you spoke to them first alone, Memsahib. Or take Miss Emmaline with you. I will attend to the princess."

Emmaline thought this was odd. Lal Singh knew which spoon went with every dish. He polished silverware until it glowed. He did not usually make a habit of telling Aunt Lucy that she shouldn't introduce Princess Purnah to visitors who called for her.

Aunt Lucy nodded thoughtfully and tapped the side of her nose in a most unnatural way. Emmaline thought this must be a signal that she understood.

"I am sure you are right, Lal Singh. Come, Emmaline. We will meet these gentlemen from London."

Rubberbones was stuffing his face with a huge slice of cake (Aunt Lucy allowed them to have cake for breakfast) when Lal Singh shut the kitchen door quietly and gestured for the two youngsters and the professor to follow him into the scullery. He had one finger to his lips, a signal even Princess Purnah understood.

"Walls are having ears," he whispered. "And I am most suspicious. These men are perhaps not who they are pretending. Rab-sahib, would you slip out of the back door and observe for strange personages? Return with news as swiftly as possible."

Rab crushed the rest of the cake into his mouth. If Lal Singh thought something was wrong, it was.

"O princess Purnah," the Sikh continued. "We must disguise you as some person quite unlike your actual self. We may be leaving swiftly in the appearance of an alternative individual, such as Rab-sahib. He keeps spare clothing here in case of explosions."

The princess scowled. "I don't wishing to dresses in Errand Boy's clothes. He sweat too much and stinky up! I Chiligriti princess, much royalty!"

"Yes, and that is why these men from London wish to take you away. Now shush, thy majesty! Go silently upstairs and get things you are needing. Put pins in your hair for raising it under boyish hat. Be swift about it, for time is short."

(If you had been there, you'd have been impressed by the lack of proper English grammar in the conversation so far. But, then again, you wouldn't have had time to think because Lal Singh would certainly have put you to work as a decoy, and—if you were a boy of around twelve or so— borrowed your clothes and left you standing about in your underwear.)

Princess Purnah did as she was told. Which proved that there was something unusual going on.

Emmaline followed Aunt Lucy into the drawing room. She was trying to remember what she knew about her aunt's dealings with the India Office.

Emmaline and Princess Purnah had met at St. Grimelda's School, an institution so harsh and repressive that it boasted it was "the strictest school in England," and quite possibly the whole world. Princess Purnah had been delivered there under circumstances she didn't really understand herself— she'd been nine or ten at the time—and had pretended that she didn't understand any English. This was actually true, so the pretending wasn't hard. Over time she had picked up the language in her own bizarre fashion, but had kept this a secret. One day she had tried to escape. To her surprise, because she didn't have much of a plan, she succeeded when Rubberbones (who was hiding in the back of a grocer's van) had lent her a helping hand. After that it all got a bit complicated with pursuing teachers and flying monsters and Purnah getting kidnapped and eventually escaping again—but the point was that Aunt Lucy had ended up in charge of a strange girl who happened to be a princess from a tiny country in the middle of nowhere. Even Aunt Lucy understood that escaped princesses aren't like stray kittens or lost puppies; you can't just keep them and give them a new name. So she had written to the authorities.

Princess Purnah was the daughter of the late Mir of Chiligrit, a tiny mountain kingdom in the middle of Asia. Anything to do with Chiligrit came under the India Office because Chiligrit was nearer to India than to London. Emmaline had looked it up in the *Encyclopaedia Britannica*:

Chiligrit: small country of Central Asia, under the high Frizzibuttok Mountains. Population: unknown.

*Area: never surveyed. Religion: an ancient pagan faith
with many gods, mostly angry. Ruled by hereditary
"Mir." Economy based on rearing sheep and bandit
raids. Chiligrit lies in a poorly mapped region where
the borders of Russia, India, Tibet and Norway are
unclear. It is believed that mountain passes not shown
on existing maps may lead from Russian outposts to
the north into Chiligrit, and then on to India via
Yargarwar and H'rippp. In recent years the royal
family have been involved in much bloodshed
between rival princes, and foreign influences have
been believed to be behind these events.*

The account went on to describe the country itself—
"mountainous, with deep valleys and ravines"—and the
climate, which was "sub-zero during the winter months;
extremely hot and dry in summer; and a brief but not
completely unpleasant spring and autumn." The language
was a variant of something called "Rootitooti," though
some people spoke ancient tribal dialects that nobody
outside their own valley could comprehend, and the
rulers of the whole region talked to one another in
Persian. (Emmaline thought they probably needed a way
of threatening each other with kidnappings and
strangulation.) There was a list of names of Mirs of the
past fifty years, which were things like Garottee and
Muchclubbo; all of them had been murdered by
somebody they had known their whole lives, usually
because they had the same grandmother.

Emmaline had looked up Chiligrit in the old leather-
bound atlas in the study. It was about the size of a toenail,
had no towns, rivers or anything with names listed, and
seemed to consist of three mountains, four valleys and a few
ravines and gorges to throw your enemies into.

It seemed like a dreadful place. Princess Purnah planned

on reconquering it as soon as she could muster an army. So far she had recruited Rubberbones and Stanley.

Aunt Lucy had written to the India Office about what to do. She was happy to keep Princess Purnah, of course, but she thought that there might be relatives who had no intention of strangling the girl. And there were "political considerations." Emmaline wasn't sure what that really meant, but it had to do with Purnah's late father (beloved, but still strangled), her wicked uncles, her despicable cousins and the Russians.

The India Office had written back to say that an official was coming on Friday.

And this was Thursday.

———⟨⟩———

Emmaline watched the men from the India Office as they sat stiffly at attention. The first was short and stout and cheerful; the other was tall and thin and looked as if he'd just dropped his wallet down a drain. They wore black frock coats, striped trousers and silk cravats. It was the short man who spoke.

"Ah, Mrs. Butterworth, I presume! Excellent! I am Mr. White; this is my colleague, Mr. Black. We've come to take care of Princess Purnah."

"Take care of?" said Aunt Lucy.

"Yes. Take charge of. Make arrangements for. Proper arrangements. Foreign royalty. Yes."

Mr. Black, who seemed to Emmaline more like a skinny bloodhound than a human being, uncoiled himself to his full height. He was as tall as the room itself. He didn't say a word.

"Gentlemen, I apologize for my rudeness. Please take a seat. I shall arrange for some refreshments." Aunt Lucy rang a bell for Lal Singh.

"Er, is this young lady our princess?" asked Mr. White,

smiling at Emmaline. In truth, Emmaline did not look like a princess from a wild mountain kingdom in Central Asia. Then again, Emmaline knew that in the far northern parts of India, there were people with blue eyes, pale skin and red hair. Aunt Lucy ignored the question as Lal Singh entered, bearing a tea tray. Emmaline noticed that the tea smelled funny, and the cake was the leftovers of Aunt Lucy's most recent experiments with dandelions and slugs, which even Rab had not been able to finish.

Lal Singh loomed impressively. Aunt Lucy asked, "Cake, gentlemen? And a nice cup of tea?"

Aunt Lucy made sure each got a big chunk of cake, strong on slugs, and a delicate little cup of tea that smelled like something the sea had washed up. Emmaline wondered for a moment whether Lal Singh had decided to poison the visitors. She decided he wouldn't do that. But he might want to make them … uncomfortable. Yes, that would be it.

"Very nice," said Aunt Lucy as she sipped the tea. "My own special blend."

Mr. White took a big swig of tea, spluttered, tried to swallow it and finally collapsed into a fit of coughing. Mr. Black took a sip and turned slightly green.

Emmaline simply swirled her tea around in the cup.

Aunt Lucy leaned forward. "Do tell me about your plans, gentlemen."

Mr. White replied, "We intend to make sure that Princess Purnah receives the finest, ah, lodging and education that the taxpayers' money can provide. She will be treated according to her royal status and trained in the manners and protocols suitable for a future queen. I can assure you, madam, that Princess Purnah—the future Mirana of Chiligrit, as she will be known—will be nurtured, cosseted and treated with the utmost—"

"Of course, Mr. White. You say that she will be, what did you say, 'Mirana,' of this odd little country?"

"Yes. The female form of 'Mir,' which is the title her late father held. All the male heirs are deceased or missing or being held hostage somewhere, so Princess Purnah is the legal heiress. And you must appreciate that Chiligrit is not simply an 'odd little country' as you put it. Although small, isolated and backward beyond belief, Chiligrit stands at the head of the Skafrizbum pass, which connects with the outposts of the Russian empire. If the Russians control Chiligrit, they have an easy route to invade India. At present, the murdered Mir's uncle Bakkistabbo sits on the throne. He is in cahoots with the Russians. But the people of Chiligrit hate him and want their lawful ruler back. That being Princess Purnah."

Emmaline had looked at the maps. What he said was true.

"But the princess knows that, of course," said Mr. White, looking at Emmaline with an oily sort of smile. So he *did* think she was Purnah.

"Er, yes," replied Aunt Lucy. "Of course, she doesn't really speak much English, you know. Mostly just threats of one kind and another."

Emmaline took this as her cue. If they thought that she was Princess Purnah, that was what she'd be. She put on her best impression of Purnah's voice.

"Chiligrit good place! Those pigs of Hoolgar! Those goat-stealers of Rootitooty! I curses them alls!"

Mr. White looked a little surprised. Mr. Black's jaw dropped.

"I see what you mean, Mrs. Butterworth. I must admit, I expected the princess to look more, um, eastern. Perhaps more Indian."

"It's the English clothes and hair. And the corsets. Corsets make you look different. I am against them myself. If she were wearing Indian clothes she'd look quite Indian, I'm sure. And Chiligrit is not in India, Mr. White. It's just on the same page of the atlas. At the top, near the page number."

"Glekk!" shouted Emmaline. She was enjoying herself. Mr. Black dropped his plate.

"More tea and cake?" asked Aunt Lucy. She seized Mr. White's cup and poured tea into it. She forced another piece of cake into Mr. Black's hands. Mr. White took another sip, very cautiously indeed.

"This tea is very good for you," announced Aunt Lucy. "Cleanses the bladder. Most people don't have very clean bladders, you know."

Mr. White turned bright red and, in an effort to swallow, began coughing uncontrollably. Mr. Black's hand was trembling as he held his piece of cake. Emmaline couldn't resist the chance to point out a really big slug protruding from the side of the slice where Mr. Black hadn't noticed it.

"Lookkee! Nice big slug, Mr. Black! Chewee!"

Mr. Black turned white, and the cake fell from his fingers.

———

Rubberbones stepped silently out the side door and into the bushes. It was useful that the garden was so desperately overgrown. Even without leaves on the trees, there were enough evergreen bushes and ditches to conceal a lad who wore mostly old, muddy clothing and only washed his face when he was specifically told to. Rab crawled through the garden on all fours. He knew right away that he was not alone.

For a start, Stanley was right behind him. He should have made sure the door was closed properly. Stanley was not the creeping sort of dog. He was the "rushing about like a mad thing" sort of dog.

But that wasn't it. There were people around. Strangers.

There was a man by the old stone wall, watching the upper stories of the house. There was another across the road, smoking a pipe.

Rubberbones moved carefully around the edge of the garden, toward the hollow places at the bottom of the hill. In his twelve years in and around Lower Owlthwaite, Rab had spent a lot of time hiding from gamekeepers, running from dogs, farmers and bulls, and generally living the life of a frontiersman. He was like Davy Crockett, only small and not dead, and with a Yorkshire accent.

At the foot of the hill, hidden from the house, was a coach and team of four horses. It wasn't the sort of thing you saw every day, being a closed-in coach with shiny varnish and glossy paintwork, and the most beautiful black horses, all matching. The driver, in a top hat and fancy long coat, sat on the high seat. Rab crept closer.

Until this point, Stanley had behaved perfectly. He seemed to think that Rubberbones was playing a game where the rules involved being very quiet and slinking about under cover. So he was playing, too. But seeing the horses was too much for him. Stanley loved horses. He wanted to run over to them, to frisk alongside, to pass the time of day with them. So he did. Yipping and panting, he rushed from the bushes.

The horses reacted to the small dog racing toward them by whinnying in complaint; their reaction stirred the driver back into life. He called out to calm them. "Settle down, my beauties!" He gave Stanley a dirty look. "You clear off, flippin' mongrel!"

A hand pulled back one of the curtains inside the coach. A white shape appeared at the window, scowling. Rab, hunched motionless behind a tree, turned pale. He could feel his knees weaken. He felt his throat tighten.

It was the Faceless Fiend.

CHAPTER 8

The Faceless Fiend Foiled Again

Aunt Lucy let the two visitors settle down once again. Emmaline could see that she was enjoying this chance to torment these shifty men who were surely not who they claimed to be.

"I'd very much like her Royal Majesty to stay with me. She seems to be happy here. We have a private tutor—an American gentleman, Professor Bellbuckle, very scientific—and the fresh air and good food will do wonders for her." Emmaline tried to stifle a giggle at this last suggestion.

Mr. White sucked in his cheeks. "Ah, no, dear lady. Can't have that. Policies and procedures. No, we'll take her away immediately. Perfect place already arranged. If you could get her belongings—if she has any, for I know she left that school in rather unusual circumstances—we'll be off right away. Of course, you can write to her. We'll make sure you have the address."

"Oh," said Aunt Lucy brightly. "I'm not sure she's here. She might be off on … on a nature walk with the professor. She adores nature walks."

Mr. Black's jaw dropped. Again. Mr. White pointed at Emmaline. "But this is—"

"Oh, no. This is my niece Emmaline. I can't imagine you

really thought that Emmaline was a Chiligriti princess. I mean, does she look Chiligriti? No more than I do."

"But you said—"

"Don't be silly, Mr. White. Have another cup of tea, and I shall ask Lal Singh to look for dear Princess Purnah."

"But she spoke like the princess—in some sort of eastern gibberish!"

"That's a very unkind way of referring to the beautiful Chiligriti language." Aunt Lucy frowned. "We are all learning it and can curse one another quite comprehensively. I am surprised that the India Office permits you to be so disparaging of the many lovely tongues spoken throughout our empire."

"Glekk! Porok! Harroomph!" added Emmaline.

Aunt Lucy rang the bell once again.

———

Lal Singh did not seem surprised by what Rubberbones had to tell him. The professor listened, dumbfounded at the villainy of it all.

"Why, I have a good mind to tell 'em off and send 'em away with a flea in their ears. It's a danged dirty low trick!"

Lal Singh replied, "I do not think that they are willing to go away with fleas in ears. There are at least six men outside who wish harm upon blessed majesty Princess Purnah. Deceit and trickery will serve us better than combating them directly."

"I was good at fisticuffs in my schooldays," said the professor obstinately. His little beard stuck out and he looked quite fierce.

"I once captured a hill fort in Waziristan with only a shovel and a pointed stick," said Lal Singh. "But still I am proposing trickery and deceit."

Rubberbones thrilled to hear this mention of heroism on the far frontiers by a younger Lal Singh—Rab thought it was probably before he became a butler, but decided this was not the time to ask.

The kitchen door opened, and a small boy in ill-fitting, muddy clothes came in. His cap looked a lot like Rab's own cap. This was because it *was* Rab's own cap. Beneath the brim, Princess Purnah grinned savagely, her eyes glowing like hot coals.

"Lookit mee! I am Errand Boy from Yorkishire! Ey-oop, lad! I can bounce off the roof, see me—"

"Sh!!" whispered everyone.

"Oople!" said Princess Purnah, remembering that it wasn't all a big joke.

"Now," said Lal Singh. "Rab-sahib must put on the princess's own clothes."

Rubberbones was about to protest and Purnah to burst out laughing, but Professor Bellbuckle shushed them both and gestured for Rab to get on with it.

Lal Singh answered the bell from the front parlor as the youngsters went upstairs to dress Rubberbones in a bizarre impersonation of "an Eastern princess as English schoolgirl."

When Rab looked in the mirror, he was certain that nobody would think he was anything but a rather grubby youth dressed in a skirt, a straw hat and a dark pinafore thingy over the top. Nobody would say, "Look! That's Princess Purnah!" They'd say, "Has Rab lost a bet of some sort? What a fool he looks!"

Purnah thought so, too. Then an idea occurred to her.

"Why you dressing in my school clothes? You Chiligriti princess! Look like Chiligriti princess!"

So saying, she pulled the coverlet off her bed—an ornate piece of fabric in purple and blue—and threw it over Rab's head. She pulled down a curtain (red velvet, moth-eaten in spots), and soon Rab was swathed in a strange outfit that covered him from the top of his spiky hair to the bottom of his muddy boots. She used pins to hold it all together and wrapped a scarf around his waist three times to stop the whole thing from unraveling. As a finishing touch she found bangles and bracelets that actually were her own—"You looking after these or I cut your gizzard out! Pulkh!"

"I look a complete flippin' idiot," said Rab from under it all. His voice was muffled, and his whole face was concealed by the drapes in the bedspread.

"Yess!" Purnah shrieked with joy. "Always looking idiot! Now looking like what people in England thinking Chiligriti girl wearing. Ho ho!"

Rab looked at the princess in his cap and the scruffy boy's clothing. "You don't look nothing like me."

"I knowing that. Not ugly enough!" She stuck out her tongue and crossed her eyes. "And not near dirty enough!"

Just then the professor hurried into the room, and they

remembered this was no time to be playing. He looked serious. "Princess, you have to get to safety. There's six men out there who mean you no good."

"And a Faceless Fiend," added Rab helpfully from under his drapery.

"And a Faceless Fiend."

"You could go to my gran's house in t'village," suggested Rubberbones. "Number fourteen, Mill Street. Go down the High Street, turn left at the grocer's, fifth on the left. Tell her you're a friend of mine and need to come in until I get home."

Princess Purnah nodded thoughtfully as if she were memorizing the instructions.

Professor Bellbuckle was puzzled. "How is Her Majesty supposed to get past these dangerous men?"

"I attack them! I beat them down! I slice headses off and fight through to Granny Errand Boy's hut!"

"It's not a hut, it's an ordinary house," sighed Rab. "But don't be daft. You can't fight your way through. You've got to be sneaky."

"I can be most sneaky," asserted the princess.

"Just pretend to be me—an errand boy. Tell 'em you brought a note up from t'village about something. Keep your cap down over yer eyes and put yer 'ands in your pockets. Whistle a bit. And just walk past 'em."

"Where is the girl?" demanded Mr. White, looking at his pocket watch.

"Oh, you know these young girls," replied Aunt Lucy. "Probably packing everything she owns. Five suitcases and a trunk. Books, keepsakes, jewelry, letters from home, that sort of thing."

"I understood she ran away from school with just the clothes she was wearing?"

"Well, yes. But she's acquired all sorts of things since. You know these young girls. Clothes, books, jewel— "

"Yes, yes. Can't you hurry her along?"

"I'll go and see what she's doing," said Emmaline, standing up carefully. Her foot still hurt.

She went gingerly out into the hallway. Lal Singh nodded for her to go upstairs. Professor Bellbuckle was coming down. "I'll fetch some stuff from the workshop. Might come in useful."

Lal Singh looked at him sternly. "No fireworks inside the house, Professor."

The professor frowned a little.

Before she could climb the stairs, Emmaline met a small boy with dark, flashing eyes, attended by a piece of rolled-up drapery with feet. "Ey-oop, Miss Em," said the drapery in a muffled sort of way. It was descending the steps in little bunny hops.

"Into the hallway, Rab!" commanded Emmaline. She was the oldest, so she ought to be in charge. Anyway, Lal Singh was in the corridor, and he'd know what to do. At least, she hoped he did.

To Emmaline's relief, Lal Singh swiftly took control. "Rab-sahib, I will show you to our most unwelcome guests. Say nothing. As long as they believe that the princess is here, we chance to deceive them. Princess, peace be upon thee. You must flee. Be safe and we will recover yourself shortly."

"I can go with her," said the professor. "We'll walk down to Robert's granny's house. I can fend 'em off if we need to." There was a bulge under his arm that Rab assumed to be something dangerous and probably illegal. "Rab," the professor continued, taking something from his pocket. "Take this and tuck it away under your, er, curtains." It was the odd little device Rab had seen when they'd all got lost.

Some sort of radiophonic what-jer-mer-callit that hadn't worked.

"Er, thanks, Professor!" Well, it might work. Perhaps.

Lal Singh steered him toward the front parlor.

———

Emmaline looked out of the window to see the mad inventor and the "errand boy" walk toward the muddy lane to the village.

A man appeared from nowhere. Then another. They were talking to the professor. He pointed toward the church steeple, half a mile down the lane. They seemed to talk some more. Suddenly the "errand boy" attacked the nearest man with blows to the stomach and kicks to the shin and an effort at biting his arm off. The professor pulled something from his coat, and there was a puff of pink smoke. Then the pair raced back to the house.

———

"This is Princess Purnah," said Emmaline. "She doesn't speak English very well. She has only just begun to pack, and may be some while."

"Princess Purnah" lurked behind Emmaline so that she could barely be seen. Lal Singh managed to place himself so that he stood respectfully as a butler should, while at the same time blocking the draped figure from Mr. White and Mr. Black.

"What the deuce has she been up to all this time?" asked Mr. White, clearly annoyed at the delay.

"She is extremely religious and prays for an hour and a half. Nine times a day," replied Emmaline. "She always faces toward the shrine of the God of Fierceness, Stikko, in, ah, Yellunscream." She pointed firmly toward the kitchen. "Yellunscream is that way."

Rab thought he ought to confirm this, so he made a gargling noise under his curtain.

"And now we will pack," said Emmaline. "Probably an hour at the most." They went upstairs.

The professor and the "errand boy" were quarreling in the upstairs hallway. "I can't believe you attacked that man!" hissed Professor Bellbuckle.

"He disrespectful to me! I Chiligriti princess!"

"Consarnit, Princess Purnah, Your Blasted Majesty. He thought you were a boy from the village. He offered you a piece of candy. You fooled him good, right until you started screaming and punching and kicking!"

The princess snorted. Emmaline could see that she realized she had made a mistake. But princesses do not admit mistakes.

"What to do, then?" asked Rubberbones from under his swaddling. The professor smiled. "Kites!" he replied.

"Excuse me," said Emmaline, not liking the sound of this. "You mean my experimental kites?"

"Why, yes," beamed the professor. "I brought 'em upstairs when we came in. Princess Purnah, you and I are going flying!"

"Fantastic!" said Rubberbones from under his haberdashery.

"Trikk! Folocky Gripp!" said the princess incomprehensibly.

"Oh, no," said Emmaline. "No!"

"You can come, too!" said the professor. "That leg's almost better, isn't it?"

"This is mad!" said Emmaline, shaking her head. "You are going to take two kites, which only Rubberbones can fly, and somehow escape from these people—who are these people, anyway—by sailing away from here?"

"Three kites," corrected the professor. "We mustn't leave out Stanley!"

And so, five minutes later, three kites appeared to hurl themselves off the roof of Mad Mrs. Butterworth's house. If you had been watching the house—and there were several burly men doing just that—you would have seen one of them plummet almost immediately into the trees below. You would have seen one of them, apparently barking, float over your head. And you would have seen the third catch a gust of wind and soar into the gray November sky and off toward the distant woods.

"Criminy! Tarnation!" complained Professor Bellbuckle. "I just fell like a stone."

Which was what Emmaline had expected, really. But it wasn't the professor she was worried about.

CHAPTER 9

Things Go Wrong — A Lot

"Is that blasted girl ready to go, or not?" demanded Mr. White once again. "It's been three hours."

Aunt Lucy looked at Emmaline. Emmaline looked at Lal Singh. Lal Singh looked at Aunt Lucy. None of them had thought this part through.

"Ah, yes. Mr. White, I've thought it over," replied Aunt Lucy. "And I have decided that the princess will stay here with us. Thank you for your kind offer, but we are going to keep her. Sorry for the inconvenience and all that."

A nasty—well, a nastier—edge came into Mr. White's voice. "I didn't suggest that it was a matter of choice for you, Mrs. Butterworth. We are taking the princess with us. Our carriage is outside."

"I must make myself clear," replied Aunt Lucy. "You will leave my house immediately, without the princess. You can each have a piece of cake to take with you, though. I'm not an unreasonable person."

Mr. Black uncoiled himself from his chair. "Let's grab the girl!" he barked. This was the first thing he'd said.

Mr. White began to scramble out of his seat. A firm hand pushed him back down again. Lal Singh had moved silently behind him.

Mr. Black tried to push his way past Aunt Lucy. The widow stood her ground. "Get out of my way, you stupid woman!" yelled Mr. Black. He raised his hand as if to slap her. Aunt Lucy raised her teapot, newly filled with a fresh, hot brew of the disgusting liquid, and poured it carefully down his shirtfront. He screamed.

"That was very rude of you, Mr. Black." She poured the rest of it over his head as he hopped about tugging his clothes, hot tea scalding his skin. "Very rude, indeed."

Lal Singh thought so, too. He continued to pin Mr. White to the chair with a steel grip. The short man had not been rude yet, but Lal Singh sensed that poor manners were only moments away.

Emmaline was astonished. She'd never seen anything like this before.

"Stop gawking, Emmaline!" shouted Aunt Lucy. "And get the princess out of here!" She had now broken the teapot over Mr. Black's head, which showed how serious things were. It was a valuable antique teapot. It was not an everyday sort of breaking-over-visitors'-heads teapot.

Emmaline started from the parlor, hopping a little on her good foot and using one crutch. "Run!" she shouted to Rubberbones, who stood behind the scullery door in his wrappings.

"I can't run in this lot!" he replied. "I can't hardly walk."

"Bellbuckle to the rescue!" shouted a voice from the kitchen. "Come this way!"

Princess Purnah was screaming loudly as the howling west wind buffeted the kite far across the sky. The gales of November blew strongly.

"Harroo! Porok! Glekk! Glekk! Glekk!"

The princess decided that when she took her rightful place on the throne of Chiligrit, all her uncles and cousins would be forced to fly in kites just like this one.

The relatives she *really* didn't like, well, she'd have the kites set on fire as they were pushed off the palace roof. She was going to do that bit herself. Oh, yes.

A strange machine whirred outside the back door. It was the size of an open carriage and had started life as one. But most of the body of the vehicle was filled with a huge steam boiler, a brass funnel and an engine with pistons and rods and revolving gears. It was a sensational machine. It would have been the most marvelous invention of, say, 1794. It was unlucky that it was actually 1894, and other inventors were building machines that weren't so … strange.

"The Bellbuckle Steam Carriage, Mark II," announced the inventor. "Not ready quite yet. This is a test!!"

Rubberbones shuffled to the side of the contraption and just managed to topple forward into the open cockpit.

A determined-looking man rushed into the yard. "Stop right there!" he yelled. The professor leapt into the machine and hauled on the levers and cranks. The machine bucked into activity, and strange devices whirled about with enthusiasm. Smoke burped out of the funnel. The man grabbed for the carriage.

Emmaline, hobbling across the yard with her crutch, had been shocked by the sudden violence that had burst into her quiet country life. But it was only right to join in activities, so she hooked the top end of her crutch around the beefy man's ankle and hauled back. He went over like a drunken sailor, one hand flailing against the boiler as he fell.

"Aaagggh!" he cried.

"Don't touch that. It's hot," replied the professor.

Emmaline scrambled over the side into the cockpit, and the machine started forward. They turned out of the courtyard and down the driveway, only to see another burly fellow rushing at them, yelling, "Stop right there!"

The professor was pulling levers and twirling handles so he wasn't about to stop. Indeed, Emmaline wasn't sure whether the machine had any brakes—they were something Professor Bellbuckle would have installed only if someone had ordered him to. She swiveled around to see Mr. White running after them, with Aunt Lucy on his heels throwing dinner plates. He kept on running, his stumpy little legs pumping despite the crashing around him. Mr. Black followed, with Lal Singh in pursuit, smacking him fiercely with an embroidered cushion.

Then the steaming contraption was bouncing along the lane toward Lower Owlthwaite. A narrow, muddy lane with a high bank on the right and a deep ditch to the left. Firmly in the middle of it stood the largest, beefiest, most muscle-bound man of all.

Suddenly the hulking brute was attacked by a large brown paper parcel. It launched itself at his ankles, and he kicked at it. It hurled itself upward at his ample posterior; the giant slapped at it. But (because he was huge and the lane muddy) he tumbled into the ditch, trousers torn to reveal dimpled pink buttocks. He shouted phrases that we won't repeat here, and even over the sound of the coughing, wheezing engine, Emmaline was embarrassed. Then, as the steam carriage plunged onward at a sizzling ten or twelve miles per hour, the large brown paper parcel leapt up into the cockpit.

"Woof!" announced the parcel. The brown paper had ripped away from the wooden frame, and Emmaline realized it was the remains of a kite. Stanley peered out of the wreckage, held in place only by some string that had caught around his middle.

Rubberbones looked out of his wrappings. "Hello, Stanley. I wondered where you'd got off to." He looked around. "Can I take off these togs now?"

The professor turned around at the controls, almost upsetting the machine. "I'd keep 'em on, son. Just for a while yet."

Emmaline agreed. "They might have another man out here. The longer they think you are Purnah, the better for the real princess."

The sound of galloping hoofbeats in the rhythm of a well-trained team came from behind. It was a thing of beauty. A thing of terror. A coach and horses, racing down the lane toward them.

Her Royal Majesty was unhappy. She was alone, stuck in a tree. There was a kite wrapped around her, broken and tangled. This was disrespectful to her position as a royal princess. The mad professor who had promised her safety and his company as her servant—or something like that—had dropped to the earth like a stone, without her consent. Even the little dog "Stan-leee," whom she liked despite his being a filthy, unclean animal not fit for a princess to have dealings with, had not escorted her on her passage through the heavens.

Not really "the heavens," she thought. But certainly, above the ground with wind and rushing and hanging on very tight indeed. The kite not doing anything she ordered it to, like going to the house of Errand Boy's ancestor in the nasty English village, but transporting her wildly into the forest. Where there might be wolves. Bears. Or wild chickens. Purnah did not mind wolves and bears, but chickens were accursed creatures in her homeland.

She reached into the coat she had taken from Errand Boy and pulled out a blade, a simple, English buttery-toast sort of knife, ground sharp against a brick. She cut away the brown paper so she could see. Glekk! How many trees were there? In Chiligrit there were only some nasty pointy evergreen trees at the bottom of steep ravines, just right for impaling your foes. And there were apricot trees in little orchards. Purnah licked her lips at this thought and decided she was hungry. She wielded the knife deftly, slicing the kite into pieces like a goat for the stewpot. It fell away into the undergrowth.

Purnah peered around, looking for bears or chickens or horrid men who were after her for reasons she didn't know. Not that this worried her. When you were a Chiligriti princess, you came to expect enemies at every turn. England was normally very dull in this respect.

The princess was used to climbing mountains, but trees were something new, and she had only managed to swing a few feet, like some form of royal monkey, when she fell.

"Glekk! Turok!" cursed Purnah, dusting herself off and deciding to kill something woodlandish for dinner.

CHAPTER 10

In Which Things Get Even Worse

"Go faster!" shouted Emmaline. The coach was galloping toward them, outpacing the professor's steam oddity. "Go faster!" mumbled Rubberbones through his layers of muffling. "Woof!" barked Stanley, which meant the same thing. And the professor was *trying* to go faster.

The problem was he hadn't designed the steam carriage to go faster. Not faster than a sleek team of fine horses pulling a superbly built coach at full gallop. The law in Great Britain was still that a horseless carriage could not go faster than a walking man, and that there should actually *be* a walking man—with a nice red flag—in front of it as it puttered about the highways and byways. So the fleet twelve miles an hour that they were doing—downhill, with the wind behind them—was actually a rapid, tearaway pace for this sort of vehicle. And illegal, as well.

Still the coach came closer. Rubberbones recalled the time he and the princess had escaped pursuit from cruel teachers riding a giant bicycle, a "trilocopede," by throwing provisions at them from the back of a delivery van. But this time there was nothing to throw, and he was wrapped so tightly he could barely move his arms. The professor was wrestling with the controls. "Gosh-darn it! The pressure's rising in the boiler and the steering handle's come loose in my hand!" Indeed, the handle had broken off completely, and the professor waved it about helplessly.

"Brakes!" yelled Emmaline.

"Yes, indeedy!" shouted Professor Bellbuckle as he pulled at a lever. "Can you release the drag boot?"

Emmaline had no idea what a drag boot might be and looked around frantically.

Not that it mattered either way, because the lane took a sharp right turn a whisker ahead, and everyone knew that without a steering handle it was just a few moments before disaster struck.

"Aaagh!" screamed the professor as the vehicle lunged forward into a hedge, plunged through it, spun around in midair and landed in a soggy part of a ploughed field.

"Eeekkhh!" cried Emmaline as the carriage teetered from one side to another.

"Woof!" added Stanley as his vocabulary was limited.

Nothing came from Rab because he was nowhere to be seen. One moment he was wrapped up like an Egyptian mummy in the back of the conveyance—and then he was gone!

Princess Purnah looked at the tree. Again. It was the same tree she had examined fifteen minutes before. They all appeared the same in this cursed English forest. At least when she was up the tree, she had known where she was. Porok!

She carved a symbol, mystical in her mountain kingdom, on the tree in front of her. Then she retraced her footsteps, slashing that same symbol on every fourth tree. She had a great deal to say about it all: "Tlokk! Haroki Pilchit Gasoma Porrik Porik!"

But I can't tell you what that means until you are twenty-one.

Rubberbones couldn't get up. He tried to move his arms and failed. The Chiligriti princess costume had become a prison. Somehow the combination of bedspread, curtains and scarf had wrapped around him so tightly as to swallow him whole. He couldn't see a thing because the cloth completely covered his face. Flippin' 'eck.

From somewhere in the distance, muffled by the drapery, he could hear their voices. The professor's American drawl. Emmaline's sensible tones, even when she was screaming. Stanley's yap. But the voice he heard now was chilling. It was Mr. Brown.

"Pick her up and put her in the box. And do be careful, Number Three. She may be a dashed nuisance as far as you are concerned, but there are people in high places who do not wish her to come to any harm. Not today, anyway."

Rough hands seized Rab, lifted him up and then deposited him inside something long and narrow. And, with the squeak of wheels and the clatter of hoofbeats, he was moving.

Purnah had made a bow. It was just a bent stick with a kite-string tied between the ends and a smaller, sharpened stick as the arrow. People in Chiligrit didn't use bows much anymore. They liked a type of big, old-fashioned musket called a "jezail," which you paid the local blacksmith to make or, better still, stole from your friends and neighbors. Then you loaded it with a big lead ball like the egg of a Fhnorkk bird and sat on the roof of your hut (or palace) and shot at those friends and neighbors as they went about their daily chores. Happy days!

Princess Purnah choked back a wail, but Chiligriti princesses don't cry; she decided to find something to shoot instead.

Professor Bellbuckle stood next to his steam carriage, and he *was* crying. Not for the machine, which had sunk up to its fenders in the mud, but because he had no idea what to do next. He hadn't felt this bad since the day he'd blown up his family's ancestral home.

Emmaline looked at the wreck. Where was Rubberbones?

Had he been flung from the carriage? Had he been captured? She knew, instinctively, that he had. This was very bad, indeed. Stanley set up a pitiful howl for his missing friend.

She was heartened to see the dogcart, with Lal Singh and Aunt Lucy, coming down the hill. "We'll get it all sorted out," Emmaline assured the blubbering professor. But she had no idea how.

—————

Rubberbones was worried. He was a bit concerned by how things were turning out. He seemed to be in a coffin with airholes drilled in the top. He couldn't hear much through the plush padding, but he knew that he had been hoisted onto the top of the coach and strapped down to stop the box from falling off the roof as the vehicle moved. Mostly he could hear the wind as the coach galloped along, and the horses clip-clopping on a cobbled road as they left behind the muddy surface of the country lanes. The motion bounced him around inside the box, which made it more confusing. Of course, it was pitch black. He had no idea where the coach was going or who the Faceless Fiend really was or what the Fiend would do when he found out that the body in the coffin was not Princess Purnah. He might laugh and hand the boy sixpence for playing such a hilarious practical joke on him. But that seemed unlikely.

But even though it was frightening, Rab told himself, he didn't have to turn to jelly. He'd see what turned up and act as seemed best. It would be all right, he told himself.

Still, that Faceless Fiend . . .

—————

Rubberbones was gone. Aunt Lucy and Lal Singh had watched the boy being captured and taken away by the coach, too distant for them to prevent it. Now they must save the missing princess. Lal Singh had taken Stanley out toward the woods beyond Lower Owlthwaite in the hope of scenting Purnah. She'd last been spotted drifting in that direction. The girl had to be found tonight, before darkness set in.

Professor Bellbuckle remained at the house with warnings not to use fireworks indoors. He planned on firing some rockets off as signal flares if Purnah hadn't returned before nightfall. This was actually a good idea, and Lal Singh had looked at him oddly, as if he hadn't expected something so sensible from the American scientist.

Aunt Lucy and Emmaline were at the village police station. Constable Skelp was a kindly man, as wide as he was tall, but not known for his keen grasp of information.

"Mrs. Butterworth, you mean to tell me you have mislaid two children?"

"Yes, Constable. Lost separately this afternoon."

"Separately? That seems a touch careless, if you don't mind my saying so, ma'am. Losing one is a bit unfortunate, but two—well, seems like you wasn't watching 'em well enough. I gets me eldest, Sarah, to keep an eye on the little 'uns— "

Aunt Lucy had already told him the story, with much left out or made simpler. You can't just tell a village bobby that foreign agents have tried to abduct the eastern princess you have staying at your home but have ended up kidnapping your errand boy in a mix-up involving the upstairs curtains. It sounds crazy. So Aunt Lucy had told a shortened version in which Purnah (being a stranger to the village) had wandered off and Rab had been taken away on top of a coach, in a box. Some sort of game he was playing. The coachman must not have realized Rubberbones was there. All the same, he was twelve years old, trapped inside the luggage and had last been seen traveling at a fast clip.

"Ah, the lad's probably fine," said the constable. "Stuck in a trunk by accident. Happens to everybody. No, he'll turn up. Probably have to walk back from Grimethorpe!"

Emmaline thought that if Rab had to walk back from

anywhere, it was better than being a prisoner of the Faceless Fiend. But she couldn't tell the constable that.

"And the other young 'un, the girl. Friend of Miss Emmaline's from school, you say?"

"Ah, yes," replied Aunt Lucy. "She doesn't know this area at all. She doesn't know England, really. She's from a place called—"

"France," said Emmaline, thinking it wasn't a good idea to let everyone know who her missing friend was and where she came from. "She's French. Only speaks a bit of English. Her name is … Glecque!" she announced as inspiration struck her. "G-L-E-C-Q-U-E. A common name in France. You say it 'Glekk.' Her last name is Poroque. P-O-R-O-Q-U-E." Emmaline knew that if she told the policeman that Purnah was a Chiligriti princess, word would get back to the Fiend's underlings and ruin the plan. Although it seemed ruined enough already.

"Oh, yes," said Constable Skelp. "Funny names them foreigners got. We'll get some people out looking for her. Though we might have to wait 'til morning to get a proper search going."

Next they made their way to Rab's gran's house, walking slowly, as Emmaline was trying to get about without the crutch. She knew where the house was, but she'd never actually been there. Emmaline felt ashamed about this; Rubberbones was her friend, yet she had never seen his house or met his grandmother. And now she was going to tell her that Rab had been kidnapped.

It was a narrow brick house, two rooms upstairs and two down. Aunt Lucy rapped on the knocker.

"Mrs. Burns?" she called out. "I am Mrs. Butterworth. I am here about Robert."

A woman with white hair and a lined face opened the door. "What's that little monkey been up tae, then? Is he making a mischief of himsel'? Ah tell't him tae mind his manner around the gentry—people like yersels. Ye are ower-payin' him, ah don't mind telling ye, if ye dinnae ken that already."

She was a mite Scottish. Emmaline wasn't sure what Mrs. Burns was saying, but Aunt Lucy seemed to understand.

"No," replied Aunt Lucy. "He's not making a mischief of himself. The fact is, he's been abducted. Taken away by, ah, bad people who think he is somebody else."

"Ach, away wi' ye, Mrs. Butterworth. Yon laddie's always takin' aff. He's probably oot in the braes. He'll gang hame right soon, mark my words."

Mrs. Burns picked up a plump tortoiseshell cat. "Prudence wants her supper. She aye lets me know. Ye'd best come in the hoose."

They followed her into the hoose—sorry, the house. It was scrubbed clean as a pin, and there were sepia-toned photographs on the mantelpiece of people frowning at the camera in their Sunday best clothes. In one of them, a mother and father sat proudly with two small boys and three daughters, one an infant. The older boy was perhaps seven years old. Emmaline instantly recognized the freckled face of Rab. She knew just a little about Rab's parents. His mother was a Londoner who had married Rab's father and moved to this village in the north. When her husband had run away from home (to make a fortune that somehow never materialized), she had taken the younger children and gone back to her family in the city. Rab had stayed with his grandmother to help her out, so he said. Emmaline knew that he sent some of his earnings every week to his mother and gave the rest to his gran.

It brought a lump to her throat.

"Mrs. Burns, my name's Emmaline. Rab may have mentioned me to you. What my aunt says is true. Rab was disguised as ... well, as an eastern princess, and these men believed that he was the princess, and they are chasing the princess, and they took him instead. By mistake. We are doing everything we can to bring him back."

Mrs. Burns continued to stroke the cat, but her face seemed to grow pale.

"Och," she said. "Will ye let me know any news as soon as ye get it?"

"I promise," said Emmaline. "As soon as we hear."

————

Purnah recognized where she was. At least, she recognized the great oak tree where she and her friends had taken shelter on the night — it seemed ages ago! Turok! — that it had rained so much. She scrambled up what looked like a pile of rocks and fallen branches to avoid a muddy patch. Looking carefully, she realized it was the remains of an old shed. Then she tumbled through the roof.

But it was only a short fall, and there was moss underneath. And she had found a piece of chocolate in the pocket of Rab's coat. Hrriing!

————

Lal Singh had returned with Stanley, muddy and wet. They'd found no trace of Princess Purnah. Both were hoarse, one from shouting, the other from barking. It was dark, and a cold rain had set in. Professor Bellbuckle had fired off rockets at five-minute intervals to help the princess find her way home. It was to no avail, but he shot fireworks off until he ran out. Wearily and with hearts cast low, everyone went to bed. They'd be up early to start the search. Both searches.

Rubberbones could tell a little of what was going on. They had reached a railway station. He could hear the rattle of trains and the steam whistling. The coach had been wheeled inside a railway carriage. Rab could hear the squeak of wheels and feel the pull of gravity as the vehicle mounted a ramp.

Then they were off, headed in an unknown direction. And going quite fast, it seemed to Rab. He'd been on a train once in his life, to visit his other grandmother in London in the days when his parents were together. He'd been about eight, which seemed a very long time ago. But he remembered the sounds and the smells. Like every other boy in the world, he'd watched, fascinated, as trains passed by. He knew, for instance, that the nearest station was Grimethorpe Halt, and this was probably where they'd boarded the train.

Not that this changed anything, of course. But Rab told himself that he might have a chance at escape, and if he did, it would be good to have an idea of where he was.

Even though he was worried stiff, the rhythm of the train worked its magic. Rubberbones fell asleep.

CHAPTER 11

Things Don't Improve Much

Princess Purnah awoke as the morning light streamed through the hole she'd made when she fell through the roof of the abandoned shed.

"G'terkk!" she said to herself. She had slept soundly, huddled down with Rab's cap as a pillow and his shirt collar pulled up over her head. Still, a Chiligriti princess must not sleep late, alone in the great forests with only a butter knife, a bow and a piece of chocol—no, she'd eaten that. Turokk! She'd wash her face in a stream, shoot a buffalo for breakfast and walk through the woods to Auntilucy's house. She could find it today, doubtless. England was surrounded by water, so she would simply walk to the edge of the island and march around it until she found the house. She'd have to watch out while passing her old school—she had set fire to it, and the teachers might want vengeance—but, aside from that, it would be easy. And there'd be English peasants who would be honored to assist her. It would bring joy into their sad, peasanty lives to help a royal princess.

Or perhaps she'd go to the hut of Errand Boy's grand-mother. Purnah didn't understand exactly who these people were she'd had to run away from. No doubt it was some sort of plot against her. Every Chiligriti prince or princess knew to run from bandits, assassins and uncles. Yes, perhaps Errand Boy's aged ancestor would hide her in her mud hovel.

Then she heard the sound of human voices. Purnah did what any sensible person would do. She fitted the arrow into the string of her homemade bow.

———◦◦◦———

The searchers had met at the Stick and Ferret a little after dawn. The pub was serving beer already.

Constable Skelp had appointed himself as leader. Aunt Lucy and Emmaline stood next to him as the losers-of-the-missing-child. Professor Bellbuckle remained at the house (again forbidden to use fireworks indoors). Lal Singh and Stanley had gone in search of Rubberbones. The faithful servant had taken the dogcart and a hamper full of Aunt Lucy's sandwiches, which Emmaline knew he would feed to the first ducks he came across; Lal Singh was no fool.

Emmaline had surprised herself by addressing the assembly. "My friend doesn't speak much English because she's from—from France. You must call out her name, which is 'Glecque Poroque.' Perhaps she'll hear and reply."

The crowd thought about that for a moment. Some of them mouthed the odd-sounding words. Others mumbled about taking orders from a girl—a "lass," as they called her. But they decided it must be all right since she was the missing child's friend, even though they didn't really hold with foreigners coming to their village at all. Still, there was beer at breakfast-time, and you couldn't beat that, all agreed. Constable Skelp, full of cheerful self-importance, formed them into a long line at the edge of the trees, and the whole party advanced into the woodland shouting "Glekk! Porok!" in Yorkshire accents, while the dogs chased one another and forgot their mission.

Aunt Lucy seized Emmaline by the arm. "Why did you tell them that Purnah was a French girl called Glecque Poroque?" she asked in a whisper that could be heard fifty feet away. "I wondered that last night. I mean, it's not safe to let anyone know who she really is—those horrible men might still be around—but why such an outlandish name?"

"I thought if people called out in Chiligriti, she might reply. Come out of hiding."

"But couldn't they just say the Chiligriti words for 'Come out, Princess Purnah,' or something like that?"

"I don't know the words for that. I only know the things that Purnah shouts out when she's excited or angry, which is most of the time. I don't really know what they mean."

"I have always assumed they were curses, insults and threats of violence," said Aunt Lucy.

"Like when the professor says 'Criminy!' and 'Tarnation!' when he's upset?" replied Emmaline.

"Possibly, although they might be a bit more rude."

Emmaline hadn't really thought about that. Meanwhile, the village crowd continued through the woods, shouting possible curses, insults and threats of violence in a strange Asiatic tongue.

Princess Purnah was alert. There were people in the great forest. A band of brigands, no doubt. Or perhaps hunters, seeking wild beasts to slay and make vile English cookery out of.

The sound was coming closer. They seemed to be chanting. Perhaps they were monks. She remembered a procession of monks from Tibet coming through Chiligrit once. They were strange men from the high plateau to the east, followers of the Buddhist way. They had chanted. Something about "Ommmm," as she recalled. The good people of Chiligrit had thrown donkey dung at them. Lots of donkey dung. Donkey owners had come in from across the mountains and valleys to sell their extra manure. Purnah had not been allowed to throw donkey dung (being a member of the royal family), and the disappointment of that day stung her still.

She could make out what they were shouting. "Glekk! Porok!" Such savage accents! Barbarians! What a thing to shout in the presence of a princess!

Princess Purnah seized her bow. She would shoot down the chief of these intruders! That would show them, as their leader writhed in his death agonies! How they would rue the day they had insulted a princess of the house of Chiligrit.

Aha! Suddenly a thought struck her like a ball of donkey droppings! It was all a trick. Princess Purnah knew it, as any cunning and resourceful thirteen year old would. These bandits were deliberately trying to make her angry, so that she would reveal her hiding place by rushing out screaming bloody murder. That was what they wanted. Some might fall victim to her mighty wrath and homemade arrows, not to mention the scything blade of the butter knife, but others would seize her and bear her away in shackles and possibly chains with heavy steel balls, as she had seen in books.

But she would foil them. She would hide like a mountain urkkilbag—which is like a fox, but better in every way, and native to Chiligrit—when pursued by hounds. They would not find her!

The ruined hut was excellent cover. From a few feet away, it looked like a heap of forest debris, all fallen trees and bushy growths. Princess Purnah crept inside, deliberately pulling branches over the doorway behind her.

She peered through a chink in the wall. One of the bandits was close, a big man with a stick and a bottle of ale. He was poking the ground with his stick and swigging freely. He was very near, indeed. She could see his red, jowly face and smell his sweat and his beery breath. She held her own breath.

He looked like the nasty men who had been at Auntilucy's house earlier. But all English people looked alike, thought Purnah; you had to concentrate to tell one from another. He might be a completely different nasty man. If he came any closer, she'd shoot him. She only had

one arrow, so it would have to be a good shot. Princess Purnah drew the arrow back against the string, feeling it tighten. She aimed at his middle, his hugely protuberant stomach. It would be hard to miss. Just a step closer—

The man stepped back. Distant barking attracted his attention. He finished his beer and slung the empty bottle into the bushes. He poked his stick one last time in the leafless bushes next to the hut, turned and moved at what might have been a run—a very slow, waddling sort of run—back through the wood.

Princess Purnah let out a sigh of relief. She wasn't sure that shooting a man with her bow and arrow would have been easy to do. It was all well and good to chatter on about slayings and stranglings as if they were nothing—well, in her family, these things were actually quite common events—but to murder passers-by unawares was something else. She was glad to avoid it.

Besides, he was a very large man, far too big for her to drag into a ditch, and having a dead body lying around can be a nuisance. You had to be practical.

Rubberbones heard voices. A man and a woman.

"Number One will be back tonight?" said the woman.

"Yeah, on the Dover train. He'll take the boat over from Calais this afternoon and be 'ere before midnight," replied the male voice.

"What about the girl?"

"Oh, she 'ardly understands English. We don't need to worry about that." Rubberbones recognized the man's voice as that of a Londoner, a "cockney."

"No, I mean, we can't just leave her in that coffin. She's not a piece of luggage. She has human needs."

"Oh, yeah, right. I suppose so. Do you want to get 'er out, then?"

The coffin was opened with a certain amount of effort. Light streamed in, and Rab scrunched up his eyes in response.

"You can 'ardly tell there's a person in there, with all them clothes," said the man. "Ridiculous costume to be going about in."

"Be quiet," said the woman sharply. "She's a princess in her own country and deserves a bit of respect."

"Turok!" said Rubberbones through the layers of cloth. "Hey Ho Nonny No." These weren't real Chiligriti words, as I'm sure you can tell. Unlike Emmaline, who listened carefully, Rab had never bothered to remember the odd words that the princess sprinkled into her conversations. He was making them up as best he could.

"See what I mean?" said the man. "All foreign."

"Hush! The people who pay us are foreign, and you don't grumble when you take their money. Besides, who else would employ an old jailbird like you? Come on, my girl. Let's 'ave you out of there."

Rab needed some help to get out of the coffin, and he felt a little dizzy when he stood up. "Wee Willie Winkee!" he said. "Ilkely Moor Bah Tat."

"Probably wants something to eat and drink," said the woman. "And the lav, too."

Rab looked through the narrow slit between the layers of cloth that engulfed him. The woman was old, maybe forty, and tough-looking, somebody you didn't want to argue with. The man was a runty sort of fellow with big ears and greasy hair ending in mutton-chop whiskers. He looked embarrassed at the mention of "the lav"—the lavatory. Perhaps princesses weren't supposed to go. Rab needed to, though. The woman helped him toward an open door. He shut the door behind him in case she wanted to follow him in. "Pry-vitt!" he called out, and that might be a Chiligriti word, mightn't it?

It was a tall but tiny room with a water closet and washbasin. Above the basin was a small, high window, and it

was a moment's effort for Rab to climb up for a look outside. Through the panes he could glimpse a stone-flagged courtyard far below and red brick walls with tiny windows like the one he was peering through. The kind of windows that only opened a few inches. No way of escaping here, he thought.

"Are you all right, dear?" came the woman's voice.

"Wirrik a minick!" answered Rubberbones. He straightened his costume, looked into the mirror to make sure he appeared exotic, or at least tucked in, and that his face was mostly concealed by a wrap of bedspread. He found the professor's "experimental radiophonic device" inside his undershirt and pressed the buzzer that attached to the main handle part by a spring and a piece of rubber. As he expected, nothing happened. He'd have thrown the thing away, but it probably wouldn't flush down the lav, and his gran had told him off about doing that in the past. He missed his gran.

"Would you like breakfast?" asked the woman when Rab returned. She said it slowly and loudly. "What do princesses eat in your country?"

Rubberbones knew what this princess wanted to eat.

"Grokk! Wunting sossidges!"

And so the abducted princess was served a big plate of sausages with fried bread, a bowl of watery porridge and a mug of tea with sugar.

"They aren't supposed to eat sausages," said the man. "It's against their religion."

"Who? Princesses?"

"No, foreigners. I knew a foreign bloke as 'ud never touch a pork pie or a bit o' bacon."

"Don't worry. I know the butcher as sold them sausages. I bet it's mostly old 'orsemeat and a bit of sawdust."

Which put Rubberbones off, a little. Still, he wasn't supposed to understand English and, anyway, he was ravenous.

Emmaline was exhausted. She'd been out all day with the search party, which had grown smaller as the hours went by and people lost enthusiasm. Her injured foot hurt like mad. Constable Skelp was still busily encouraging the searchers, but even he had stopped shouting the name of the missing French schoolgirl.

"She's not here," said Aunt Lucy. "She must have taken off in another direction. If she'd been hurt, we would have found her by now. The woods aren't very big, really—just a few acres."

Or maybe, thought Emmaline, she was hiding. You never knew with Purnah.

CHAPTER 12

The Other Man from the Ministry

The professor did not answer the door when Aunt Lucy and Emmaline returned to the house. Somebody else did.

"Hello!" said a tall, thin man wearing goggle-like spectacles. "I let myself in—the door was open. I assumed you'd be back before long. Not been here long myself—took a cart to bring me from the station."

He stooped to peer at Emmaline. "You'd be the princess, then. How d'you do, Your Majesty?"

Emmaline was surprised at the number of people who seemed to think she was Princess Purnah. They looked nothing alike. "No, I am Emmaline Cayley. Who are you, sir?" she demanded.

"Botts. Winthrop Botts of the India Office. Here to inquire into the matter of Princess Purnah, heiress to the throne of Chiligrit, presently vacant. As arranged by letter, last week, with, ah, Mrs. Butterworth, who would be, ah, you!" He pointed at Aunt Lucy triumphantly, as if he had finally guessed correctly.

Aunt Lucy agreed that she was and invited herself into her own home. Mr. Botts followed her down the hallway. She turned on him. "I suppose you can prove you are who you say you are?"

"Yes, indeed, good lady. I carry proper identification on my person, should you care to inspect it."

"I do. Hand it over and be quiet a minute. You can sit down over there if you don't mind." Aunt Lucy was touchy, thought Emmaline. Evidently she was not happy to find yet another strange man in her home.

She examined his papers. "I suppose you are who you say, then."

"Why would you doubt that? I mean, who would possibly—"

"Two men yesterday with a group of their friends outside. They claimed to be a Mr. White and a Mr. Black, from your office," replied Aunt Lucy.

"Good grief! I have been with the India Office for fifteen years and I have never heard of either of them."

"No, I very much doubt anyone at the India Office has. They seem to work for a man with no face."

Mr. Botts went visibly pale. "No face?"

"More or less. Apparently he lost most of his face in some accident."

"Oh, my giddy aunt!" said Mr. Botts. "Oh, golly gumdrops!"

Emmaline had thought that "tarnation" and "criminy" were silly, but this was just ridiculous. "You know this man," she demanded. "Who is he?"

"He is a very dangerous man, indeed. He is known sometimes as Count Alexei Vilanovich, and at others as Baron Drexler," explained Mr. Botts. "I have also heard him referred to as the Duke of Piacenza, as Monsieur de la Patisserie, and once as Marko Plipp. In England, he affects a British name, like Jones or Smith or Blenkinsopp."

"Or Brown," said Aunt Lucy quietly.

"Some say he is a senior operative for the Ochrana," Mr. Botts continued. "That's the Czar of Russia's secret police. Some say he is a master criminal who works for the highest bidder. We know that he has worked for the Russians in the past, but he got his face blown off trying to assassinate one of the Czar's ministers. On a visit to Vienna, in Austria, some years ago."

"That doesn't sound like working for the Czar," said Emmaline, who knew that "Czar" was the same word as "Caesar" and meant the Emperor. Emmaline knew a lot of things.

"You wouldn't think so, dearie, no, but the Ochrana is fond of setting up what they call 'agents provocateurs,' which means having secret policemen go undercover among the enemies of the government—anarchists and revolutionists of all sorts—to encourage them to commit terrible acts. Then they nab 'em. Of course, quite a lot of people get hurt, but the Ochrana doesn't care about that. His underlings call him 'Number One.' We have no idea what his real name is or where he comes from. We are just glad he got his face blown away—no disrespect meant, of course, horrible thing, horrible—but at least we know what he looks like now. Before that happened, we couldn't trace him at all."

"But why is he interested in us?" asked Aunt Lucy.

"Why don't I tell you what we've learned," said Mr. Botts. "Right from the time Princess Purnah left that nice school we put her at."

It was getting dark, and Princess Purnah knew that the brigands had left the area. At least, the crashing noises of men tramping through the woods had ceased, and the barking of dogs had faded off into the distance. They hadn't found her hiding place in the ruined shed. All this was excellent! Trikk!

What wasn't so good was that she had long ago finished the remains of Rab's chocolate and was very hungry. All this brigandage had prevented her from getting out and shooting the buffaloes she had planned on eating. There was water, probably nasty, in a little brook, so there was no chance of horrid death through thirst or heating-stroke. It was cold, though nothing compared to winter in the mountains of her beloved Chiligrit.

All she could do was settle down and wait for the sun to rise again.

———

Rubberbones was alone in the room. The man and woman, whose names he had learned were Ted and Biddy, had left him with a jug of water and a blanket. Biddy had curtsied as she left the room. The boy looked around for the first time; eating had been the immediate thing on his mind.

It was a large, shabby room. High ceilings, flowery wallpaper, sepia photographs of people who didn't smile for the camera.

There wasn't much to work with. A table and a moth-eaten old sofa. Two battered copies of *The Strand* magazine. A rug that smelled funny. Curtains that hung limply from a slightly bent rod. They might be useful.

Rubberbones pulled back the curtains and looked out of the window. It was securely protected by iron fittings like those barring the lavatory window. But it was a different view from the window in the privy.

Outside it was a gray, wet day in a place quite unlike the Yorkshire dales. He'd been to Grimethorpe, dirty and industrial, and to rescue Emmaline from the school on the cliffs overlooking the sea. And once he'd been to London to see his mother's family. They had lived in a narrow street in a dingy part of the city. Yet, he remembered that London had great huge buildings—palaces and cathedrals and sweetshops—and massive bridges, and a river as wide as …

As the one he could see below him, a few hundred yards away.

———

Emmaline was furious with Mr. Botts. "It was *you* who put poor Purnah at St. Grimelda's? *You* personally?"

Mr. Botts smiled at her in a glassy sort of way. "Why, yes. We always use St. Grimelda's for our, ah, 'sensitive' cases. Girls who need an education in England. Girls who need protection from unwelcome visitors. They are very security conscious, you know. Never let any of our girls come to any harm from outside forces."

Emmaline exploded with rage. "Outside forces! What about inside forces? What about the cruelty of the teachers and the horrid food and the fact that you aren't allowed any letters or visits with your friends and family? And the pterodactyls?"

"Well, we can't expect every school to … did you say 'the pterodactyls?'"

"Never mind the pterodactyls! The school is terrible! Purnah never learned anything there. She pretended she didn't speak English at all—she didn't to begin with—but the staff never made any effort to teach her. As long as she was quiet—as long as any of us were quiet and followed the rules and did what we were ordered—Mrs. Wackett was happy. It wasn't a school; it was a prison!"

Mr. Botts wiped his glasses. "I am sure you have your opinions. But the India Office expects Princess Purnah to return to the safety of St. Grimelda's. We've made arrangements to transport her there. Where is she, by the way?"

"Ah," said Aunt Lucy. "It's all a bit complicated."

———

The sky was darkening over the river, and a steady rain beat on the windowpanes. Rubberbones felt the strange instrument that the professor had given him buzz against his chest. That was a surprise.

It was even more of a surprise when a little voice inside his undershirt said, "Hello. Anybody there? Hello?"

"Hello," said Rab. And then, remembering what he'd heard about telephones—there was only one in the village, and he'd certainly never had the chance to use it—added, "You've got the wrong number."

<hr />

Mr. Botts had left the house in extreme displeasure that "his" princess, his responsibility, had so thoughtlessly disappeared into the clouds above Lower Owlthwaite when he had made an appointment to see her. This was unreasonable behavior, he said. What Emmaline suspected was that nobody at the India Office would accept this explanation, and Mr. Botts would get blamed. In fact, they'd probably laugh at him.

Still, it was his fault that Aunt Lucy had thrown him out by his ear. Literally. She had just told him about Rubberbones and the disguise and the coach and the steam carriage going through the hedge, when he said, "My dear lady! I don't have time to listen to your servant problems! If this boy has got himself in trouble with Number One, that's hardly my affair. I am simply concerned with the well-being of Princess Purnah!"

Aunt Lucy might have argued with him that Rubberbones would not have been abducted if he had not been trying to protect the princess. But she was tired, and Mr. Botts was tiresome, so she reached up and grabbed him by the right ear.

"Eeek!" he said.

"Out!" she said.

Bang! went the front door as he passed through it at considerable speed.

"I didn't care for his manners," explained Aunt Lucy to Emmaline.

"Wasn't he going to tell us more about this Faceless Fiend and his plot?" asked Emmaline.

"Hmm," replied Aunt Lucy. "I don't suppose we can ask him back in now, can we?"

Probably not, they both agreed.

Lal Singh returned. He shimmered into the room, perfectly dressed despite the mud and rain that were evident on Stanley, who reveled in wet dirtiness. They were back from Grimethorpe Halt, where persuasion in the form of five shillings and a hot beef-and-onion pie had led the inspector on duty to make inquiries. There had been a private train yesterday, arriving from York at 11:34 a.m., standing most of the day before leaving at 4:08 p.m. on the London line. The telegrams confirmed that the train— which was just a locomotive, a passenger carriage and a goods van large enough for, say, a coach and horses—had passed through Sheffield, Nottingham and Watford Junction on its way to—

"London!" shouted Professor Bellbuckle. "I just talked

to Robert, and he's in London. Unless you've got another city with a big river and a bridge that opens for ships to go through, and a church with real loud bells." He appeared, suddenly, from his workshop in the old barn. He had missed luncheon, tea and dinner and was very excited. "My radiophonic oscillating device—"

Bow bells, thought Emmaline. The City of London. Tower Bridge. St. Paul's Cathedral. Jellied eels. Pie and mash. She'd heard so much but never been there.

"Well, then," said Aunt Lucy. "London it is. Although I expect we shall have to sort out this Princess Purnah matter first of all."

"He'll see you now," said Biddy. "Your Majesty, I mean." She wiped her nose on her sleeve and ushered Rubberbones out into a hallway. Rab followed her, carefully adjusting his Chiligriti princess costume as he did so.

His heart was beating wildly. On the one hand he had just spoken to Professor Bellbuckle. The voice was small and tinny through the professor's odd little device. "Hello, Robert! Are you there? Where is there … I mean, where are you?"

Rab had held the thing in front of his mouth and, keeping his voice low, had said that he was in London. It must be London because there was the opening bridge that let the big ships through. The device had made some crackling sounds, the professor had said, "Can you hear me?" and then there was just a sort of low hum.

This was very exciting, and he hoped the thing would speak to him again.

On the other hand, he was about to go and see the man they called Number One, and Rab had strong suspicions who this might turn out to be.

CHAPTER 13

Face to Face with the Man with No Face

"Come!" boomed the voice from behind the polished oak-and-brass door.

Biddy led Rubberbones into a massive, expensively decorated library much different from the shabby room he'd been kept in. There were bookshelves covering one entire wall, a tiger-skin rug on the floor and heads of animals stuffed and mounted above the fireplace. Maps and photographs were encased in glass. Rifles and shotguns hung in a rack. Rab understood it was the room of a dangerous man.

That man himself sat in a leather armchair, facing the roaring fire. Biddy pushed "the princess" toward him. Rab said nothing. The man did not look up. From behind, Rab could only see that he wore the kind of expensive dressing gown called a smoking jacket, a silk scarf at the neck. His head was completely bald.

No, it was completely ... naked. Empty of features. The man without a face had no hair or ears.

He did not turn around, nor did he seem to expect his guest to come around to face him. He spoke toward the fireplace.

"So, Princess Purnah. You are completely in my power."

Rab said nothing.

"Come, now. I cannot believe you don't understand me."
Still, Rab said nothing.

"I cannot believe that after three years at a fine English girls' school you do not know what I am saying."

Rab decided that Chiligriti was the answer. Not that he spoke Chiligriti. "Glekk! Bah Bah Blacksheep! Wee Willie Winkee!"

The man paused for a moment. "You know, I speak twelve European languages and nine Asiatic tongues. Sadly, as yet, the language of Chiligrit is not one of them. Still, I believe that you understand me perfectly."

Another pause. Rab kept silent, although he had another bit of nursery rhyme if needed.

"You are my honored guest and will come to no harm at my hands. You will be treated well. We shall not stay long in this house, but will soon travel to the continent. There will be a very long train ride to—to meet those who commissioned my work. If you are sensible, there will be no need for you to travel in the way that I brought you here. I cannot imagine the coffin was comfortable."

"Threee Bagsfull!" replied Rubberbones.

The man without a face, Number One as they called him, or the Faceless Fiend, as Rab preferred, sat for a moment. Then he spoke in a quiet tone. "I wish for you to come and see my face. It may frighten you, child, but I think it is necessary for you to know that I am not a man to be trifled with. Come around and stand in front of the fire. Look upon me, and know that your fate is in my hands."

Trembling, despite his efforts to keep calm, Rab did so. Perhaps the disguise would work. Who would connect the Chiligriti girl with the Yorkshire lad? It was a hope, anyway. Rubberbones edged his way around to the fireplace, stood on the tiger skin and looked into the face he had seen twice before. The face that had all its features smoothed away. The face with glittering eyes full of malevolence, a gaping, lipless mouth, nostril holes and ... nothing else. Rab squealed without meaning to.

"Yes, my dear, I am terrible to look upon. I had tried to kill a man with a bomb, you see, but the explosives proved ... unreliable. Still, enough about me. Pull down your coverings a little, if you would. Let me look at your face."

Emmaline had decided she was going to find Princess Purnah. Her leg felt much better, and she would take Stanley with her. After all, if Purnah was hiding from the search parties—and she might be, since most of them were strangers to her—then perhaps she'd come out for a friend. Alone.

She set her alarm clock for five in the morning. It was a normal, sensible alarm clock—not one of the professor's inventions. He was a wonderful man, but she didn't want to be woken by anything that exploded, or spat flame, or caused her to require any more medical attention. She had important things to do.

Turokk, it was cold tonight. Perhaps it was that she hadn't eaten all day, or that she had no blankets, or that the hole in the roof let in an awful lot of rain. H'rikk! She would have liked to go back to the house of Auntilucy, but no doubt the bandits had burned it down by now—there were many of them in the war band that had been through the forest yesterday. Auntilucy should have built a proper fortress with high mud walls, a stout barred gate and holes to drop boiling oil down on the enemy. Now she must surely have fallen heroically, sword in hand, with brave Lal Singh fighting beside her. The young people, Emmaline and Errand Boy, must have been taken for slaves. The professor was too old for keeping as a slave; he was a magician, too, so the bandits would have hurled him into a chasm, as was the custom. It was hard, but Princess Purnah knew that raids by brigands were part of life. She would avenge them all! Today she would find her way to the hut of Errand Boy's aged ancestor, and together they would plot vengeance and eat cake. Purnah was very hungry.

Rubberbones did not want to pull down the veils of old curtain and bedspread that covered most of his face. He shook his head. He tried to convey an expression of feminine modesty with his eyes. That was difficult.

"Don't waste my time," said the Fiend impatiently. He lunged forward and yanked the cloth down from the lad's nose and mouth. If the "princess" had been a genuine eastern lady, that would have been a deadly insult and might have started a feud that would spill blood for generations to come. As it was, Rubberbones simply grinned in a way that he hoped might resemble an actual princess. Actually, he looked completely gormless.

"*You!*" screamed the Faceless Fiend. "The boy from the Black Bull! What trick is this?"

So much for hoping that the Fiend would simply think he was a very ugly princess. He clearly had an excellent memory for faces. Then again, faces were of special interest to him, since he didn't have one of his own.

Rubberbones *ought* to have laughed and said, "Aha! So we meet again and I shall foil you once more!" Then he should have somehow overpowered his adversary, stolen some secret plans and escaped by a scheme so daring, so breathtaking, that nobody could prevent it.

Instead, he just said, "Er …"

Two minutes later he was back in the dingy room. Biddy told him that he could sleep on the ruddy sofa, nasty cheating lout that he was. (She seemed to take the fact that he was not the princess personally.) Number One would decide what to do with him. Rab thought it probably didn't involve a comfy train journey across Europe. That part was definitely off.

CHAPTER 14

If You Go Down to the Woods Today

Emmaline was up before dawn. She dressed and crept carefully downstairs. She was silent. Stealthy.

Lal Singh was waiting in his long blue kurta and perfectly tied lunghi.

"Breakfast is ready," he announced in a whisper. "Since you have a busy day ahead, I am taking the liberty of making proper English bacon and egg, and none of Memsahib Butterworth's vile weedings and snippings."

Emmaline was taken aback. "But how did you know I'd be up at … er, five in the morning?"

"I am Lal Singh," he replied with a hint of a smile. "It is my business to know such things."

Lal Singh had also prepared Emmaline a packed lunch, avoiding Aunt Lucy's preference for nettle salads and jellied snails in favor of a dozen cold chicken sandwiches, a bottle of ginger beer and lots of chocolate for Princess Purnah. He'd fed Stanley and given him his best collar. "Be early, before the princess stirs herself."

Emmaline bolted down her breakfast and set out to find Princess Purnah, Stanley scurrying at her heels.

Dawn had come, and Biddy had brought something resembling male clothing for Rubberbones. No sausages this time, though; just lumpy porridge that stuck to the bowl. Apparently sausages were for actual princesses, not frauds pretending to be royalty.

"That was a dirty trick to play!" said Biddy, slamming down the bowl. Rab could have replied that being taken hostage, thrown in a coffin and whisked to London against his wishes was an even dirtier trick. But he didn't, in case there might be sausages later.

Fog hung low in the valley, and bare trees loomed like skeletons. Stanley raced up to trees, fallen logs and anything else that appeared before him. He sniffed and sometimes barked at them.

It occurred to Emmaline that she might get lost again, but this time she was prepared: she had sandwiches and a raincoat and a waterproof hat. She knew these woods a little from her walks with the professor and tramps with Stanley. It was just a question of searching thoroughly, and not frightening Purnah into bolting or going further into hiding. The countryside was quiet and wet, and squelchy underfoot. She could hear nothing but her own cries: "Purnah! Princess Purnah! It's me, Emmaline!" There was a hint of an echo. And then there was another sound. A distant call that touched her to the marrow.

A shriek, or a scream. Not a human shriek. Not an animal. A bird. *The* bird.

The pterodactyl.

There had been two. They had lived in the ancient Black Tower at St. Grimelda's. Nobody knew how they had got there or where they had come from—at least,

Emmaline hadn't known. The headmistress and her staff had used the threat of "the birds" to keep the girls in a state of terror. The birds were foul, savage flying lizards—no, that was wrong. They were raptors related to dinosaurs, extinct for sixty million years. Except that these ones weren't. One had carried Purnah off struggling. Both of them had smashed Rubberbones and his kite against the castle walls of St. Grimelda's. And they had pursued Emmaline's flying machine as she escaped from the school roof, clawing and biting at her as she soared over the cliffs.

One had been shot and fallen into the sea. The other had shied away under rocket fire.

Now it was flying again.

Emmaline ducked low, beneath a tangle of fallen branches.

Unfortunately, Stanley decided this was an excellent time to bark.

The fog was growing thinner, as Emmaline had hoped. Only now she wished it wouldn't.

———

Rubberbones barely had time to eat the cold, lumpy porridge—or to ask for more, as anyone who knew him would have expected—before he was hustled out of the room. "Move," said Biddy harshly. "Yer Majesty!" chimed in Ted from behind. He, at least, thought it was all very funny. He chuckled to himself as he once again led Rab to visit Number One.

The Faceless Fiend sat in the same armchair in his library. There were two men with him: one short and stout, the other tall, thin and with a sad face, like a bloodhound that had received bad news. Rubberbones knew them; they were Mr. White and Mr. Black, or it might be the other way round. He was fairly sure that these were not their real names.

"Ah," said Number One, as he styled himself. "My little Asiatic princess. Who are you, anyway? Some urchin boy? Some servant? Some sneaky thieving boy?"

"Nawwsir," replied Rubberbones. "Me name's Robert Burns." He was an honest lad.

Mr. Black and Mr. White chortled unpleasantly. "The Scottish poet! I thought he was dead!" said the stout one.

"It's me name, sir. I'm not a poet. I'm a—I'm a pioneer aviator." That was what Emmaline called herself when she was experimenting with flying machines.

The men laughed again. Number One did not.

"I don't care what you might be," he snapped. "Clearly you are a tool in a plot to deceive me. You are a mere peasant. A pawn. A nobody. Where is the princess?"

Rubberbones said nothing.

"It will be the worse for you if you do not tell me, boy! You will die a hideous death if you do not reveal what you know!"

Rab looked the Fiend in the eyes. Since he had so few other features, they were easy to find. The face was ... monstrous.

"Don't know nothing, sir."

The Fiend's mouth turned up in a scornful smile. "You were disguised as the princess."

"Oh, nawssir. It were a game. I were dressed as, er, Sinbad the Sailor." Rubberbones knew he should not tell lies. It was wrong, and he was very bad at it.

Number One snorted heavily. He was like an angry bull deciding whether to toss you a few times on his horns before trampling you into the dirt.

"You *will* tell me where the princess is." The remains of the Fiend's nostrils flared.

So Rab told the truth because he knew there was nothing they could do about it.

"She were tied to a great big kite and blew away in the wind. I don't know where."

They didn't believe that, either.

"To the dungeon," hissed Number One. "We have ways to make him talk. Meanwhile, Number Two, take the first express train back to Yorkshire. Those thugs we hired—hire them again, and tell them it's on their heads if we don't have the correct result this time. In fact, send a telegram and get the hooligans over to that ghastly little village immediately—an extra shilling per man. Greedy devils will do anything for beer money. Number Three, you stay and help persuade young Master Burns to tell us all he knows. We'll let him spend some time in the cells first. I have business to attend to now. My Masked Minions arrive shortly, and we'll no longer need to rely on local hirelings."

The thin, sad-faced man smiled. Rubberbones did not like that smile in the slightest.

Princess Purnah could hear a human voice followed by the throaty bark of a dog. There had been dogs yesterday, but they were too busy playing in the woods and scampering about to scent her. A single dog with a tracker who knew his business was another matter. Glokk! Glekk! Her Uncle Pilkiwoo, a fine scout, had once followed a Nepali bandit for six days over a glacier just to steal his gold tooth.

Perhaps this tracker was as good as Uncle Pilkiwoo.

She fitted the arrow to her bowstring once again.

And then she heard the scream of the pterodactyl—she just called it "the bird," or sometimes "Khark" (which was a flying monster that ate children in a much-beloved tale

Chiligriti mothers told their toddlers to stop them from wandering too far). She knew that sound. The bird had seized her when she was carrying a tray of cocoa to beloved Professor Bellbuckling. It had carried her (despite her demands to be set down) all the way to the Black Tower at the wicked school and had most certainly thought of eating her. It hadn't, but that was only because foul schoolteachers wanted her alive.

Princess Purnah was angry now. Wojjid! The tracker could wait. She would slit his gizzard at her leisure. The filthy bird must be dealt with first.

CHAPTER 15

The Khark

Emmaline felt fear rising within her. Circling somewhere above the trees was that scouting pterodactyl. The beast's senses were far better than her own. It had razor-sharp talons to seize her or, worse, rip her flesh into shreds. It had gaping jaws, lined with jagged teeth—

"Get a grip on yourself, girl," Emmaline told herself.

She remained crouched, grabbing Stanley by the collar. "Quiet, boy!" The pterodactyl would detect any move she made. It was like a hawk seeking out a juicy rabbit for supper. If the rabbit stayed still, it might be safe, but if it ran the hawk would spot the movement and be upon it. She had no illusions that a running girl could outpace a diving raptor, and her leg—though improved—wasn't up to more than a gentle walk.

So she huddled close to a tree, wishing the leaves were still on it. Her raincoat was a dull brown, and she pulled the hood up as far over her face as she could. She had to blend in with the forest.

The bird must be looking for Purnah. Mr. Botts had undoubtedly let St. Grimelda's know that Purnah would not be returning to their tender care. The headmistress, Mrs. Wackett, would not have just accepted that. No, she would want the princess back as soon as possible. After all, Purnah had burned down part of the school in her escape, and the wicked Wackett wouldn't forget that. She must have sent out the surviving pterodactyl. They had probably given it a piece of Purnah's clothing—she'd left most of her belongings at St. Grimelda's—so it would have her scent.

Emmaline remained motionless.

Stanley wrestled free of her grip and, with a succession of enthusiastic yips and yaps, ran playfully for open ground.

Emmaline broke into a run as she pursued him. Pain shot up her leg. She gasped and hobbled forward. Stanley turned and looked at her. He smiled, his tongue flapping at the edge of his mouth. Idiot dog! But she had to save him. She urged herself forward again. "Come here, boy!" she called, as low as she could manage.

Stanley wagged his tail. A shape wheeled over the line of trees.

Biddy and Ted had escorted the prisoner to the dungeon. It wasn't as bad as Rubberbones had expected. For one thing, it was in the attic. Dungeons aren't supposed to be in the attic, as anyone with the slightest knowledge of these things knows; they are supposed to be in dark, dank cellars with water dripping down the walls and the skeletons of past inhabitants hanging from rusty chains.

Apparently a proper dungeon was part of the Faceless Fiend's orders. Ted and Biddy were arguing about it.

"He thinks you arranged the cells downstairs," Biddy complained.

"What's the difference? The attic's as good as the cellar. Besides, I'm using the cellar."

"You were too lazy to clear out the cellar, you idle beggar. You've got it all messed up with that jumble of crates and barrels in there."

"It's convenient! You try rolling barrels up to the attic. He'll be fine up here with the old bikes."

"Not really a dungeon, though, is it?" snapped Biddy.

"You can't have everything," replied Ted.

"Number One can. You'll have to explain it to him."

It was a tiny room with an angled roofline. A mattress with a blanket that had seen better days. A jug, a chamber pot and a bowl. A small dormer window with only the view of another slate roof. No candles, no sausages. No shackles on the walls to make it more like a proper dungeon. Rubberbones thought that Ted was probably too lazy to have put them up—they were probably in a box in the cellar marked "Rack and Gibbet: Instruments of Medieval Punishment, established 1206," waiting to be unpacked.

There were other things in the attic as well:

Most of a penny-farthing bicycle, wooden, circa 1870 or before.

Parts of a lady's safety bicycle, newer model, but with no front wheel.

Random bits of old bikes with chains, gears, brakes and handlebars, and about nine very uncomfortable-looking saddles.

And a box of tools, which Biddy pointed out to Ted. "You'd leave the little devil with a screwdriver and an 'ammer and either he'd break the lock and run about the 'ouse or he'd brain me when I brought 'im 'is dinner." Ted took the tools, although there were some small items he ignored as being too insignificant for braining or lock picking.

Rab could hear them still arguing as they locked the door and retreated down the staircase. Biddy was yelling, "He'll 'ave your hide, you idiot! Just because he's not 'ere 'alf the time doesn't mean you can do what you like. My son'll be back from work in an hour, and I'll get him to 'elp with the barrels and boxes. If we don't 'ave a proper dungeon and a kid 'anging up by 'is thumbnails ... well, I wouldn't want to be in *your* shoes."

Rubberbones decided he had a few hours before he would be "'anging up by 'is thumbnails." Rab was not about to let this time pass by while he counted the floorboards. He still had his strange invention from the professor: nobody had searched him when they took his princess outfit away. (Number One was terrifying, but his helpers were bone idle and hopelessly inept — not at all Master Criminal material.) He pulled the device from his undershirt and pressed the buzzer. If anyone knew how a pile of old bicycle parts could help him escape, it was Ozymandias Bellbuckle, Ph.D.

Princess Purnah listened intently. She had her head cocked to one side to make it easier to tell the direction of the sound. That was something her favorite uncle, the tracker, had taught her before he was faithlessly slain by her other favorite uncle. Pilkiwoo had shown her much. She would honor his memory with cunning wit and pitiless shootings and stabbings.

She heard the scream of the Khark once again. It was closer now. And there were the crashings of branches, the barkings of curs and the tracker saying things like, "Come back here, Stanley, you stupid dog!"

Stan-lee! Her friend Stan-lee! The fine, tongue-waggy unclean doggy Stan-lee!

Purnah poked her head cautiously out from the cover of the ruined hut. Stanley bounded toward her, eyes merry, yapping in excitement. Emmaline followed, stumbling, tree branches snagging her clothes and the bag that hung from her shoulder. The bird—the Khark—was crying in anticipation of the kill. Talons at the ready, it was poised to dive after Emmaline. Or perhaps after Stanley, who might provide a nourishing snack.

The sight of the Khark sent a chill through Purnah. She remembered the scaly, leathery skin—yellow like disease, dry to the touch—and the rank smell of rotting breath. She recalled the grip of the talons on her body, protected only by luck and Victorian underwear. Purnah gripped the bow and drew back the string. Emmaline staggered onward, yelling for the dog to stop, her hood up, unable to see the bird. She must know it was pursuing her, though.

But it wasn't chasing Emmaline. As Purnah emerged from the hut, the bird surged forward, darting away from the hooded girl and toward the princess. Glekk!

She released the string of her bow.

The arrow flew true, straight toward the diving pterodactyl. It struck the leathery scales in the centre of the body, where the heart must be.

And bounced off.

The Khark shrieked in annoyance. Princess Purnah shrieked in annoyance. The monster slipped a little to one side, its diving attack disturbed by the glancing arrow, and clipped the roof of the hut. Turning, the creature flapped upward to circle once again.

Purnah waved her fist in anger, yelling at the pterodactyl. "Torok! Hanjji Pok!"

The bird attacked again, its savage beak aimed like a torpedo at the raging girl. Wings spread, the creature lunged forward, and Emmaline darted toward her friend. Pain shot through her foot, but she crashed into Purnah, flinging her down. The grasping talons missed the princess, sliced through Emmaline's hood and seized upon the satchel that swung from her shoulder.

The pterodactyl hurtled upward, the satchel in its claws, the strap still bound to Emmaline. The bag fell open and a wrapped sandwich fell out. Stanley, heroic and noble, ignored Emmaline's plight as he raced for the sandwich.

"Is foodings!" shouted Princess Purnah, standing up. A bar of chocolate fell from the bag as Emmaline struggled with the monster. "Is chocolates!" she shouted.

Purnah leapt forward. Something flashed in her hand. Emmaline was lifted into the air as the satchel strap pulled tight against her chest. She was wheezing, her eyes darting about desperately. Purnah had a knife. A butter knife.

The princess leapt up and grasped the foul creature by the leg above its talons. Her sudden weight pulled the pterodactyl lower, and Emmaline gasped as she touched ground again. Princess Purnah seized the moment. She plunged the knife into the pterodactyl's thigh. The

monster shrieked in an agonizing jolt of sound. Purnah stabbed again, muttering, "Eeky! Trikk tick klik! Kar-ver-eeee!" She did not let go, despite the spray of slimy black blood that shot from the creature's hide. "Handings over me chocolate, wretch! Porok!"

The enraged pterodactyl flapped its batlike wings furiously and rose again, this time lifting Purnah off the ground, jabbing with her butter knife and cursing roundly in Chiligriti. Emmaline, pulled to her feet once again by the satchel strap, grabbed Purnah's legs and hung on for grim life. She was not going to let a wounded, angry pterodactyl take her friend. Stanley, having finished his cold chicken sandwich and remembering his duty, jumped, landed on Emmaline's shoulder and wriggled upward to bite the monster.

The strap broke with a sudden rip. Everyone except the pterodactyl tumbled in a heap. The bird hissed and screamed, flapped its great wings and rose upward. Circling above the trees, it turned once with an expression of pure evil and flew away.

"Good!" said Princess Purnah. "Not stealings chocolate. I am not eatings in days. Ravenous!"

She was filthy, dressed in the ragged remains of Rab's clothes and splattered with the filthy, oily blood of the pterodactyl. A huge grin spread across her face. The butter knife dripped black ooze onto the wet leaves below.

"Excellent. We showing him! What else you got in bag for eatings?"

Emmaline wasn't sure what to say. She was terrified, triumphant, exhausted and hurt. So she answered truthfully, "Chicken sandwiches, ginger beer and quite a lot of chocolate." Then her injured foot gave way beneath her, and she collapsed.

CHAPTER 16

Up on the Roof

Rubberbones was trying to get Professor Bellbuckle's device to work. He rattled it. He tapped it. He twiddled it. Just when he had decided that the thing was dead, it crackled into life.

"Hello! Hello!" creaked a disembodied voice. "Robert, my boy, is that you?"

"'Allo, Professor," said Rab. "I'm in a pickle. I thought you might help."

"Right," said the inventor after Rab had explained his situation. "So you have the equipment to make" —He thought for a moment— "what we call a 'bicycle.' That's the scientific term."

Rubberbones sighed. "I've seen bicycles before, Professor. I've rid on Bert Jenkins's. It were grand."

"Excellent. You know what they look like, then! And 'was grand' is the correct term, Robert."

"Yessir. Only problem is, I'm in a little room in the attic, up the stairs. Steep 'uns."

"Aha. Then you must get out onto the roof. Do that, have a look round and call me back."

The device clicked in a final sort of way.

Rab examined the window. It was just an ordinary window, glued shut by a thick coat of paint.

Rubberbones leaned on the window with all his weight.

The layers of paint burst, and suddenly it was open. He wriggled through the window and onto the roof. He moved carefully, for yesterday's rain had made the slates damp and slippery. The roof wasn't steep, but he was at least four or five floors up. The building was a little taller than those on either side. They were big old houses, probably prosperous in their time but a bit scruffy now. Rab looked down into the stone courtyard that he'd seen from the window in the first room he'd been in; it was not a fall that even he, the rubber boy, would want to risk. The roofs extended in every direction—red tile, gray slate, the lead roofs of churches. Nearby he could see the streets—narrow alleys for the most part, with horse-drawn vans and wagons splashing through the mud—and tiny people looking like toy soldiers. He could glimpse the River Thames flowing toward the sea, with the great gate of Tower Bridge and London Bridge upstream. To the left Rab could make out big ships; those must be the docks his mam had often talked about, where her father and brothers had stood in line for work. There were church steeples and domes—that one must be St. Paul's Cathedral! And one of the steeples had to be the famous St. Mary le Bow, but which one? It was all very interesting and wonderful—

But he was trying to escape from the clutches of the Faceless Fiend, and Rab had no time to be gawking at the sights of London Town. He tried the buzzing device again.

"'Allo, Professor! It's me!"

"Hello, Robert. Miss Lucy has telegraphed a man in London who might be able to find you. They say he's famous—so what can you see from the roof? Make it as detailed as you can."

So Rab told him, at great length.

"Can you get down from the roof?" asked Professor Bellbuckle.

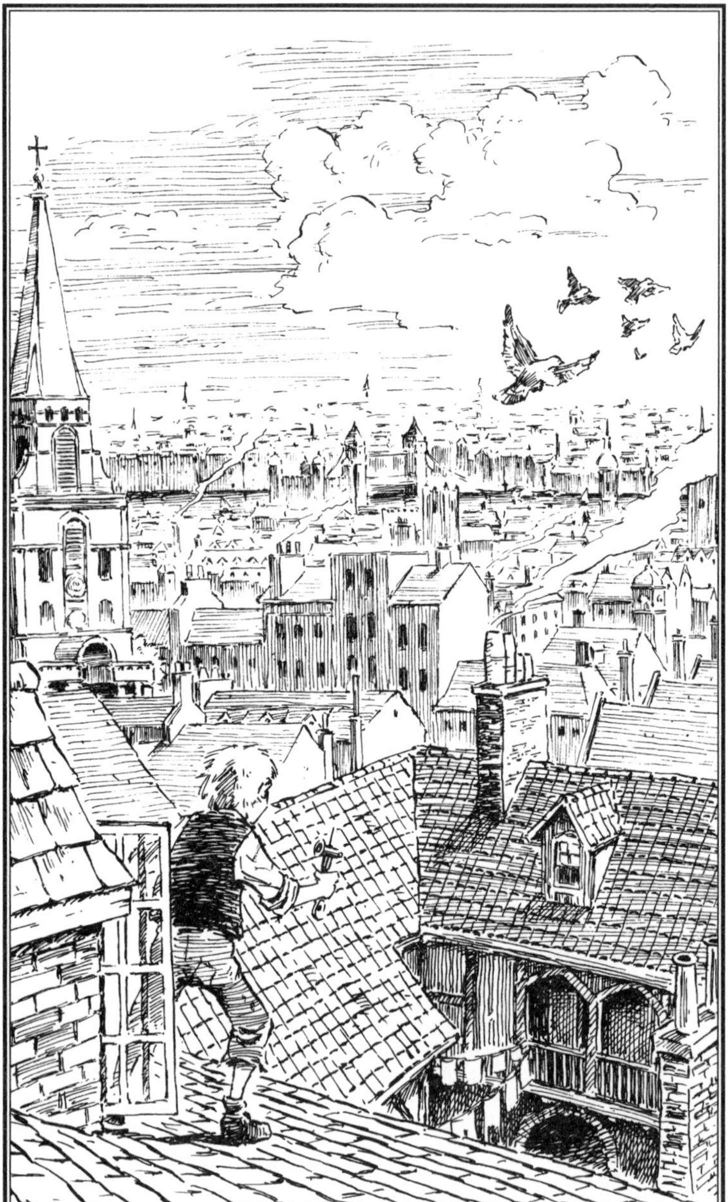

Rab walked carefully to the edge, standing almost on the gutter pipe. "The next roof is mebbe, er, ten or fifteen feet away. More than I could jump. And, er, it's a long way down."

It was.

"Well, get inside and see what you can find to help you."

Emmaline's head swam, but she was awake and something warm was licking her face. Stanley's tongue.

"Emmaline Cay-lee!" It was Purnah's voice. "How happy is I that you are not deadings!"

"Dead," said Emmaline. "The correct word is 'dead.'" Her injured leg throbbed in pain, and there was a bloody scratch on her forehead where the pterodactyl's talon had pierced her hood. But she was not dead.

"How long have I been unconscious?"

Princess Purnah flashed a huge grin that was whiter than usual since her face was so smudged with dirt. "Six sang-wiches time. Not countings chocolate!"

Emmaline didn't know how long this was—more than a minute, probably, but less than what? Ten, fifteen minutes? More?

"Is allowed in my religion to eat foul unclean chicklings if sliced roastly in sang-wiches. No cake, though. Gritt! Now, Emmaline Cay-lee. You able to walkings?"

She was able to limp. The princess cut a stick for her to lean on. Stanley yapped about, in his usual way, and they made their way through the woods. Emmaline moved slowly, hoping she'd done no serious damage to the twisted ankle.

The princess was chattering. "You good friend, diving on me like that. I not really thinking 'bout the evil Khark dangerishness—I so angry with horrid bird not slain by mine arrow, I forget is still trying to eatings me or carryings off again."

She thought about it some more. "Also, helping bringly me down. I stabbing fervently. Not good to be stabbings thing what have you high above ground. Fall doomish! Porok!"

So they walked, the fog lifting and Princess Purnah listening as Emmaline told her about Rab's abduction. "Poosh! We gets him back, easy as pies!" pronounced the princess. Emmaline shook her head at Purnah's disregard of danger; in this case, Rab's danger.

The heiress to the throne of Chiligrit was finishing off the remaining "sang-wiches" (the chocolate had already been eaten). Emmaline was glad she hadn't wanted any for herself because Purnah ate the lot.

Then, suddenly, Stanley stopped. He slunk low and growled in the quiet way of a dog faced by a danger too big for biting. Emmaline held her hand up for Purnah to be silent, but the mountain princess was already kneeling, her homemade bow at the ready. She'd taken her one and only arrow back and was ready to use it again.

There was a man in front of them, like one of those big, hefty bullies who had chased the professor's steam carriage two days ago.

Oh. They were back. "Tarnation," said Emmaline. "Criminy."

Rubberbones was rummaging through the attic. He had hoped there might be rope or even a big umbrella. After all, Ted and Biddy weren't the most careful jailers in the world. But, then, most prisoners weren't looking for ways to fly off the roof. He looked at the bicycle parts that, as Professor Bellbuckle had cleverly suggested, were ideal for putting together a bicycle and some very small tools Ted had missed. He picked up the mattress. Even the famous aviator Rubberbones couldn't make a flying machine out of a lumpy mattress. He tried the professor's buzzing device once again. The connection was bad.

"Professor. There's nowt here."

"There's the bicyc — *(crackle)* — it together on — *(crackle)*"

"It's no use in here, I told you. There's loads of stairs. Steep 'uns, wi' sharp corners."

"Not inside — *(crackle)* — the roof — *(crackle)* — next roof — roof after that — down."

The conversation ended in a splutter.

Rab thought he understood. He was to assemble a bicycle and ride it across the roofs. He could jump the gaps between buildings, hopping from one roof to another, until he could escape.

It was the stupidest, most ridiculous, absurdly dangerous idea he'd ever heard. He'd have to get started on it right away.

CHAPTER 17

A Good Time to Run Away

Emmaline watched in horror as the big man turned around. He must have heard Stanley growling. But, no, he was just lighting a cigarette.

The man faced away once again. Emmaline relaxed a little. Stanley was silent, wary, ready to spring if he had to.

Then someone called out to the man. "Got one to spare, Jackie? I smoked me last 'un." Another of the beefy men appeared. Emmaline thought he was the one who had stood in the roadway, taunting the professor to run him down.

"No sign of that flippin' girl, then?" asked the newcomer.

"Naw. Another day's pay for standing in a wood. Not bad. And there's a reward for 'im as catches her. Five pounds from Mr. Brown 'imself."

"Five quid? I could do a lot wi' five gold sovereigns. That Mr. Brown. Is 'e coming up again? 'E's a bit of a frightener, that 'un."

"Oh, aye. Som'at evil abaht 'im, I'd say. Don't never show 'is face. No, it were the fat bloke—White—as spoke of a reward."

"I thought we'd already caught that wench! The girl in the coffin at Grimethorpe. Was that someone else then?"

"Dunno. Mebbe there's two of 'em. If I see any girl at all, I'll grab her first and sort out 'oo she might be later on. Five pound is five pound."

The second man faded off into the woods again.

Emmaline hoped the first one would finish his cigarette and go somewhere else. Then she and Purnah could sneak toward the house and see if it was safe to go in. But perhaps they should stay away from the house completely. What to do?

The question was solved when the man finished his smoke and turned to throw the cigarette end into the bushes. Stanley saw the motion and, being an enthusiastic beast not renowned for his brainpower, leapt to retrieve it. The man looked up, astonished. He saw the dog. He saw the girls. He leered in a way that Emmaline found very unpleasant, indeed.

"Oh-ho, my pretties! Come to Uncle Jackie! There's five pounds with my name on. Mebbe I'll buy you a bunch of flowers!" He stumbled forward, arms out as if ready for a bear hug.

Stanley snapped at his ankle, seizing the leg of his trousers. The thug went to kick the dog, but the boot never connected with the fur because the bow twanged and Princess Purnah shot him in the leg. He screamed like a small child, hopped once and fell over.

So much for quiet! thought Emmaline. Stanley barked at the fallen bruiser, who was whimpering in pain.

"Trikk! Can I be cuttings his throat?" asked Purnah. "That will silence the pig for goodness! Hrrkkk!"

"No," said Emmaline. "We don't cut people's throats in England. It's considered very rude. Besides, I think it would be a good idea to run away now."

Which was true, so they did.

Rab opened the dormer window again. He was no fool; he knew that there was no point in assembling a bicycle inside the room if he couldn't get it out of the window. He looked at the pieces available to him. The one-wheeled lady's bicycle would do, and he pushed it through carefully. The back wheel would come from the penny-farthing, although it was much smaller than he'd prefer. He picked up the box of spare parts and chains and rusty bits and slid those out onto the roof as well.

Suddenly he heard footsteps on the stairs. In a moment the door would open. Rab had two choices: in or out. All his instincts told him that an open window is an opportunity not to be refused. But, without assembling the bicycle, there was no escape from the roof. He shut the window quickly and flung himself onto the mattress.

It might, after all, simply be lunchtime.

It wasn't, of course. It was Ted, taking him for another interview with the Faceless Fiend. "If he asks, tell 'im you was in an 'orrible dungeon wiv chains and suchlike." Rab didn't like his captors' keen interest in medieval torture.

He'd have to find a way out of all this—what would Miss Em call it?—"unpleasantness." And very soon.

Rubberbones walked down the stairs, two winding flights of them, and then along the hallway to the Faceless Fiend's study. He mentally abandoned the scheme where the bicycle leapt off the roof. They wouldn't send him back to the attic. He'd have to devise another plan.

If the house was either four or five stories high—Rab couldn't be sure which—then the Fiend's lair was one or two floors above the ground. The bare steps down from the attic were at the back of the house. There was another much grander staircase in the middle of the building. Rubberbones tried hard to memorize the layout. There were doorways that opened into bedrooms, and others that probably led into cupboards or lavatories, or those rooms where rich people took baths.

But now they had come to the door of the Faceless Fiend's lair. Escape was out for the moment.

The two girls and the small dog fled the way they had come. Purnah ran, Emmaline limped and Stanley rushed about in circles, growling each time they heard the sound of the grown man wailing like a child because of the sharp stick stuck in his leg. "Pooh!" said Princess Purnah, an opinion that Emmaline shared. "Is slightest woundings! If Chiligriti man howl like that, all family dishonored forever. Probably slicing his throats their own selves."

As they emerged into a clearing, they spotted a brightly painted Gypsy caravan parked ahead, the horse in traces nibbling grass. An elderly man in the distinctive costume of the Romany nobility greeted them with the dignity of his station: "Worro, Emmaline! Hop in the back. Norah's got the teapot on, but we've got to get cracking. You'd be the princess, then? And Stanley as well!"

Emmaline beamed with joy. Her friends Sid and Norah had arrived in the nick of time, like the cavalry in a western story. The Gypsies were uncanny in that respect.

As they entered the caravan—Stanley jumping, Emmaline helped by Princess Purnah—muscular men appeared through the screen of trees. They cursed and waved their fists. The vehicle lurched into motion, the horse surprisingly quick for its advanced age.

"We have to be able to move sharpish in our line of work," said a voice from inside the caravan. "Some people don't like Gypsies." Norah's crinkled face leaned forward to greet the new arrivals. "I'll pour the tea. I can do that while we move. Been doing it for fifty years and more. We knew about your trouble and came as quick as we could."

"How you knowings about much troubles here?" asked Princess Purnah. She was suspicious. "We not knowings ourselves."

Norah smiled. "Madame ZaZa knows all. Least, I consults me crystal ball regular to check up on Emmaline and young Rab. So I saw it. Rab's locked up in a room, you know. He was wearing the funniest costume. Nasty people there. A bloke so wicked that I can't 'ardly make him out. Can't see his features at all."

Emmaline explained to Princess Purnah. "Norah's professional name is Madame ZaZa. She's a fortune-teller. A very good one, too!"

"Oh, a seeress! A sorceringness! We have those in my country, too. Sometimes we keeps them as trusted advisers to Royal House. Sometimes we burnings them like witches. All depend on if they predictings rightly!"

"Mmm," said Norah, pursing her lips. "You aren't from Yorkshire, then."

"Where are we off to?" asked Emmaline.

"We're going to meet your aunt at Groansby Station. There's a train to London at 8:17, and she'll have the tickets."

And indeed she did. Aunt Lucy was there with Lal Singh and a pile of luggage. She looked at the two girls fondly, as if they had just returned from a visit to the village sweetshop rather than a dangerous series of misadventures.

"You look a little wild, Purnah, dear. I suppose it's the dirt and Rab's clothing, but there appears to be more blood on you than usual. It's not human, is it? It looks awfully dark and sticky. I've packed some clothes that you might change into before we get to London. We are meeting a man at King's Cross Station who has agreed to help us find Robert. Quite a well-known person in his field, as I understand, so everything will sort itself out quite soon, I expect."

She twittered on as if nothing was wrong at all, although Emmaline noticed that Lal Singh was looking around carefully, and he carried something heavy in his right-hand pocket. Also, there appeared to be some sort of knife slash across the shoulder of his kurta.

"Where is the professor?" asked Emmaline.

"Ozymandias is at the house," replied Aunt Lucy. "He was chatting with Robert on that strange device of his, so we left him in charge of things there. Oh, and that annoying Mr. Botts came back with a legal warrant for the princess. So Lal Singh and I caught a lift with a farmer in his hay cart—it seemed the best thing to do, and it's quite jolly burrowing down in the hay at my age."

"But the professor—will he be all right?"

"Oh, yes, dear. He has lots of rockets to fire off, and some small bombs he wants to try out. I did tell him not to use those inside the house, if at all possible."

There was a whoosh of steam and a squeal of brakes, and the 8:17 to London was awaiting them.

The Gypsies were ready to say farewell, for now. "We'll go to your aunt's house," said Sid to Emmaline. "We'll see if the professor needs a hand. If we can get rid of all the unwelcome visitors, we might see you in London. I hear the

137

lawn at Buckingham Palace is ideal for camping. I can be there in a week if the horse feels up to it!"

Norah had something for each of the girls. For Emmaline, she had a pendant on a chain. It was a tiny silver eagle, wings outstretched. "It'll help you talk to the winds, dearie. This has been in my family for hundreds of years, waiting for somebody who needed to fly. Keep it on you all the time."

She turned to Princess Purnah. "Something for you, my lovely." Purnah didn't seem to mind this term of endearment, even if it wasn't exactly how royal princesses were normally addressed. The gift was a silver ring, beautifully made and clearly very old. It was embossed with a symbol of a standing figure, an animal, paws raised in a fighting stance. "This is from the east, from the time when our people were fleeing from great peril."

"What do it do?" asked Purnah, puzzling over the figure.

"It keeps bears away," said Norah. Then she was inside the wagon and gone.

Lal Singh tossed the luggage into a train compartment, and the whistle blew. London!

CHAPTER 18

The Excitement of Trains

The Faceless Fiend was in no hurry to deal with the boy who had so rudely interfered with his plans. He was on the telephone. A normal telephone with a crank and an ear-horn and a separate piece to speak into rather than one of the professor's devices. Somebody at the other end of the line was getting an earful.

"Those dolts must not fail this time. You say they left as soon as I contacted you? Don't lie to me! It's an hour's journey to Little Owlthwaite. They must be at the house by now. If not, heads will roll—literally!" He banged down the phone.

Rab stood quietly by the door. There were two other men in the room. One was the bloodhound-featured Number Three or "Mr. Black." Rubberbones thought he was probably a very dangerous character, and his humiliation at the hands of Lal Singh and Aunt Lucy two days ago couldn't have made him any sweeter. The other was a muscular figure dressed from head to foot in black leather, beautifully tailored to fit, with a hood and mask. Both were standing at attention. If Number One didn't tell you to sit, you didn't sit. Rab didn't sit. Nobody seemed concerned about him being there; they must have considered him insignificant. He looked at the clock—it was ten thirty-two—and the stuffed animal heads.

Number One told the men to sit. They gathered close to the fireplace and began a discussion that Rubberbones couldn't hear. The man in leather fascinated him. His costume shone in the firelight. Must be ruddy hot wearing that next to the hearth, thought Rab. Who was this masked man?

The clock read eleven-oh-four. Would they keep him waiting forever?

"Anyway," said Aunt Lucy, "I'd got the bags all packed when Lal Singh returned. Dear Ozymandias was talking to Robert on that radiophonic device he invented—he's so clever! He mentioned something about being on a roof and the sound of Bow bells and a bicycle. Then that horrid pterodactyl appeared again, flying as if it were injured. And those nasty teachers from St. Grimelda's showed up on that funny contraption they own—'trilocopede,' isn't it? It was the thin one I'd seen before and a muscular woman. Not the huge headmistress, thank goodness."

Emmaline knew who she meant. The thin one was Miss Scantcommon, the wicked matron who tended to the "birds." During her escape from St. Grimelda's, Purnah had fired a rocket at the teacher, setting fire to her skirt and sending her hurtling down a flight of stairs. Scantcommon was mean to the marrow. Her companion had to have been Miss Sharpelbow, the hearty games mistress, who was as cheerful as she was brutal. The headmistress, the horrible Mrs. Wackett, must have sent them to follow the pterodactyl after it was set loose to pursue Purnah. They must want her back badly.

Aunt Lucy continued. "We'd arranged that Lal Singh and I would hop into Farmer Jenkins's cart when he came past. The professor would cause a diversion—something he learned from his American friends who rob banks for a living, he told me. Of course, what he did was spectacular."

Emmaline was filled with excitement. And fear. What had Professor Bellbuckle done?

"Well," explained Aunt Lucy, "he climbed out of the attic window with a basketful of his rockets and aimed one of them at the bird, which was perched in its unattractive way upon the chimney pots. It was probably twenty feet away. I assume the professor was trying to hit it, but—well, you know how he is—he missed completely, accidentally dropped the match into the basket and fell head over heels down the roof."

Emmaline gasped in horror. Princess Purnah's eyes lit up. "Horrible manglings?" she asked.

"No, no. Ozy—the professor—caught the gutter pipe as he fell. I noticed him swinging precariously for a moment, but he managed to pull himself back up onto the roof tiles. He's really quite acrobatic, that man! But the basket of fireworks went flying off the roof with the pterodactyl after it; I expect it thought it was chasing Professor Bellbuckle. The thin woman called out to the creature. So the pterodactyl caught the basket and brought it directly to its mistress."

As Stanley would have, thought Emmaline. She made a mental note that Stanley must never be allowed to fetch flaming fireworks.

"There was a tremendous set of flashes, then a huge bang. I was helping Lal Singh get the luggage into the hay cart at the time, but I looked up to see the professor standing on the roof trying to put out his coattails, which were smoking rather fiercely. He didn't look too badly singed, though, and he waved at me, and then we were off with rather a jolt and I didn't see anything else."

Princess Purnah shouted "Aieeee!!" in an exultant sort of way and jumped on her seat in a little dance. Emmaline was full of questions. Was that the end of the pterodactyl? What about the teachers? They were strict—cruel, in fact—but she hadn't wished for them to explode; although Purnah clearly thought this was a fate they deserved. What about the beefy men? Had they run away? And the house—had it fallen down? It always looked as if it might tumble to the ground if someone so much as sneezed loudly.

"Sad about the pterodactyl," murmured Aunt Lucy.

Emmaline nodded. "It should have been studied by scientists. They could have built a place for it at a zoo. If it was killed, it could be stuffed and put in the Natural History Museum."

"Actually, I was thinking of making stew from it," said Aunt Lucy. "We've never had that."

"I wanting its head," said Princess Purnah. "Make excellent

decorations for Chiligriti royal palace. Or bringings out for parade on my birthdays."

Lal Singh smiled. Emmaline thought that he enjoyed living at Aunt Lucy's house, assuming it was still standing, because it was full of mad people, and he could entertain his many relatives in the Punjab with long letters about their lunatic behavior.

It was at this moment that something quite ordinary happened. The train slowed down to a halt as a second train, heading north on the opposite track, passed it.

They looked out at the faces of the people on the other train, as normal people do, and saw children waving in one compartment. Princess Purnah waved back and pulled faces, as Emmaline was rather afraid she might.

"Ooh! Look-eee!" she shrieked.

Of course, they all did. And they saw Mr. White looking back at them.

He stared back in recognition and leapt to his feet. His face turned crimson red as he opened the carriage door and flung himself across the gap between the rails in a single bound. Emmaline was astonished that a man so short and stout could move so quickly. Princess Purnah continued to pull faces, this time at Mr. White, now with her thumbs to her ears and waggling fingers to anger him further. Lal Singh gently lifted her aside, ready to deal with the raging henchman of the Faceless Fiend.

"My turn, if you don't mind, Lal Singh," said Aunt Lucy with a steely voice.

"As the Memsahib wishes," he replied with a smile.

As Mr. White hauled open the door, Aunt Lucy stepped back to allow him to step up into the compartment. This was a trick, of course, because as soon as he came forward she struck him over the head with her umbrella. With his hat crammed down over his eyes he didn't see the firm jab that poked him in the chest and sent him head over heels onto the gravel between the tracks.

Aunt Lucy would have finished with a final, brolly-busting thwack across his ample buttocks, but the train to London started to move again.

She flourished the remains of the umbrella in a swashbuckling fashion—like one of the Three Musketeers, thought Emmaline—and sat down.

"That'll teach him," said Aunt Lucy. "Well, it might not. But I enjoyed it."

Mr. White was floundering on the ground as his own, northbound train, disappeared into a tunnel.

CHAPTER 19

"Any Luck with Escaping?"

The Faceless Fiend finally turned toward Rubberbones.

"So, we meet again. I trust you are enjoying the hospitality of my dungeon?"

Rab tried to look like a prisoner who had been hanging by his thumbs.

"No marks on your wrists," observed the Fiend. He turned to his colleagues. "Number Three, Number Four. Give me your opinions."

"No scratches at all, Your Excellency. No bruises, burns or other signs that he has been chained up. Nothing on his ankles, either. Your jailer must be far too kind," hissed the man in black leather. The mask had openings for the eyes, the nostrils and the mouth. Rab was impressed, in a terrified sort of way.

"The jailer's an idle beggar," declared Number Three. "This boy's been no more chained up than I have. Well, I actually have been chained up, but not today. I tell you, Number One, we need better people."

"Silence, Number Three," said the Faceless Fiend. "The Masked Minions have arrived from their operation in Berlin, so we'll no longer need the fools I have been forced to employ." He looked into Rab's eyes. "You, boy, must tell what you know, immediately. I have no time for foolishness. Again, where is the princess?"

Rab told the truth. "Dunno, sir."

The Fiend slapped him across the face.

"Where was she when you last saw her?"

"Flying in a kite off the roof of the house," replied Rubberbones. It was the exact truth as he knew it. Another slap.

"Do not take me for a fool, boy! I must deliver the princess to my ... clients, and I brook no delay. Where can I find her?"

Rab was about to say again that he didn't know when the radiophonic creation of Professor Bellbuckle's, concealed beneath his shirt, crackled into activity. "Robert! Hello! Hello!"

The Fiend ripped open Rab's shirt (it was one that Biddy had given him, so he didn't care much) and grabbed the device as it buzzed and whined at him.

"Hello, Robert! Bellbuckle here again! Any luck with escaping?"

The Fiend's face would have blazed in fury if he had had one. "Bellbuckle!" he shouted. "The mad American! The inventor of gimcrack machines and engines of destruction!"

Rab nodded, then silently cursed himself for doing so.

Number One held the device in front of his face, staring at it as the tinny speaker sounded out "Hello!" once more. Then he spoke with a false calm. "Professor Bellbuckle. You will recognize my voice. We met once before, in Vienna, and your interference cost me dearly. I will avenge myself on you when we meet. But, for now, I have your young friend in my ... hospitality."

"You gosh-durned scoundrel!" replied the small voice from the device. "You're the thievin' galoot who stole a jug of my experimental Nitro-Glycerine Hair-Restorer and used it as a bomb! If you hurt that boy, I swear that I will personally—"

What the professor would personally do was left unsaid, as the device spluttered and went dead.

"Number Three, please escort this boy down to the dungeon and ensure that he is treated … as I would wish. Number Four, let us speak of your mission in Germany."

Rubberbones would learn nothing of what the leather-clad man and the rest of the—what? Masked Minions?—had been up to in Germany because the thin, frightening man they called Number Three escorted him to the door by the scruff of his collar.

Despite a lingering fear that Mr. White had clambered up on the roof of the train and would drop on them as they stepped down at King's Cross Station, Emmaline found the rest of the journey very pleasant. She was able to get cleaned up from the mud and pterodactyl blood, and Aunt Lucy wrapped her injured foot in a poultice of roots and vegetables she'd brought along crushed up inside a sock. Princess Purnah turned herself into a reasonable imitation of a Victorian schoolgirl by a liberal use of soap and a set of fresh clothes. Lal Singh discreetly disappeared while the girls washed and changed, which was impressive as the train had no corridor. Emmaline didn't see him leave or return, but suspected he had climbed on the roof for half an hour. Perhaps he'd been watching for Mr. White.

Neither Emmaline nor Princess Purnah had ever been to London before. Purnah had never been to a city at all and thought that Lower Owlthwaite—a place of four hundred people—was a teeming metropolis. Settlements in Chiligrit were clusters of mud houses huddled in the shadow of defensive towers. Emmaline had been raised in the vast, broiling sprawl of Calcutta, in India, where the calm British architecture of the government buildings sat cheek by jowl with jostling bazaars, narrow alleys and crowded slums. Of course, London had the same things (although the street markets weren't called bazaars, and there were no elephants doing the heavy work), but it was different in so many ways. So she'd read. Now she would find out.

Remembering Calcutta made Emmaline think of her parents. With a jolt, it occurred to her how seldom they were in her thoughts. Mrs. Cayley had always seemed to want her daughter to be more ladylike, more decorative, more frilly; her father had always seemed to be oblivious to his only child's existence. She hadn't sent a letter in weeks, since escaping from the school they'd arranged for her. She must write. Perhaps something like *"Dear Mother and Father, I have a tutor who makes me jump off the roof. Today I fought an extinct flying lizard. I find myself running from hired thugs on a regular basis. Hope you are well. Love, Emmaline."*

"Are you daydreaming, dear?" asked Aunt Lucy. "We are pulling into London."

Nobody jumped down from the carriage roof as they climbed out of the train. The big, muscular man awaiting them appeared kindly; it was something about his eyes. Emmaline thought he was quite old, since there was gray in his mustache.

"Mrs. Butterworth?" he asked.

Aunt Lucy nodded. "You'd be Mr. Watson, then."

"Doctor, actually. I'm a physician. But proper introductions later. My colleague has a balloon waiting for us."

The dungeon! Rubberbones wasn't about to be locked up again if he had a choice in the matter. But getting away from Number Three would be tougher than escaping from the lazy caretaker. The bloodhound-faced man was professional and efficient; he reminded Rab of a game-keeper guarding his lordship's estate from trespassers.

Should've done a runner when Ted was behind me, he thought. I'd have lost him in a moment. This man would not be as easy to get rid of. He kept his grip on Rab's collar as they marched down the hallway. Rab wriggled a little, just to see what Number Three did. The hand tightened, and the lad was jerked off the floor.

"Don't test me, boy!" he hissed viciously. Rab pretended to go limp. Number Three prodded him in the back with his knee. "No tricks!"

"Sorry, sir," mumbled Rab and shuffled forward at his captor's command. They reached the top of the cellar stairs. The steps were steep, the stairwell winding.

"I'm hanging on to you, my lad. Don't do anything silly. You'll break your neck."

But, of course, he was Rubberbones. Everybody in Lower Owlthwaite knew about the rubber boy. If this bloke didn't, he'd soon find out. Rab set his feet against the top step and gritted his teeth. If Number Three wouldn't let go, they'd both find out what the bottom of the staircase had to offer a falling human.

Rab leaned forward as if to look before climbing down the stairs. The man's hand on his collar allowed him to stretch forward a few inches. Then the boy kicked his feet against the wooden upright of the step, and launched himself into space. He heard a startled voice behind him shriek, "Wait—a—aaaggghhh!" He plunged forward with a body thumping into his own as they hit a step. Then another, and another.

And then he was up and running with no hand on his collar and a furious voice shouting at him in an agonized fashion. The kind of shout a man who had broken a leg or two, or perhaps an arm, or all of the above, might make.

CHAPTER 20

The Balloon

Emmaline had never ridden in a hansom cab before. It was a carriage for two people, pulled by a single horse, with a driver standing up behind them leaning over the roof. She and Purnah shared one cab; Dr. Watson and Aunt Lucy were in the cab ahead, while Lal Singh and the luggage followed in a baggage cart. Emmaline thought that it was unfair to Lal Singh because he wasn't really a servant. He was more a "resident hero." Still, Stanley rode with him, and that was good.

The convoy passed through city streets of stone and red-brick buildings with colorful names like "Jockey Fields Street." Princess Purnah was astounded at the number of buildings, their size and regularity, and the fact that none were made out of mud. They pulled up at a park crowded with people. What made it interesting was what the people were gathered around gaping at. A balloon.

Emmaline had never actually seen a hot-air balloon. There were pictures of them in books she had read, but they were quite rare in everyday life. This one was a white ball the size of, er, a really big white ball, covered in netting and tethered to the ground, apparently against its will. There was a basket beneath it with apparatus that controlled the hot air inside the balloon, or the "envelope," as Emmaline knew it was called. She had always been so interested in her great-great-uncle's concepts of gliders and "heavier than air" flying machines that she'd never spent much time studying balloons. Was there a chance she could go up in this one? She hoped so.

The balloonist was inside the basket, adjusting the gas burners, and another man, a tall, slender figure with the kind of long nose ideal for looking down on people, stood close by. Emmaline was excited to see that he was wearing a cape and a deerstalker hat, as he did in the popular illustrations. She was not sure what one should say to such a great man, a hero to millions, idol of rich and poor. Aunt Lucy had no doubts, though.

"Hello, Mr. Holmes. I thought you were imaginary!"

Sherlock Holmes smiled—a thin sort of smile. "Yes, I have heard that about myself. And I've put some effort into pretending to be dead, as well. Still, here we are."

The man inside the basket indicated that the balloon was ready whenever Mr. Holmes was ready. Mr. Holmes spoke with Aunt Lucy while Emmaline examined the balloon and Purnah threw sticks at passers-by. After a few minutes, the great detective came over to speak to the girls.

"Your aunt has told me all she knows about the whereabouts of your missing friend. This communication by radiophonic device is most interesting. We will ascend to such a height as makes it possible to scan the city for the house your friend, Master Burns, describes as being his prison. He apparently describes it as old, although we cannot know what he means by that. Very few buildings in the city have survived the fire of 1666, but a house built a mere hundred years ago might seem ancient to a boy. He believes that it is four or five stories in height, and that the neighboring houses are lower. That is most useful. He can see what he believes is the new Tower Bridge, and London Bridge, as well. He can see something of the docks, possibly at Wapping, where the river turns southward. He identifies St. Paul's Cathedral, although the area has a number of impressive churches which the boy might have mistaken for the great cathedral; frankly, I am surprised that a village boy would have heard of St. Paul's at all."

He cleared his throat and continued, "The evidence suggests that this house is within a mile of the river, possibly some distance north of the Tower of London, or a little to the west. It could be the area known as Smithfield, or perhaps Spitalfields beyond it. I have my associates scouring the area, but I thought we might take advantage of Mr. Pettipas and his balloon to examine London from the air. Who knows, Master Burns might accommodate us by actually being on the roof of the house in question, although that seems a lot to presume. We will observe the skyline by use of this telescope."

Sherlock Holmes pointed to the basket, then toward the two girls. "Pettipas says that he can take two persons of your weight. I assume you would both like to ascend in a balloon?"

"Yes!" said Emmaline breathlessly. "Yipp!" said Princess Purnah, which might have been a "yes," or possibly a "not if I can help it."

"Princess Purnah, you must understand that your safety is of tremendous concern to Her Majesty's Government. I would rather that you remain in my company, or with Dr. Watson, who has a revolver, than risk your falling into the hands of people who wish you ill. Believe me, you are in as much danger in London as you were in Yorkshire. However, you will be in no danger as long as the balloon is tethered; indeed, probably less so than on the ground, where disguised foes may approach in the crowd. Which is it to be?"

Purnah looked very suspicious. "You no takings me back to horrid schools?"

Holmes laughed, briefly. "My dear princess, I have no interest in returning you to any school you do not wish to attend. But the government is certainly concerned that you are kept from harm; you can argue the details with their officials at a later time."

Princess Purnah mumbled something about being referred to as "Your Majesty," but beneath her breath so that only Emmaline caught it. At least there were no threats of strangling made.

Holmes helped both girls into the basket as Mr. Pettipas, a small, swarthy man with an intelligent gleam in his eye, adjusted the gas jets for the balloon to rise. As it did, Stanley broke away from his seat among the luggage, evading Lal Singh's efforts to stop him, and jumped into the basket.

In fairness to Lal Singh, it should be mentioned that he was holding a picnic hamper, a steamer trunk and three umbrellas, one broken. Otherwise, he'd have caught the dog.

Pettipas said something uncomplimentary about Stanley and small dogs in general. Stanley bit at his trouser leg. Aunt Lucy called out, "Break a leg!" as if they were acting in a play.

The balloon slowly rose above the trees and rooftops of London.

Rubberbones was running like a madman. He ignored the injured yells of Number Three, lying in a heap at the bottom of the stairs. He leapt down the hall toward the grand staircase that ran up the center of the building. As he reached the stairs, he heard footsteps running up from below.

Tarnation! Criminy! Rab thought it sounded like a dozen gamekeepers after him.

This staircase was out. He ran for the steps at the rear of the building. He just *had* to get there.

The footsteps on the stairs pounded closer, but Rab was racing down the hall. He bounded along the worn green carpet toward the back stairs.

A man in the same head-to-toe leather uniform as Number Four appeared from nowhere.

Rab swerved to his right, head down. The man turned, ready to grab. Rab charged and hit the wall, then cannoned off past the leather man's outstretched hands. Rubberbones didn't stop running. The man was behind him, turning fast.

The back wall of the building loomed ahead. Surely there was a doorway to the steps?

There was, and he hurtled through it, dodging like a rabbit pursued by hounds, onto a darkened landing where the steps that would take him down to the ground floor were … were filled with the sound of footsteps coming upward at a clattering run.

Rubberbones could only go in one direction. He started up the stairs toward the top of the house. Maybe he could double back on his tracks and make it to the kitchen and out the back door. But right now he was running up, not down.

Emmaline was astounded at the view from two hundred feet above Lincoln's Inn Fields. Aunt Lucy and Lal Singh were like toy figures. To the south was the River Thames. To the west was Westminster Abbey, and Big Ben towering over the Houses of Parliament, and Mayfair and Hyde Park, places she'd only read about. Mr. Holmes was not interested in those places; he preferred to focus toward the east, to the area where he believed that Rab was being held. He was, however, willing to point things out.

"That dome is St. Paul's Cathedral, of course. Built by Sir Christopher Wren after the great fire, which burned down most of the city in the year after the Great Plague, as I am sure you know."

Emmaline thought that Mr. Holmes had no idea how to talk to young ladies. He probably seldom had to, except when they came to tell him about their fathers going missing, or their uncles trying to murder them for their inheritances. Not normal conversations, anyway. So she said, "Yes, sir," and prodded Princess Purnah to agree as well. Purnah burped in the traditional Chiligriti sign of agreement.

Mr. Holmes fell silent as he scanned the horizon with his telescope. Pettipas fussed with his apparatus and spoke occasionally to Mr. Holmes, pointing and apparently complaining about something, using the word "eh" a great deal. Emmaline thought he might be a Canadian.

A gust of wind struck the balloon suddenly, causing it to judder against the lines tethering it to the ground.

"Trikk! Hooty-hoot!" announced Princess Purnah. Pettipas glared and spoke again to Mr. Holmes. Emmaline could hear the conversation.

"I promised you nothing of the kind, Mr. Holmes. Not with the wind picking up like this, eh. We'll have to descend. It's not safe to be up here. It's certainly not safe to be drifting across the city. I need the balloon in tip-top shape for the exhibition tomorrow."

"Mr. Pettipas, I find I cannot observe the building in question owing to the taller structures between our current location and the dwelling I seek. In simple terms, I can't see the house from here. I'll give you another ten sovereigns to fly over the City itself."

Pettipas gulped because ten sovereigns—ten pounds in English money—was worth having. But the wind was picking up, and Emmaline understood that ten pounds is no use if you have plunged two hundred feet onto Charing Cross Road or Chancery Lane. She didn't know the geography of London, but one street looks much like another when you are smashing into the cobblestones.

Princess Purnah understood the situation very well, also. She knew that Rab's safety was at stake. While Mr. Holmes and Mr. Pettipas argued about whether to remain aloft for a while longer, the heiress to the royal throne of Chiligrit drew out her sharpened butter knife from under her skirts.

And, grinning at Emmaline, she cut the ropes that tethered the balloon to the ground.

CHAPTER 21

Up on the Roof, Again

Rab raced up the back stairs. Behind him he heard a flurry of footsteps in pursuit. He leapt upward, two steps at a time, until he arrived at a landing with a door. Should he open it? No. The Fiend had his study on this floor. It was a terrible place to look for a hidey-hole. Up another floor. The same sort of landing with another door. The first room he'd been held in was here. He'd duck down this hallway and find a place to hide—maybe there was a cupboard with sheets and blankets and—

The door opened, and there stood another of the leather men. The Masked Minions. Rubberbones slammed into the man with his shoulder, then kicked him in the shin. The Masked Minion howled, hopping on one leg. Rab rushed up the stairs again. He reached the top; the steps ended. There was a single door without a landing, and Rab realized that he'd reached the attic, the very top of the old house. Which meant that he was not getting out of the kitchen door or the scullery window any time soon. Still, he knew where to hide.

No, criminy and tarnation! He knew where to escape.

He flung open the door into the room with the bits of old bicycles and was out of the window in a flash.

The wind caught the balloon in a vast billowing gust and swept them eastward. The basket was spinning. Pettipas frantically operated the burners, and Stanley barked in delight. Mr. Sherlock Holmes smiled, in a grim sort of way, at the princess.

"Mrs. Butterworth told me that you are a strong-minded young lady, Your Majesty. The phrase she used was 'mischievous scamp.' I would ask you to restrict your enthusiasm a little and hang on tight. Hold onto your dog, also. I don't wish to preserve you from a Master Criminal only to drop you into the Thames from several hundred feet up. Important people would be displeased."

Princess Purnah was about to reply that she, too, would be displeased, and that there might be beheadings or stranglings, or possibly something nastier still, but Emmaline stepped on her foot to silence her. The aerodynamics of the balloon, the balance, the control of altitude by Mr. Pettipas's burners enthralled Emmaline. The only time she'd flown before was in a homemade glider with pterodactyls in pursuit and the North Sea below her. Now she could appreciate the flight, rather than simply hope that it ended soon.

The brisk wind, fresh out of the west, had not turned into the gale that Mr. Pettipas had feared. He'd come to an agreement with Mr. Holmes, too, about the extra money for the flight; after all, since it was already underway, he might as well get paid for it.

"You see that building there?" demanded Holmes. "Not the big one. That's the British Museum. No, across the road, there's the Adelphi Inn where I spoke to the innkeeper about his geese in 'The Case of the Blue Carbuncle.' You've read Watson's account of it, no doubt?"

Mr. Holmes regarded the flight above London as a chance to point out items of interest, many of them places where he had pursued criminals or been hounded by his enemy, the late Professor Moriarty. Emmaline tried to pay attention but found herself fascinated by the aeronautical aspects of ballooning. Princess Purnah, however, was looking out for her friend, the Errand Boy, who was somewhere out in this strange world of slanting roofs and chimney pots. It all looked to her like some sort of mad mountain range, the peaked roofs of tile and slate like the summits of crags. So it was only right that she would be the one who saw a boy climbing on one of the peaks.

"Look-ee! Is himling! Over there."

Mr. Holmes seized his telescope and scanned the skyline to the northeast. "Spitalfields. The old silk-weavers' houses around Fournier Street. A fine old London neighborhood, now falling into slums. And, yes, you can see that the house in question is higher than those on either side. A very tall house, probably dating from the early part of the eighteenth century. Note the distinctive architectural features. A most perceptive boy."

Emmaline was less interested in the architectural uniqueness of the house. "But he's on the roof! Can he get down?"

"That, my dear young lady, is the question. Mr. Pettipas, is it possible to maneuver our way in that direction? Oh? A matter of the wind, you say? That's most inconvenient."

Emmaline realized that Mr. Holmes, although an expert in poisons, stains and footprints, among many other things, did not know that a balloon goes only where the wind takes it.

And the wind was taking it along the edge of the river, where they would pass the house at quite a distance and not even be heard by Rubberbones if they were to shout at him.

Emmaline was afraid. Rubberbones was on a roof, a very high roof, above a very hard stone street, and he didn't have a kite to fly with.

"You are worried your friend will fall," said Sherlock Holmes.

"No," said Emmaline. "I am worried my friend will jump."

Emmaline clutched the side of the basket in one hand and the pendant that Norah, Madame ZaZa, had given her in the other.

At that very moment the wind shifted to blow from the south, and the balloon began to drift northward.

———

Rubberbones wrestled with the bicycle parts. If he could take the small wheel from the ancient penny-farthing and fix it to the broken safety bicycle—and fix the handlebars and straighten out the saddle—he might have something he could ride. If he had an hour, he could work it out.

He thought he might have two minutes.

Rubberbones dragged the various bicycle parts toward the crest of the roof so he couldn't be seen from the attic windows. He was so engrossed in fixing the chain and watching to see if any heads popped out of the windows that he didn't notice the balloon drifting his way. He was testing the assembled jumble of bicycle bits to see if they would pedal forward when he heard a voice that he knew well.

"Aieeee! Errand Boy! Why you so foolishly bikings on rooftop?"

At the same time, he heard a window creak open.

Rab looked up, and the handlebars fell off.

He saw a balloon not fifty yards away, carrying his friends Emmaline and Princess Purnah and two unknown men. The balloon was approaching slowly, and the princess had a rope in her hands. A small face bobbed up above the edge of the basket, barking happily.

A Masked Minion emerged through the window of Rab's recent cell. A second followed. Their eyes, visible through the holes in their full-face masks, darted around looking for him. Then they spotted the balloon. Rab saw both men dive back inside the house, shouting; he didn't think they were scared.

No. They were alerting the other minions. Even if they hadn't spotted him, the balloon had attracted their attention.

"Robert Burns!" shouted Emmaline. "Stop messing about with that—that broken bicycle and prepare to be rescued!"

Rubberbones was unwilling to abandon his plan, ridiculous though it might be. The professor had told him to cycle off the roof, and he was going to do as he was told. Gosh-darn it.

"Throw me a screwdriver and a pair o' pliers and I'll have this thing fixed!" he shouted back.

Emmaline could not believe that Rab could be so wooden-headed. "We're going to throw you a rope. You will grab onto it. Drop the blasted bicycle and listen to me!"

Sherlock Holmes whispered to Princess Purnah, "Your friend can be quite determined, can't she?"

"Oh yess, Holmslock Shears. Emmaline Cay-lee is completely bossy-boots!"

Emmaline tossed the rope down as the balloon veered forward toward the chimneys. "It's secure enough—take it, Rab!"

Rab might have argued, but Masked Minions came bursting out of the attic window. The first one lunged forward up the tiles toward him. Rab hoisted the bike and threw it with full force. The man took the seat in his teeth and staggered backward onto his comrades.

Princess Purnah leapt excitedly. "Throw more bikings, Errand Boy!" She was tremendously disappointed when the Minions collapsed in a heap on the roof rather than falling to their spattered deaths fifty feet below. "Make slaughter of enemies!"

Rubberbones seized the rope and inched his way up. He swayed precariously as the wind gusted again and the balloon skittered above the roof. Emmaline leaned forward, hand outstretched. Stanley pranced, and Princess Purnah shouted encouragement. "Hekki-troo! Ezzeekh! Hopti-oop!"

"Stop leaning like that!" yelled Mr. Pettipas. "You'll upset the basket."

"And then where would we be?" asked Mr. Holmes dreamily. As the others grew more excited, he seemed calmer than ever. "But I would draw your attention to that man with a pistol. I believe he means to shoot at us."

Emmaline looked down at Rab, climbing hand over hand up the rope. She saw a Masked Minion with a revolver, aiming upward. Then she saw him pitch over backward as a girl's ballet shoe struck him full in the face. A second hit him a moment later.

"Trikk!" shouted the now barefoot Princess Purnah.

Pettipas opened the burners to make the balloon rise. The basket lurched wildly, and Rab stopped climbing. Emmaline leaned far out over the side of the basket. One of the Masked Minions was clutching Rubberbones by the feet, and both were swinging at the end of the rope as the roof sank away below. She could also see the other Masked Minions forming into what could only be termed a firing squad, aiming pistols upward. They were commanded by a man who pointed fiercely —

A man who had no face. So now she had seen him for herself.

A volley of shots rang out, and the balloon staggered across the rooftops.

Emmaline heard Pettipas tugging and pulling at controls and cords, yelling all the while that he'd not been paid for this kind of work. Mr. Holmes told him to get a grip and behave like a gentleman. The balloon drifted faster across the rooftops of London. It was dropping, as well. Had the bullets punctured the gas-filled envelope of the balloon? Was a horrible death mere moments away?

CHAPTER 22

A Masked Minion and an Artistical Model

Rubberbones was having a hard time climbing the rope with a muscular opponent swinging from his legs. The man was twice his weight. Rab thought he should pick on somebody his own size.

"Come on, Robert! You can make it!" shouted Emmaline.

"Kick off villainous bandit and arising to us!" yelled Princess Purnah.

"Woof!" barked Stanley. "Woof!" He was very supportive.

Even so, Rab's efforts to wriggle free of his captor—or step on his head, as he'd once done to Farmer Brumbley's lad Tam in a village football match—weren't succeeding. Despite his silly leather outfit, which must be as slippery as anything, the man held on. Rubberbones was getting quite cross with the Minion. Flippin' cheek!

The balloon was still dropping, and on either side Rab could see into the upstairs windows of houses. The ground was not so far now, and if he could spot a soft patch of grass or a wagon of hay, he was going to jump. It couldn't be more than thirty feet, and that was hardly anything for a rubber boy. But then the balloon jerked upward and sideways, and he began to swing like a pendulum, the Masked Minion clinging beneath.

"Watch out!" shouted Emmaline.

"Be careful, Mr. Pettipas," cautioned Sherlock Holmes. "Just because we are under fire does not excuse carelessness. That fellow hanging underneath seems to be shouting for his mother in Russian. He seems rather upset about the situation."

Mr. Pettipas growled that he was just trying to save their lives, when the basket began to spin madly. Stanley hauled Emmaline back to safety as she leaned over to call out to Rab. When she looked down again, the rope was still swinging. But there was nobody holding onto it.

The window was large, as attic windows go. Sherlock Holmes would have explained to Rubberbones that it was made that way when the house was built for a French silk-weaver around 1720 to allow plenty of light for his workshop. Sherlock Holmes was not explaining architectural matters to anyone right now, since he was spinning about and being shot at. But it was lucky that the builder of the house had gone to so much trouble because Rab was about to crash into the window. There wasn't much he could do about it, so he closed his eyes before breaking the glass. The Masked Minion couldn't do much either, so he dug his fingernails into Rab's leg. "Ruddy nerve!" thought the boy.

The last time Rab had swung in midair outside a window had been the night he had used his kite to float around the tower at St. Grimelda's, trying to contact Emmaline. He'd been very shy about it, closing his eyes in case he disturbed any of the girls in their nightgowns or glimpsed anything unsuitable.

He was certain that what he saw now, as he crashed through the window, was not at all suitable. He shut his eyes again. But he opened them as he landed among a spray of glass shards, on his back, behind a sofa. The Masked Minion had swung his legs up to clear the window ledge, and between them they performed an accidental trapeze act where the minion flew forward into the room, feet first. Which might have been quite impressive. Except for the artist, and the canvas and the naked lady.

Rab didn't really take much notice of the canvas, ripped where the flying Minion had careened into it. Neither did he take any interest in the painter, who was small and angry and kicking the Masked Minion in the ribs. He was concerned with not staring at the plump, middle-aged woman holding a bunch of grapes above her head and posing theatrically. Rab was relieved that she wasn't entirely bare to the world; she had a garland in her hair and a bit of thin white sheet draped around her, like a tiny bath towel on a large bather.

"*Sauvage! Idiot! Assassin de la culture!*" yelled the painter as he pummeled the dazed Minion.

"'Allo," said the almost-naked lady to Rab. "Want one of these grapes, then? You look a bit flushed. Oh! You're blushing! Never seen an *artiste* in the altogether before? Go on, 'ave a grape."

Rubberbones gulped. The artist was jumping up and down in rage and swearing in French at the Masked Minion, who still hadn't gotten up.

"Don't mind 'im. 'E's a bit excitable," said the lady. "We don't get a lot of people busting in through the winders. That bloke with you—looks a bit funny, dun'ee? All that leather. Still, takes all sorts."

Rab was relieved that she had put on a dressing gown.

"Er, I have to go," he said. "There's strange men after me."

"You've got to watch out for strange men," replied the almost-naked lady. "Some are more trouble'n others. Let's go out while Pierre knocks the stuffing out of the bloke in the

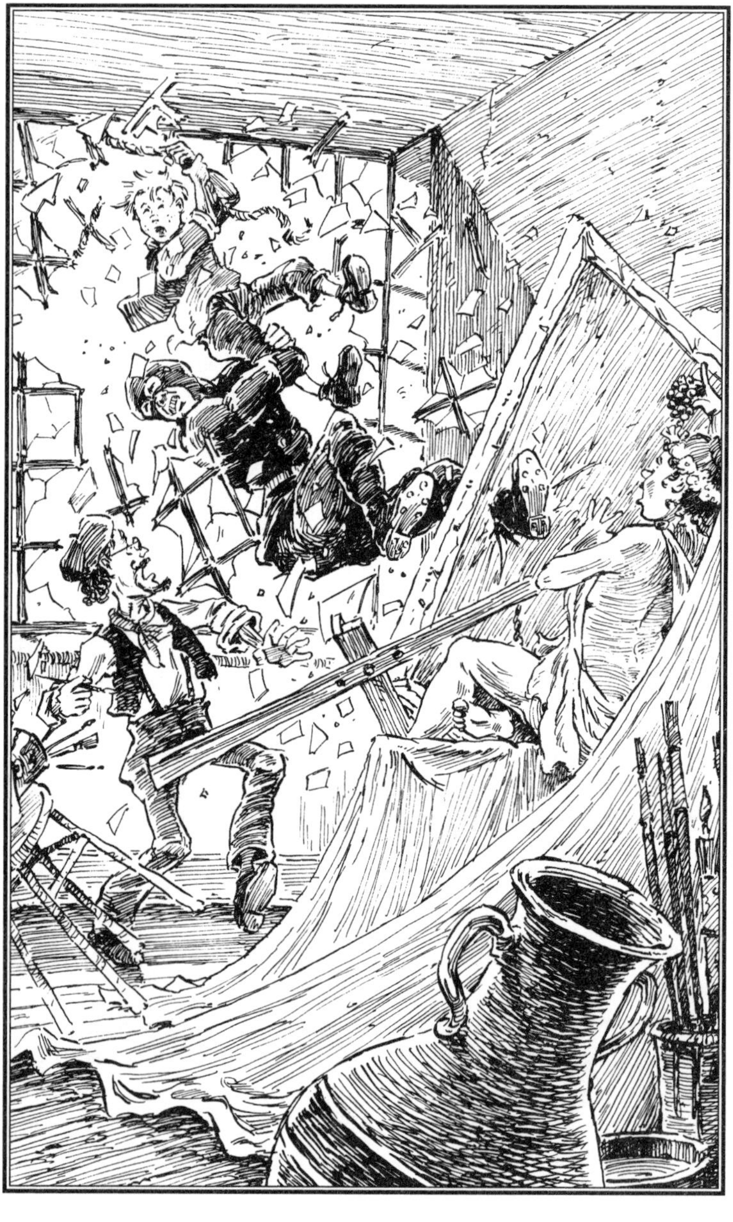

mask. 'E's a bit annoyed with the picture being damaged an' all. I don't care, meself. I'll get paid for posing again in the morning."

They made their way down the stairs. The yelling continued from the upstairs studio. Rab tried not to look at the woman's substantial wobbling bottom under the dressing gown. It made him nervous, somehow.

"Where are we?" asked Rubberbones. "Me mam lives in Bethnal Green, 27 Old Nichol Street."

"Oh, that's 'ardly no distance at all. Go up Commercial Street, down Wheler Street, across Bethnal Green Road and arsk again. Ten minutes' walk. Just 'ang on and let me look out the door for yer. Might be more of them leather blokes wiv the masks. Can't trust a man wiv a mask, in my experience."

She opened the front door and looked both ways. "Nah, just some lads at the end of the street, kicking a ball about."

"Thanks," said Rubberbones. "I've lost me friends in a balloon. I've got to find 'em. But first I think I'll go and see me mam."

The woman looked at him fondly. "Yeah, go and see yer old mum. Take this sixpence in case you need anything. If you ever need any 'elp, my name's Mademoiselle Rosalie DuGarde, Actress and Artistical Model. You can call me Rosie. Blimey, bit chilly out 'ere, innit?" She pulled the dressing gown around her ample advantages. "Cheerio then!"

Rab began walking down the street. One of the boys playing football shouted out, "There he is!" and all the lads came running after him. Rubberbones broke into a sprint. He could run like the wind. Or, at least, like a boy who has escaped from Masked Minions.

"I shouldn't worry about young Master Burns," said Sherlock Holmes. "We'll have constables on the scene within minutes. Inspector Lestrade will have him safe and sound, and he'll nab this Number One and his underlings, too! My Baker Street Irregulars are already patrolling the area, so nobody can enter or leave without their noticing."

Without the added weight of two people swinging from a rope, the balloon had lifted over the rooftops, out of pistol range of the Fiend's firing squad. Mr. Pettipas had regained control over the conveyance.

"The Baker Street Irregulars?" said Emmaline. "Who are they?"

"A gang of boys under the leadership of a lad called Wiggins. They serve me as scouts and messengers. They look like ordinary London urchins, but the Irregulars are as fine a body of youngsters as you'll find anywhere."

Princess Purnah was grumbling about losing Rubberbones again. Evidently she didn't share the great detective's belief that everything was about to get resolved in a flurry of policemen and ragged boys. "Me rescuings Errand Boy. Is my sacred duties. Porok!" she said. Stanley woofed in agreement.

Emmaline rolled her eyes. "Just try to stay out of the Faceless Fiend's clutches," she said. "I'm sure he won't care too much about Robert. It's not as if he can sell a boy from Lower Owlthwaite to the Russian secret service. Rab has no influence in the affairs of great nations."

"Me not, neither," said Princess Purnah. "Although Chiligriti princess most important. Not see how internashing-null powers is wanting of me."

"Your Majesty," said Sherlock Holmes. "If the Russians have you in their power, they will place you on the throne of your own country."

"That being most excellent! Trikk!!"

"Aha! So you might think. But they would surround you with Russian advisers so you had no choice but to obey them. There would be armies garrisoned in your country. And then, one day, the Czar would announce that Chiligrit had become part of the Russian Empire, and you'd find yourself freezing in a dreadful cabin in Siberia. With guards to make sure you stayed there."

"Me not liking that."

"No, indeed. But that's the way the bear goes about his business."

"Me have amulet against bears."

"Hmm," said Sherlock Holmes. "This bear is a very crafty animal, my dear."

Princess Purnah scowled. Emmaline smiled to herself: she'd forgotten about Russia being known as "the bear."

"We'll be landing in Victoria Park," said Mr. Pettipas. "Hold on tight."

As they landed, a hansom cab pulled up. A cart piled with luggage and a tall man in Indian costume followed.

"Good grief, Holmes!" said Dr. Watson as he ran toward the balloon. "They were shooting at you."

"Emmaline! Purnah! Are you all right? Where are your shoes, Purnah?" called out Aunt Lucy, waddling along behind him.

"Is throwing at verry bad mans," explained Princess Purnah.

"But what about Rab?"

Holmes stepped forward. "Young Master Burns effected his escape from the man you call the Faceless Fiend, whom I know as Baron Berthold Von Biebelburg, otherwise called Pieter Van Meter, and sometimes Jeb Stump. Master Burns will be found within a hundred yards of Fournier Street, Spitalfields, possibly close to the old Methodist Chapel at the corner of Brick Lane.

My associates will ensure that he is returned as soon as possible. Meanwhile, I suggest that refreshments might be in order."

Rubberbones had no idea where he was going. He cleared a brick wall and ran across a yard full of chickens; he vaulted a gate and ran down an alley. All the time the boys behind him were following, shouting. They seemed to know his name — "Stop right there, Robert Burns! Just 'old on a moment!" — which clearly proved that they were the Faceless Fiend's junior underlings. Probably waiting until they were old enough to get their own leather suits and masks. They were good runners, too. Chances were they knew these streets like the backs of their grubby hands, so Rab knew he'd have to be clever.

He ran along one lane, dived into a tobacconist's shop and out the back door — to the surprise and anger of the owner — and across a courtyard with wooden "privies" (outdoor toilets). He took a moment's breather, then saw the back door fling open and the first of a group of lads burst out. "There 'e is! Stop! We don't mean you no 'arm!"

Well, of course they'd say that, thought Rubberbones. He wriggled over the wall and took off down another side alley where he came upon a pile of old sacks, broken furniture and a load of rubbish of every description. The sign painted on the wall above the heap read "William Henry Campbell & Sons: Purveyors of Scrap Metals and Sundry Items."

Rab picked up a stone and threw it against a rusty iron fence that barred the far end of the alley. It made a satisfying clang on the metal. Then he burrowed into the midst of the scrap heap. A moment later the first of the boys came around the corner.

"Over that fence! I 'eard 'im bangin' on it!" The boys clambered over the fence and disappeared.

CHAPTER 23

In Darkest London

Princess Purnah was not satisfied. It was all very well to have strawberries and cream, chocolate cake and a whole meringue, but she wanted her friend Errand Boy returned to her.

The room at 221B Baker Street was cozy in a masculine sort of way. Purnah admired the bullet holes in the wall, and neither Mr. Holmes nor Dr. Watson objected when Stanley attacked the comfy armchairs. The doctor and Aunt Lucy made polite conversation while Lal Singh took care of the luggage, and Holmes stared dreamily out of the window.

"It was just over there," he said to Emmaline, pointing at the house opposite, "that Colonel Moran attempted to assassinate me. That window, you see? He lay in wait with a powerful air-rifle, the same weapon he had used to murder—"

There was a knock at the door. Emmaline hoped that it might be Rubberbones. But it was the housekeeper, Mrs. Hudson, bringing in a sad-faced man.

"What news, Lestrade?" demanded Holmes. "Inspector Lestrade, Mrs. Butterworth, Miss Cayley, Her Royal Highness, Princess Purnah of Chiligrit." He rattled off the names. "And Stanley, a particularly fine dog."

Inspector Lestrade of Scotland Yard appeared glum. "The horse has bolted, Mr. Holmes. The bird has flown. The—"

"Yes, yes. Get to the point, if you would!"

"The house was empty when my officers broke in. They moved pretty dashed smartly, I can tell you. No letters or papers of any sort that might serve to incriminate. No footprints. Possibly some fingerprints, although I don't believe in fingerprints—"

Holmes sighed. "What about the boy? Did you see Wiggins and the other Irregulars?"

"Those ragamuffin boys, you mean? No sign of the little bl—the lads."

The door flew open. Mrs. Hudson waved her arms in disgust as a boy of about twelve pushed past her. "Mr. 'Olmes! Message from Wiggins, sir! We chased the Burns boy when 'e

come aht the 'ouse in Fournier Street, but 'e runned away. Fair gave us the slip, 'e did. We couldn't find 'im nowhere."

Sherlock Holmes sighed again. Dr. Watson broke in. "Is there anywhere young Master Burns might make for? Didn't you say he had family in London?"

"Yes, but I don't know where," replied Aunt Lucy. "I don't think he's ever been here."

"Yes, he has," said Emmaline. "He visited when he was about seven or eight. He writes to his mother every week. He sends most of his wages to her." She felt a lump in her throat. "Only I don't know where she lives."

Princess Purnah let out a wail, which she rapidly converted into a sneeze. Emmaline knew this was as close to crying as the princess came.

"Mrs. Burns lives in a place called Beth-nell-grin," announced Lal Singh. "Rab-sahib speaks of her most often." The Sikh butler had shimmered into the room, silent and unnoticed. "Alas, I do not know the precise address. I have not been so honored as to see his letters to his maternal family. But I believe it is in an area known as Old Nick-ell."

"Good Grief!" said Dr. Watson. "How do you know so much?"

"It is my duty to know such things," answered Lal Singh.

Sherlock Holmes looked grim. "The Old Nichol is an area of great poverty and greater criminality. It is a warren of thieves, a maze of dark alleys of the worst type. I have no doubt that Mrs. Burns and her family are honest, decent people. I wish I could say the same of her neighbors. For a village boy such as young Robert, the Old Nichol offers many dangers. We must find him as quickly as possible. The Masked Minions may be the least of his problems."

He took the London Directory from a shelf and thumbed through the pages. "Alas, as I suspected, there is no listing for a Burns in the immediate vicinity of Old or New Nichol

Streets. That means nothing, of course. Mrs. Burns's home may be listed under the name of a relative—a sister, perhaps, or her parents—and, of course, many people in the poor parts of London do not list their address. Simpson!"

The boy looked up. "Return to the others. Gather all your friends. Ask all over Bethnal Green for a Mrs. Burns, a woman with several children, about thirty-five years of age, possibly with a North Country accent, probably working as a dressmaker or seamstress. Fair or auburn hair, I think, and quite tall and slender. If you are able to find her, inform me immediately."

Emmaline was astonished that Mr. Holmes could know so much about a person he'd never met.

The boy Simpson left at a run, pushing past Mrs. Hudson and racing down the stairs.

"Now we must wait," said Holmes. "I have arranged for you to stay at a private hotel close to Regent's Park. I doubt that you will be disturbed there, although Inspector Lestrade has arranged for a policeman to be on duty. I have also made arrangements for you to meet with a senior official at the India Office in the morning. Princess Purnah, Your Majesty, you must be prepared to discuss your future with these people. Your safety is their chief concern. As to their plans for you, I know nothing. My only interest is to keep you out of the hands of those who wish you harm."

Purnah made a little growling noise, but said nothing.

Rubberbones had waited among the old sacks and piles of broken knick-knacks for the searching boys to come back, as he thought they would. They took about twenty minutes to reappear. They were arguing among themselves.

"I swear, 'e came up 'ere, went over the fence and then just disappeared!"

"Nah, I saw 'im on the far side of Calvin Street."

"You did not. An' if you did, 'ow come yer never said nuffink?"

The boys passed by. After another ten minutes, Rubberbones carefully emerged from his hiding place. He climbed over the fence and looked around.

Until now, Rab had not really looked around him. *This* London, so marvelous from the rooftops with its church steeples and bridges, was desperately poor. It was a place of wretched old buildings, cramped together, with crumbling brickwork and cracking plaster. The houses loomed high and had bits built on to them in higgledy-piggledy fashion, all smeared with soot and dirt. The cobbles underfoot were filthy with horse dung and littered with old newspapers. The streets were narrow, sunless passageways. The whole place smelled of dirt and damp and something nastier. This was a kind of poverty he wasn't used to. Did his mother and his little brother and sisters live in a place like this?

It was a maze of ugly buildings tumbling into one another, without any street signs. The instructions from Rosie, the "artistical model," meant nothing to Rubberbones. Up Commercial Street, was it? And then Bethnal Green Road? He'd have to find someone to ask.

There was no shortage of people. There were burly, loud men pushing barrows in the main streets and hanging about the corners, looking rough and bad-tempered. There were grimy women cackling and drinking something that Rab thought smelled horrible.

"Giss a penny!" a beggar called out. He was an old man with no legs, pulling himself along on a cart. "A penny for an old so'jer! I lost me legs fightin' fer Queen an' country. Against the French. In America."

"I haven't got a penny," said Rab.

"Wot 'ave you got?" said the beggar.

"I've got a sixpence," replied Rab. "In case I need anything."

"Give me sixpence," said the old beggar. As Rab looked at him, he thought that perhaps he wasn't all that old. The white in his beard appeared to be flour.

"Leave 'im alone!" A boy of fourteen or fifteen pushed the beggar over so that the man rolled out of his cart and onto the paving stones, his legs unraveling from under him as he did. "Wotcha do that for?" he cried out, standing up quite easily, but rubbing his side.

"You lazy devil, Charlie! Can't even be bothered to find a decent corner among rich people to beg. Everyone knows you ain't no cripple ... 'cept this lad, it seems."

The false old soldier cursed and ambled away. The boy grinned at Rubberbones. He had a hank of red hair that fell over his eyes and a suit of clothes that might have been elegant on a man eight inches taller. "You're a stranger 'ere, ain't you? Falling for that old trick."

"Er, I'm looking for Old Nichol Street," said Rab. "I had instructions, but I got lost."

"Blimey, mate. I can tell yer 'ow ter get there. I'll make sure you gets there all right. Are you 'ungry, at all? Yer look famished. Like a nice bit of eel pie, then?"

Rab didn't know about eel pie, or jellied eels, or any of the things that the street vendor had for sale, but the boy helped him order and eat some of each. (Mostly he helped with the eating part.) "Blimey, mate, that were thruppence an' a farthing. Got to be careful with yer money!" He grinned again. "Me name's Peachey. I lives round 'ere. What's yours, then?"

"Robert Burns. They call me Rab. Me mum lives around 'ere, somewhere. Mrs. Burns on Old Nichol Street. Do you know her?"

"Don't ring no bell, but we'll find her, don't worry. Take a while, though. It's a good distance from 'ere."

"The lady said it were close by."

"Some people don't know wot they are talking about. But yer all right with me to 'elp out. D'you like dogs? You look like a bloke as likes dogs."

Rubberbones thought about Stanley and agreed that he liked dogs.

"Gimme those last two pennies, then, and we'll go see the ratting contest."

Rab had no idea what a "ratting contest" might be, or why he should hand over his pennies, but he did. They entered a dank, shadowy alley and climbed the stairs to a doorway three flights up. Then they went inside.

Holmes seemed to have decided that Emmaline was the sort of sensible, scientific young lady he could be comfortable with.

"Miss Cayley," he began, "I understand that your interest in the aeronautical aspects of our balloon journey this afternoon was more than a mere passing fancy. Would you be interested in reading Professor Chanute's *Progress in Flying Machines*? It is a recent compilation of his articles for an American journal, as I understand. You may borrow the volume, if you wish. And, if you find yourself free tomorrow afternoon, I believe that Mr. Pettipas is involved with an affair featuring a person titling himself "The Belgian Birdman." You can find the details in the newspapers, I believe."

Emmaline had heard of Octave Chanute, the French-born engineer. He was not only a pioneer researcher but also a friend to many experimental inventors. Yes, she wanted to borrow the book! Yes, she wanted to read it at one sitting!

It had been decided that they'd go to the hotel, take a bath, get changed into clean clothes and rest. Emmaline wanted to put her injured foot up on a stool and bathe it in warm water. If Rab was found and the Fiend arrested, they might find out about this alleged birdman and his public display. It sounded a bit circus-like for a proper scientific experimenter like herself.

This wasn't what Princess Purnah wanted. A quiet night with unnecessary baths and more stupid, clean English clothes, and Emmaline Cay-lee engrossed in some dull book, and no Professor Bellbuckle and his jolly explosions. And no Errand Boy. She was worried about Errand Boy. Hrikki-tikki!

Not only that, but she was in London, where there were soldiers in fine red coats and a tower for keeping traitors locked up, guarded by men who ate lots of beef. Glokk! There was a sailor man who lived on top of a column, and a new bridge that opened like a crocodile's mouth, and Queen Victoria in her palace. She must visit, since they were both royal personages, and perhaps the Queen would order some executings for her enjoyment.

All this to do, and rescuing Errand Boy, as well. And they wanted quietness! Hurkk!!

CHAPTER 24

Dogs, Rats and Horses — Mostly Rats

The room was crowded with the roughest customers Rubberbones had ever seen. Men who got into fistfights over whether one cockroach was bigger than another. Men who hadn't washed since birth. You could smell that, even over the tobacco smoke, beer fumes and the stench of dog. Dogs were everywhere—bulldogs, terriers of all kinds, dogs of unknown mixed breeds. Small dogs and, well, even smaller dogs. Dogs that were happy to see one another and dogs that clearly weren't. They were on men's laps and at their feet, in cages and baskets and running about.

Those were the living dogs. There were glass cases on the walls and along the mantelpiece, filled with stuffed dogs who had, according to the labels, been champions years before. Then there were the mounted heads, like hunting trophies, of other award-winning dogs-gone-by. Rab thought it was very strange. And not in a good way.

The men were a mixed lot. Some wore the short, tight waistcoats and colored scarves of the barrow-pushing costermongers, the market people of London. One wore a battered soldier's uniform. Older men wore huge mutton-chop whiskers. All were obsessively interested in dogs. They were checking teeth and paws, bidding for one another's animals and proposing to trade pups that hadn't been born yet. One man offered another a bottle of beer, fifteen shillings in actual money and a monkey in return for a lively looking black-and-tan puppy.

Rubberbones liked dogs very much, so he was immensely happy to see so many at once. Normally, when he'd seen that many together, they were known as a "pack" and had been chasing him. He didn't like the stuffed ones, though, or the mounted heads.

"Psst!" said Peachey. "If we're goin' to see the entertainment, we'll need anuvver shillin' apiece. You got any more gelt, then?"

"You what?"

"Money. Got any money?"

"No, you took me last pennies to get us in," Rubberbones reminded him.

"Ah, well, yeah. Thing is, we need a shillin' each. The penny just got us in to see the dogs. The main entertainment, the grand event, to what we is privelidged to be invited should we pay the aforementioned shillin', is about to occur upstairs. Chance of a lifetime, me old china."

Rab had no idea what an "old china" might be, or half of the other things Peachey had said. And he wanted to see his mother. The dogs were interesting, all right, but he wanted to see his mum and his little brother and his sisters.

"Nah, don't worry about that," said Peachey when Rab mentioned it. "They won't be 'ome yet."

Rab thought this over for a moment. There wasn't any point in standing around outside an empty house. And he wanted to see a grand event.

But he didn't have a shilling. He pointed this out, again. Peachey had an answer. "Well, tell you wot. Since you are a visitor to London, I'll arsk the landlord about loaning us five bob so we can get in and 'ave some betting money. Then we'll pay 'im back out of the winnings."

Rab thought this sounded like a good plan. But he did have

one question. "It's not dogs fighting each other, is it? I don't want ter see no dogs getting 'urt."

"Oh, no, nothing like that. Dogs getting 'urt! Perish the thought!"

So they went upstairs. The smell was even worse than downstairs, for the crowd was jammed in around a circular pit, built up from the floor like a tiny gladiatorial arena. A man in military uniform stood in the center of the pit. He had astounding whiskers, like matching toilet brushes, and a shining bald dome.

"It is my honor to present to you sporting gentlemen a veritable feast of ent-ter-tainment this very afternoon! A special, once-in-a-lifetime opp-or-tunity to see the Finest Dogs in England, here today! Handsome terriers and sportive bulldogs and everything in between, graduatified according to weight and age! And all most determined and active in their pursuivance of rodentry! The first contestant weighs in at five and a quarter pounds and answers to the name of Clarence!"

A shriveled little man brought Clarence to the fore. He was a cheery little dog of unknown breed—somebody said he was a mix of Albanian badger hound and something else—and had a no-nonsense sort of look to him.

"Let's put a shillin' on him!" said Rab. This looked like the sort of dog you might want to put a shilling on.

"Nah, 's early yet. Sixpence."

So they each bet sixpence that wasn't theirs on a dog they'd never seen before, in a contest that Rab, at least, had no idea about. But he was soon to find out.

The captain, as he was called, brought out a small cage. Opening the door, he tipped out a stream of squabbling, wriggling, furry creatures into the pit. Rats! Big brown ones and smaller black-and-gray ones, with twitchy pink noses and hideous naked tails that swished and curled. Rubberbones caught a massive whiff of the rats' powerful stench.

"Sewer rats," said Peachey. "Stink, don't they?"

"What's going to 'appen?" asked Rubberbones.

"That dog, on wot we 'ave placed sixpence apiece, is going to take on twelve of those 'orrible rats. If there are any rats still breathing five minutes from now, we lose. If, on the other 'and, our dog Clarence 'as despatched them verminious cree-turs to meet their maker, we will be better off by an additional sixpence per. Get my meanin'?"

Rab was dumbstruck. It had not occurred to him that he was gambling on the prospects of Clarence murdering a collection of rats. Peachey took this silence for interest and whispered, "The captain places the dog in the pit and the clock is started!"

The dog launched into his business, which he took seriously, as a professional in his field. He nosed into the cluster of rats, and began pulling them out by the neck, shaking them until they were limp in his mouth. These he cast aside and searched out another likely victim.

Rab's eyes were as round as saucers. The rats lay strewn around the pit, bloodied and mangled, long before the bell rang to indicate that five minutes was up. Clarence prodded one or two to make sure they were quite dead. "Make sure they ain't shammin'!" cried out one enthusiast. They weren't. The captain lifted the triumphant ratter high in the air to the acclaim of the crowd. Clarence had a good deal of blood on him, but none of it seemed to be his own. "I predict great things for this fine young dog," proclaimed the captain. His owner stepped forward to take him and was offered five pounds, there and then, for the successful gladiator. Rab thought that if Clarence proved a great success he might be lucky enough to end up stuffed and mounted in a glass case with a card that explained what a mighty warrior he had once been. He shivered at the thought.

"Good work!" declared Peachey. "A future champion. Let's see the next dog! Innit great 'ere? Piles and piles o' dead rats! What more could you ask for?"

Rubberbones could think of many other things he could ask for.

The four-wheeled cab rolled smoothly through streets far different from the slums of Bethnal Green. This was the prosperous London of fine houses, wide streets and parklike squares. There were no beggars and no rats. Dead or otherwise. They weren't allowed.

Emmaline sat with her back to the driver, looking out of the window as Regent's Park came into view. The afternoon was wearing on, and it would be dark before long; she was only now beginning to get used to the early sunset of English Novembers. All the same, she could still see the well-kept lawns and the boating lake. On her lap she had Mr. Holmes's copy of the book by Professor Chanute, together with some articles, translated from the original German, by the aeronaut Otto Lilienthal. If it weren't for the fact that Rab was still missing, she thought that this day might turn out perfectly. But, of course, he *was* still missing.

Princess Purnah fidgeted next to her while Aunt Lucy sat stiffly, with her hands tight around her purse and umbrella. Dr. Watson sat still, one hand in his pocket. Emmaline knew he carried a revolver.

The coach was moving swiftly, and Dr. Watson appeared unsettled. He seemed even more so when the horses suddenly made a rapid left turn, broke into a gallop, then cornered once again to the left. Emmaline could see the street names— "Rossmore Road," "Boston Place." Again the coach turned left, faster still.

"Good grief!" expostulated Dr. Watson. "Has the driver gone mad?"

Aunt Lucy smiled. "I expect he is just obeying Lal Singh's instructions. We are being followed. If the driver has any difficulties, I am certain Lal Singh can offer assistance. He is very good at what he does."

Emmaline remembered that Lal Singh was on the roof with Stanley and the luggage. He didn't carry a revolver, but then again, she'd never noticed that he needed one.

The coach moved at a gallop. It was an incredible pace for the quiet streets of west London. An elderly gent, out for his afternoon walk, dodged the hooves of the horses by inches. Emmaline saw him on his knees, thrown against a lamppost, his hat bouncing along the pavement.

The vehicle veered sharply to the right on two wheels. Emmaline felt herself thrown violently into Purnah, who cannoned across the little cabin into Dr. Watson. He was holding a loaf of bread, which had just flown in through the open window. Emmaline looked out to see a cart with the words "Fielding's Bakery—Best in London" in pieces against a brick wall. The owner, a big man with a mustache, cursed roundly.

Then they were back on four wheels, and racing. A crash from behind suggested that their pursuer had also collided with the bakery cart.

They went around Dorset Square twice, then up Gloucester Place at blistering speed. Emmaline wished she could see what was behind them, pursuing at the same breakneck pace.

A governess shrieked and pulled a little boy in a horrible sky-blue sailor suit back from the edge of the pavement. Then she shouted out after the coach, using the kind of language that her young charge would repeat later, in front of visitors, causing his mortified mother to faint.

Then suddenly the coach slowed down, and they were in a walled courtyard.

The driver, his face deathly pale, opened the door for his passengers to climb out. Watson was red-faced and clearly unhappy. "Was that—that sort of driving absolutely necessary?" he demanded.

"Wasn't me, sir," replied the coachman. "The Indian gent took the reins orf me. I thought I would never see me wife and five darling children ever again, sir!"

Emmaline thought she could detect a glimpse of a smile on Lal Singh's face as he lifted down the baggage from the roof rack.

Dr. Watson sighed heavily. "The St. Cletus Hotel, Madam. Very respectable. Very quiet. Very safe. Mr. Holmes prefers it that way for his clients."

"A fine choice, no doubt," said Aunt Lucy. "And just in time for tea."

CHAPTER 25

Banjo

Things weren't turning out the way Rab had expected. What he had expected was this: he and Peachey would make bets on the dogs as they killed the rats, then they'd pay back the five shillings and leave and never ever gamble on dogs killing rats again. Then Peachey would take Rab to his mother's house, and things would be wonderful.

Of course, that wasn't the way of it at all.

The next dog that entered the pit, a white bulldog with tan patches, was given the task of killing not a mere dozen rats, but a basket of fifty, all crawling over one another and climbing in pyramids up the sides of the pit. Rab thought that fifty was an awful lot of rats and bet a penny. As it turned out, fifty rats was almost nothing to this killer beast; he was removed, covered in rat's blood but triumphant, in three minutes.

"I should've put a shillin' on 'im," said Rab to Peachey. The urchin agreed. "We could've put a lot on that dog, only we ain't got it. Look for the next one, and you decide."

The dogs kept coming forward. Peachey explained that there would be one grand event at the end with a dog "famous from all over London," in which the big money would be wagered. Rubberbones bet a penny on a Skye terrier who failed to meet the time limit and a mongrel who seemed to have tremendous joy in the pit. Then an old man brought out a dog who was clearly ancient. As old as the pyramids. It had rheumy eyes, a mangled left ear and the sort of scars that could only come from a lifetime of fights. Rab could see its ribs showing through the mangy, graying skin. He saw the stiffness as the old creature moved its joints. "This is Banjo," said the owner.

"That 'un's on its last legs," whispered Peachey. "Another month and they'll be using 'im as a taste dog."

"A what?"

"A taste dog. That means a dog as is used to train young fightin' dogs to kill. You sets 'em against a dog that can't fight back proper, the taste dog, so they learns to kill anuvver dog. Then you can teach 'em to fight other fightin' dogs for money."

Rubberbones recoiled in horror. Was that what happened to these dogs when they got too old and sick to kill rats? Those that didn't end up in a glass case, or with their heads mounted on a wall? He made a decision.

"Peachey, I want that dog."

"What, to bet on? You'll lose, unless he's fighting three blind mice. If you have to bet, the smallest they'll take is a halfpenny."

"No, I mean, I want that dog. How much would the old man take for 'im, d'you think?"

"You're joking!" said Peachey. "Wot d'yer want wiv a crocked-up ol' dog like that, then?"

"I just want him. I'm going to take 'im home wi' me."

It was Peachey's turn to stare, open-mouthed. But after thinking about it for a moment, he went over to the man. He whispered in his ear, and then returned to Rab. "'E says he wants ten shillins for the dog. Seems like a lot for an 'alf-dead old animal."

"Do you think he'd take five?" asked Rubberbones.

"You 'aven't got five."

"No, but I 'aven't got ten, either. But I might get five, if he can wait a bit."

Peachey looked interested at the idea that Rab could get money. "So 'ow would you be getting this five shillins, then?"

Rubberbones actually knew several ways of getting money, but most of them involved running messages around Lower Owlthwaite. Then he remembered the scheme he'd had when he was at the Gypsies' camp last summer.

"I never get 'urt," he declared. "I'm sort of rubbery. In fact, some folks call me Rubberbones. So, if you was to push me down them stairs, or chuck bricks at me 'ead, or hit me wi' sticks, it wouldn't bother me."

Peachey rubbed his chin. Rab could see he was pondering this, working out a way to turn his rubber bones into a money-making scheme. "So, wot, people'd pay to throw you dahn the stairs? Dunno abaht that. People in these parts is used to throwing one another dahn stairs for free. Likewise, the bricks and sticks. Mostly they prefer it if the object of their chuckin' and 'ittin' *does* get 'urt, becos' that's the 'ole reason of doin' it to 'em."

Rab could see his point.

Peachey thought some more. "'Owever, it might be possible to get certain persons," he pointed at the gathered audience, "to pay for the pleasure of witnessin' a boy wot has these 'rubbery' qualities. Lemme think on it!"

His thinking on it was interrupted by the captain announcing the start of the sporting competition in question, in which the elderly dog, Banjo, was pitted against a dozen rats. It was a sad affair. Banjo could barely see or smell the rats, which scurried around the edges of the pit faster than the hunter could react. He got one, but dropped it when it wriggled. Another rat jumped up and bit him on the nose, hanging in midair with its teeth embedded in the dog's leathery nose-tip. The ancient canine whimpered a little, and knocked the rat off with its front paw. Then, as if to draw the whole sorry spectacle to an end as quickly as possible, the time-bell rang.

The captain shook his head and announced that Banjo had not succeeded in killing twelve rats—or, actually, any rats at all—in the allotted time. There was a general murmur of disgust across the room.

Peachey went back to the dog's owner, a man who had embarrassment written all over his wizened face. He came back to Rab.

"Five shillin' it is, then. If we can be back 'ere at six o'clock, you can 'ave the dog. No idea wot yer want wiv' such a decrepitated crittur, mind you. And we still 'ave to pay the landlord wot we owe 'im. So, let's go to the market in Petticoat Lane. We'll find out 'ow many people are interested in your rubberiness."

The St. Cletus Hotel was as boring as watching goats sleep, thought Princess Purnah. She had eaten more cakes and chocolate and sat looking out of a window onto the bare flower beds. Emmaline was engrossed in those silly books that Mr. Sherholm-Lock had lent her. *Glekk!*

She was ready to rescue Errand Boy.

Purnah tiptoed quietly into the cloakroom to find her hat and coat. They were ridiculous English schoolgirl clothes, of course; she would have preferred a nice pair of baggy Chiligriti trousers made of sheepskin with the fleece on the inside and a sensible hat that kept your ears warm on cold days as you waited behind rocks to fling mud at the neighbors. Still, she had to blend in, camouflage herself like the mountain gazelle, whose coat turns white when the snow falls. So the silly hat with the ribbons and the coat that was neither comfy nor warm would be best.

Princess Purnah looked for weapons. But there weren't any. She couldn't understand why British people did not carry swords and pistols with them on their daily going-abouts. That Doktirwotsun man had a pistol, but he had hidden it under his coat.

Still, she had her butter knife. *Spigg!* There was someone behind her. She turned around, trying to look innocent.

It was Aunt Lucy, a thin smile on her face. "Hello, Purnah. I understand you'd like to … take a walk in the garden, but I would really prefer it if you remained indoors. Besides, the professor will be arriving soon, and you wouldn't want to miss him. Take your coat off, please."

"Roll up, roll up! Ladies and gentlemen, please take the incredible opp-pur-tunity to see the Amazin' Rubber Boy! See 'im fall down the stairs wivout 'urtin' 'isself! Chuck rocks at 'is 'ead! It don't bovver 'im at all!"

Peachey was "pattering." A patterer, as he explained to Rab, is a man who uses his ability with words to interest the public, for financial gain, of course. And it was clear that Peachey had done this sort of thing before. Rubberbones was impressed. The Londoner had paid a signmaker to whip up a very impressive placard announcing the event, promising the man payment later that day. He'd found a nice patch of pavement with a high wall behind by cuffing the smaller boys (selling this morning's leftover fish) to get them to vacate the space and bribing the bigger ones with offers of "a free go" at Rubberbones. They were at the edge of a busy street market, full of stalls covered with colorful awnings where everything, from old clothes to cheap jewelry to questionable bits of meat, was sold. There were men pushing barrows of vegetables and little girls selling flowers. The smells of blooms and eels and ancient clothing and pickled shellfish mixed into a heady brew in Rab's nostrils. He saw a girl helping at one stand, a girl with rather wild black hair and dark eyes who reminded him of Purnah. He felt a pang. His friends were somewhere in this huge city, and he had no idea where.

Everyone was shouting out, offering bargains. "Who'll buy me oranges?" "Fresh 'addock, orf the boat today!" "Slap-up toggery, veddy nice!"

"If we make enough money," said Peachey, "You can 'ave the dog, we'll pay the landlord, get you some clothes as might fit yer, an' 'ave a proper feed o' pie an' mash."

"I'd like to get a present for me mum and my little brothers and sisters," said Rab.

Peachey smiled. "I can't believe I met you 'ere, I really can't. You'd best be tellin' the truth about this Rubber Boy act." But Peachey knew that this innocent lad from the distant north was not lying about anything. He shook his head, the hank of red hair getting in his eyes once again.

The signmaker had put up a list of prices:

Throwing a Brick: One penny
Hitting with a Stick: Twopence
Pushing off a Table: Threepence
Pushing down Stairs: Sixpence

If Rubber Boy cries out or shows Pain in Any Form,
*A **PRIZE** Will Be Awarded.*

The first paying customer was a strapping blond lad of thirteen or so who rolled up his sleeves to throw a half-brick at Rab from about ten feet away. Rubberbones stood up as tall as he could—five feet, one inch, very nearly—and smiled at his opponent. His customer smiled back.

The lad hurled the brick at Rab's chest. The crowd held its breath. Peachey held his, too, and clutched the money even tighter in case he had to make a rapid departure from the scene. Rab smiled wider.

The half-brick struck him below the ribs and sort of, well, bounced back. Just a few inches. But it definitely bounced.

The lad gaped in astonishment. The crowd gasped in amazement. Rubberbones grinned. "That were a good throw," he said. "Most people miss when they throws as 'ard as that."

Peachey smiled himself and took money from the outstretched hands of boys who wanted to throw, a girl who wanted to try out her new umbrella as a weapon and a little old lady who thought that Rab was sweet and promised she wouldn't push too hard when she tried to fling him down a nearby flight of stairs.

A fishmonger threw him off the roof of a shed. Everyone let out an "ooh" when Rubberbones hit the cobbles with his face and bounced right up, unbruised and smiling.

A "blind" beggar forgot that he wasn't supposed to be able to see and threw a chunk of fallen rock squarely and truly onto Rab's nose. Rab headed it away like a footballer nodding a ball past a goalie; not a mark was left on his face.

Within an hour, Peachey held enough money to pay for the dog and to pay the landlord what they owed him. There would even be enough left over for eel pie and mash and a quart of beer between them.

Rab said that he didn't drink beer (Peachey looked amazed) and that, if he could get the dog Banjo, please, he'd like to go and find his mother now.

"You is a source of constant astonishment to me, Robert Burns," said Peachey. "We will do that. Only, promise me you'll meet me 'ere tomorrow morning—or any morning as is convenient—and we shall make shillin' upon shillin' at this Rubber Boy lark, and make our fortunes, and perhaps go on the stage and be stars of the music halls!"

Rab just stared at him. Peachey sighed. "All right. First things first. I expect the landlord will let us off the price of admission, owing to his being my uncle, but I do insist on the eel pie and mash, for I am fair famished after an 'ard afternoon of taking people's money off 'em."

Chapter 26

The Old Nichol

"Hello, Professor Bellbuckle!"

Emmaline was excited to see her tutor. The last she'd heard of him he'd been engaged in mortal combat against the pterodactyl, armed only with his fireworks. The professor *looked* as if he'd been in mortal combat. He wore a tattered old tailcoat with burn marks and fresh slashes. His trousers were in shreds, and if it hadn't been for the fact that he was also covered in mud, he'd have been quite indecent. His face was blackened, except around the eyes. It looked as if he had been wearing goggles, which meant—

"Did you come down to London in your steam carriage? I know you were working on it in the laboratory."

The professor harrumphed like a small hippopotamus, clearly embarrassed. "Ah, no, my dear. I began the journey in the repaired Bellbuckle, Mark II, as planned, but I was forced, after a small, um … a very minor, ah, explosion, to walk the rest of the way to Groansby Station and take the train."

Emmaline could tell that the mad inventor was crestfallen. "Never mind. You'll get it right soon enough." She crossed her fingers behind her back. "It's a brilliant concept."

"I saw one of those *other* horseless carriages on my way to the hotel," the professor went on. "No future at all in gasoline engines, I tell you. You know, it was so slow that it couldn't even pass a man with a red flag who was walking in front of it!"

Emmaline knew it was the law that a man with a red flag must walk in front of any mechanically powered vehicle on the roads. This was supposed to prevent the rumbling behemoths from scaring old ladies and horses, smashing into things and all that sort of antisocial behavior. So, according to the strict letter of the law, Professor Bellbuckle ought to have had a man with a flag walking in front of his own machine, too. Although, Emmaline thought, you'd have to have a death wish to want to take that job.

The professor had rushed into the hotel, flinging small change at the cabbie—some foreign coins and one or two bottle caps. After they all sat down in the parlor, Aunt Lucy gave him a rundown of the day's events. He seemed enormously happy that Rab had escaped the Fiend's clutches. And apparently even the professor had heard of Sherlock Holmes and his masterful skills. He was sure that everything was bound to be all right.

"But where's the princess?" he asked.

"Upstairs in our room," replied Emmaline. "She's sulking. She wants to find Rab on her own. And Aunt Lucy has taken her shoes."

"Hmm," said the professor. "In that case, we might just want to check on her."

Lal Singh, who had heard the slightest of suspicious noises, was there before them—and found the princess trying to lower herself out of the window using knotted bedsheets.

The group of lads at the corner of Old Nichol and Boundary Streets saw two boys walking up the road. They were watching for a rosy-cheeked boy with fair hair, alone, about twelve years of age, last seen dressed in moth-eaten clothes that didn't fit him. So they ignored the boy with the floppy red hair and the smaller boy by his side, a flashy figure in a tight-fitting waistcoat, a sailor's jacket and a battered top hat. He carried a bunch of wilted flowers, two stuffed toy rabbits, a wooden sword and a balloon on a string. An elderly dog wheezed alongside him, attached to his hand by another piece of string.

Carrying presents for his mam and brother and sisters, with Banjo jostling along slowly at his heels, Rab happily followed Peachey through the warren of alleys that led through the Old Nichol. Deep shadows fell across the dirty cobbles. Thin cats scurried between walls and over roofs. The smells of ancient food-gone-rotten and of rats and bad plumbing and disease were strong in the air. Peachey didn't seem to notice. Rab could tell that the Old Nichol was even more desperate than the mean streets he had passed through this afternoon.

Rubberbones did not want to believe that his family lived in such a place. Perhaps he'd turn a corner and see a row of spotlessly clean, neat cottages. There'd be happy children playing in little gardens and freshly washed linen hanging out to dry. It'd be a little bit of paradise in the heart of these teeming slums.

A tiny girl with a dirty face peered out of a dank court entrance. "It's 'im, Mum!" she called. "It's our Rab."

A thin, tired-looking woman who seemed to have all the color faded out of her appeared with a small boy, a slightly older girl and a toddler all clutching on to her skirt. "Hello, Robert," she said. "We were expecting you."

Rab's heart leapt at her voice, then fell as he saw the drabness of their dress and the pinched paleness of their faces.

"Hello, Mam. Hello, Danny, Tess, Susan, Annie. I brought you all presents."

"You'd best come in, dear. There's people looking for you."

Princess Purnah promised that she would not try to escape from the hotel again. Not tonight, anyway. She swore on the graves of her ancestors that she would not go out into the heart of a strange, dark city to look for Rubberbones.

Emmaline wasn't really sure that Purnah's ancestors had graves. She thought that perhaps the Chiligritis hung their late and lamented up in the branches of trees or threw them into convenient ravines. Still, from the amount of grumbling—"Poroki-porok! Hupp!"—it was possible that Purnah was sincere. If she had been lying, she'd not have complained so much.

"Here's the plan," said Aunt Lucy after everyone, including Purnah, had settled down in the parlor once more. "Tomorrow morning we'll accompany Dr. Watson to see Mr. Drone-Tiffin, who is some sort of senior person at the India Office. It's Sunday, of course, but Mr. Tiffin-Drone is willing to see you, Purnah—do stop rolling your eyes like that—after church. We'll sort out your future; I'll tell him about your enrollment at Professor Bellbuckle's Academy for Gifted Asiatic Royalty, and I'm sure that'll suffice. Meanwhile—Purnah, please stop fidgeting—that nice Mr. Holmes will have returned Robert to us and doubtless have dealt with that Faceless Fiend fellow. And the professor has something educational for Emmaline to do while we are occupied."

"Yes, indeedy, I do!" said Professor Bellbuckle. "I have received word that a Mon-sewer De Groof, sometimes accorded the title of 'The Belgian Birdman,' is about to demonstrate his flying apparatus tomorrow. He will be ascending in a balloon above the River Thames—"

Emmaline knew about this, of course, because Mr. Holmes had told her. Mr. Pettipas was operating the balloon. She wished she could apologize to him for this afternoon's mishaps. Having a balloon must be tremendously expensive, and he hadn't agreed to have it cut loose, or shot at.

"—knew his uncle, you know," continued the professor. "Twenty years ago. Jumped out of a balloon over London. He'd built a simple gliding apparatus, just wings on a frame. I helped him with the adjustments. Killed instantly. A real shame."

Emmaline looked keenly at the American. The professor sighed. "Glad to see the nephew following in his footsteps. Hope he's used a better grade of materials than the late De Groof senior."

Emmaline wondered if De Groof's demise had really been due to his use of cheap canvas and second-hand string. She hoped her friend and tutor had not helped him to his doom.

Rab brought the presents and the dog into the grim old building as Peachey mumbled something about seeing him tomorrow and left.

"I'll show you the 'ouse while Mum gets tea ready," said Danny. Rab noticed that he didn't sound like a Yorkshire boy anymore; he spoke like Peachey. Danny was nine and the next child down from Rab; his sisters were eight, six and three years old. Rab hadn't seen any of them in more than a year, since his dad had gone to seek his fortune. He had said he would send for them all or come home rich. He'd gone to Australia, or South Africa, said Mrs. Burns. He'd write when he had the chance. But he hadn't, yet.

Rab didn't want to think too much about it.

"Come on, Rabbie. We're up on the third floor. There's all sorts living in 'ere. We share an outhouse with five other families. You 'ave to wait yer turn."

The family was crammed into a single room in the most ramshackle building that Rab had ever seen. It was an ancient house divided up into a vast number of tiny dwellings. Some were actual rooms—with doors or without—and some were areas of the hallways curtained off. People lived in the spaces under the rickety staircases. You could see where extra bits had been added on—rooms, landings, even a plank bridge across the alley from one window to another in the house opposite. Everything smelled musty and foul. The place stank of generations of misery and disease. Rab was used to being poor—eating day-old bread and wearing shoes that had had four owners before him—but this was different.

"They 'ad cholera bad in 'ere, I've 'eard tell," said Danny. He spoke like a miniature adult. "The old man upstairs says so. They was carrying out the dead 'uns by the cartload. Years ago, mind."

Cholera. That was a word that instilled terror. Rab didn't

actually know what cholera was, but he knew it meant sickness and death to everyone in an infected house.

He had to get his family out of this place.

"Come on, Rabbie. Mum'll have food ready for us," said Danny.

The Burns's family room was almost clean and almost cheerful. Mrs. Burns kept the floor swept and the dishes put away, and there were pictures in cheap frames all along the walls.

"I did that," said Danny. "Whitewashed the walls. Mam did the 'igh bits where I couldn't reach."

The little girls were playing with the stuffed toys, while Tess contemplated the hydrogen balloon in a serious way. Rab could tell she'd never owned anything like it. Like the flowers that his mother had put into water, using a jam jar for a vase, the balloon wouldn't last.

"There were boys looking for you," said Mrs. Burns. "Do you want to tell me all about it?"

And so he did, while they sipped a thin soup with stale bread and Banjo gnawed on a bone that hadn't had meat on it in a very long time.

CHAPTER 27

Masked Men at Midnight

The bed was comfortable, the room smelled of flowers, and yet Emmaline still couldn't sleep. She had every reason to be tired. Of course, she was worried about Rubberbones, but if Aunt Lucy and Mr. Holmes said that he'd be back among them tomorrow, then surely that was true. So everything would be all right, again ... wouldn't it?

Princess Purnah, for all her sulking and fretting, was fast asleep. Emmaline knew this for a certainty because of the extremely unregal snoring coming from across the room.

Emmaline tossed and turned as the snoring went on. Eventually she drifted gently toward sleep. And then she heard a scratching noise. "Stop it, Stanley," she murmured to the dog dozing at the foot of her bed. She heard the noise again—over by the window. Purnah! That blasted girl had forgotten her promise and must be fumbling with the window catch. She must have waited until everyone was asleep to climb out of the window once more. Annoyance surged through Emmaline. Then she heard the snoring again, from Purnah's bed. So it wasn't Princess Purnah at the window.

Emmaline sat bolt upright. Purnah's bed was diagonally opposite her own, closer to the window, but not under it. A thin shaft of moonlight fell on the rug in front of the window, and a shadow flickered over it. Emmaline looked up to see a human face through the glass. Well, almost a face. It was the dark silhouette of a head. Emmaline squinted to see better. The head was hooded. The features were unclear; there seemed to be a blurred shape around the nose, the mouth and the eyes.

Of course. It was a mask.

And it was time to scream. Emmaline opened her mouth, but not a single sound emerged.

Purnah kept on snoring. Stanley whimpered a little, dreaming doggy dreams, and settled again. The window opened, sliding upward.

Emmaline reached out toward her bedside table. She'd light the gas lamp. She'd find a candlestick. She'd pick up —
A book. The Chanute book lent to her by Sherlock Holmes. A nice, fat book with a solid cover and spine.

As the figure leaned forward through the window, Emmaline reared back her right arm and flung the book at the intruder.

It was the kind of throw her muscular schoolfriend Josie Pinner would have admired. The invader looked up suddenly and let out a tiny squawk of alarm as the book

took him full in the face. He sprawled backward and fell out of the open window.

The sound woke Stanley, who barked and leapt up and barked some more and looked for an enemy to bite. It woke Princess Purnah, who leapt out of bed with hair flying and something sharp glinting in her fist. Emmaline thought Chiligriti royalty must be trained from childhood to expect assassination attempts on a weekly basis.

But while one masked intruder had fallen, several more burst through the open window, one following the other like connected beings. Emmaline heard a thumping noise in the hallway as the door handle turned, then stopped. There was a sound like "oof!" or possibly "unh!" on the other side of the closed door. Aunt Lucy's voice cried, "Take *that!*"

Emmaline screamed, finding her voice at last. It was a good, full-throated scream, the kind English mothers recommend as effective against robbers, bullies and men in dirty overcoats. It didn't have any effect on the masked men, except that one of them smiled and advanced toward her. These were a more professional grade of villain than the cheap local thug who had menaced her this morning. There was an awful lot of menacing going on.

So Emmaline stood up on the bed and, having the advantage of height, kicked the grinning man in the stomach. Even without shoes (but with socks, for it was cold in bed) the blow doubled him up. Taking the advice of Josie Pinner once again—that you should never give an opponent one savage kick when you could give him two—she followed this with a knee to the nose. Alas, as knees-to-the-nose were not something she had practiced, Emmaline simply fell on her foe. Which wasn't good, for he was a masked intruder in black leather, and she was a schoolgirl in a sensible nightdress. She'd have to fight dirty.

Across the room, Stanley had his teeth in the leg of a

masked man who seemed unable to shake the plucky little dog. Emmaline noticed that the villains didn't seem to be armed, which was good; they must be abductors, not assassins. Princess Purnah, however, was brandishing a blade—that dashed butter knife again, thought Emmaline. One of the masked men picked up a chair and, turning it against Purnah, twisted the legs to disarm her. The little knife flew from her hand. "Glekk!! Porok!!"

There came another stream of curses in Chiligriti, and the princess hurled herself on her assailant, attempting to bite him.

Meanwhile, Emmaline had hooked her fingernails under the mask of the man she was wrestling with, so his eyeholes were out of line with his eyes. She'd have loved to pull his hair, but maybe that was why he wore the full-face mask, for defence against English schoolgirls.

Horribly aware that the masked intruder was gaining in strength, Emmaline gritted her teeth. He was much bigger than she was and far stronger. If he hadn't been wearing the leather mask, she'd have bitten his nose.

And, now, he was winning.

They rolled off the bed, Emmaline trying to catch the masked man with her knee as they did so. She saw Purnah being hauled off her feet by two assailants and hoisted over the massive shoulders of the bigger one. And she saw something else. A terrifying silhouette against the moonlight. The masked man trying to shake off Stanley was drawing a pistol.

Emmaline had been wrong. Of course the intruders were armed! They simply hadn't drawn their weapons to climb in the window and abduct a young girl. But now, with all the noise and fighting, there was no reason to keep quiet. The man was going to shoot the little dog still biting his leg. Her friend Stanley. And there was nothing she could do about it. Emmaline screamed again.

And then the door was flung open. The light of an oil lamp flashed into the bedroom. A small, shining thing whirled through the air, striking the man with the pistol, who shrieked and clutched at his hand. He dropped the gun and shrieked again. A large figure, topped with what must be a policeman's helmet, pulled the masked intruder off Emmaline and began pummeling him with a short club. Emmaline turned to see a short, stout figure and a taller one hurl themselves across the room and pile into the men carrying the shouting bundle that was Purnah. The shorter figure jabbed one of the masked men with an umbrella, showing an excellent ability to guess in the dark where the soft, easily hurt parts might be. The tall figure held a long, curved blade that glinted in the moonlight, and he swished it so that it danced under the other man's throat. Dr. Watson turned the gaslights on, lowered his revolver and put down the oil lamp.

There were, as Emmaline knew, four masked men in the room. The fifth had fallen from sight when she had beaned him with the book as he balanced in the window frame. Another lay unconscious in the hallway outside. The captives stood like statues, one with Lal Singh's razor-sharp saber, his "tulwar," at his throat, another with Aunt Lucy's umbrella threatening his kidneys or his spleen, or some other vital bit of his anatomy. It must have been hard for them to stand so still, thought Emmaline, since Princess Purnah, enraged, was beating at them with balled fists and screaming, "Shiirrigo bunch! Haoujjah!"

"Stop it, Purnah," said Aunt Lucy quietly. The princess stopped.

The intruder who had wrestled with Emmaline was clutching his head and moaning. The policeman had stopped pummeling him.

The man who had threatened to shoot Stanley didn't move. He clutched his hand, which had one finger less than it had had five minutes earlier. Something sharp had disarmed him of the pistol, taking the trigger finger with it. Emmaline looked down and saw an iron quoit. It looked like a bracelet but was clearly a weapon. It belonged to Lal Singh.

"Right," said Aunt Lucy, taking charge. "Line up the suspects." Despite the presence of the police constable and Dr. Watson, Aunt Lucy was the one in command here. The suspects, clad from head to toe in leather, lined up against the wall with some prodding from the policeman. They didn't seem to understand English, but they understood the officer's jabbing. Except for the man who shrieked as he looked around for his finger, none of them had said anything.

"There's another one," said Emmaline. "He fell out of the window."

"I'll send a message for Mr. Holmes," said Dr. Watson. "And I'll call for constables to check what happened to the one outside."

Lal Singh stepped forward, saying something to the masked men in a language that Emmaline didn't understand.

"Good grief!" expostulated Dr. Watson. "Foreigners!" Emmaline thought that perhaps the doctor wasn't at his sharpest when Mr. Holmes wasn't around. They were the Fiend's Minions.

Lal Singh pulled the masks off the silent intruders. The white and pasty faces were those of tough-looking men in their prime. Each had a tattoo on his forehead in the shape of a bear's paw. The Russian bear, thought Emmaline. The constable handcuffed the prisoners.

"Right," said Aunt Lucy. "Bit of a mess in here, now. Dr. Watson, could you arrange for another room for my niece and the princess? This one needs a good cleaning."

Rab wasn't sleeping well. He huddled under a blanket with his brother Danny. Across the room were two of his sisters, while the youngest snuggled next to his mother. There was no proper bed for any of them, but old mattresses pulled out across the floor. Danny snored. It was cold, the frail fire having died long ago. Next to him, Banjo snored as well; he had decided that Rab was his friend and master and lay protectively against the boy's side.

Rab stared at the ceiling, where shadows flickered as the torn curtain let in the moonlight. He had had no idea. No idea at all. Every week he had sent his family money. It was never very much, but it was all he earned except for a bit he gave his gran for board. He had assumed that his mother would have money from somewhere else. She'd do washing or stitch frocks, and her own brothers and sisters in London would help out. And maybe they were. Perhaps the best they could do, all together, was … this.

And he'd shown up in his ridiculously fancy clothes, with flowers and presents and a dog they couldn't afford to feed.

Danny had said something troubling to him. His brother was bright, the sort of boy who, with an education, could get ahead in life. Danny said that next year he'd be ten, and then he'd leave school and get a job. He'd learned enough, and now it was time to work. Rab had almost burst into tears.

Tomorrow, he'd meet Peachey. They'd do the Rubber Boy act again.

And he didn't care if those boys, the ones that the Faceless Fiend had sent after him, saw him. He'd just run again. It was a risk, but he'd have to take it.

His family desperately needed money.

CHAPTER 28

Meeting a Monster

Emmaline awoke in a strange bed, a different strange bed than the one she'd climbed into the night before, because the St. Cletus Hotel didn't allow its guests to sleep in rooms where people had lost fingers. She'd fallen into an exhausted, dreamless slumber.

It was nine-thirty. She didn't really want to think about the previous night. She dressed and went downstairs. She didn't feel like facing breakfast, but she went into the dining room. Professor Bellbuckle was there, at a table at the far end. Everyone else had finished eating and left.

"I slept through the whole gosh-darn thing," said the professor. "Miss Lucy said it was a fair skirmish in the hallway and in your room. Sounded like the Battle of Shiloh. Eighteen sixty-two."

Emmaline did not want to hear about the American Civil War. Nor was she interested in his next remark. "Excellent deviled kidneys for breakfast, my dear. Or maybe some buttered eggs. Or some of that salty fish you Britishers like to eat first thing in the day. Kippers? Nasty things, I call 'em. But I wholeheartedly recommend the kidneys."

Nausea flooded through Emmaline. She controlled her urge to run for the facilities, although she could feel the bile rise in her throat. "No, I think, um, perhaps some tea."

"Suit yourself—try not to fret about last night. They wanted to shoot Stanley, I understand, and that's worthy of punishment in itself. A man who'd murder a perfectly fine dog like that deserves punishment. The police took 'em away, finger an' all.'"

That part about the dog seemed only right. Stanley was a member of the family. But she was concerned about the man she had hit with Mr. Holmes's book. He must have fallen three stories from the window. She hoped she hadn't crippled him. But the professor reassured her. "No sign o' the fella you beaned with the book, nossiree. I 'spect he just fell a coupla floors onto the grass below and dragged his sorry—his bee-hind away. Don't you worry none, Miss Emmaline."

Professor Bellbuckle reached over and lifted the lid of the silver salver containing the deviled kidneys. The smell was appalling; Emmaline tried not to gag. The professor helped himself, generously.

"Today, while Purnah and Miss Lucy deal with the bureaucraticals of the government, you and I will go and see young Mon-sewer De Groof. You'll like that. Maybe he won't be killed, either, and we can go out to dinner together. And we'll be seeing Robert later. No doubt about it."

That thought cheered Emmaline up, at least a little. But she still didn't want the deviled kidneys.

Peachey was waiting outside the Burns's house. He might have been there for ages. He tried to act as casual as he could. "There you are, chum! Feel like goin' down the market again? Always a good crowd on Sunday mornins, wiv lots of the spending stuff!"

Rab knew that Peachey thought that the "Amazing Rubber Boy" act was a money-spinner. The cockney boy wanted to be in on any money that was spun. He'd be the manager, the accountant and the one who ended up with a good chunk of the proceeds. Rab wasn't stupid. Not as stupid as yesterday, anyway. He was unhappy that Peachey had never told him the landlord at the ratting tavern was his uncle, at least until later on. Peachey had taken advantage of the village boy in the city. Still, Rab thought it was worth having a partner. London was a strange place, even when there weren't people after you.

Mrs. Burns kissed her older boy on the cheek. "Be careful, Robert."

Peachey and Rab struck out for Petticoat Lane. "Hey! Wait a mo'!" shouted a voice from behind. It was Danny, hurrying along, with Banjo wheezing at his heels. "We're coming as well."

Peachey had their sign from yesterday tucked beneath his arm. "Let's see if we can find a decent pitch. They start early, so let's 'ope we're lucky."

They found the same spot as the day before. "Roll up! Roll up!" shouted Peachey in a confident voice. Rubberbones could tell he took pride in his work. And, very soon, the public did, indeed, roll up.

At first it was the same as yesterday. A boy lobbing a brick. A coal merchant's helper throwing lumps of his boss's finest grade at the Rubber Boy. A little girl who simply launched herself at Rab, hitting him with her rag doll; Peachey gave her penny back to her. She was only three.

There was a crowd gathering to watch. A big crowd.

"The Amazin' Rubber Boy!" pronounced Peachey. "Directly from 'is 'ome in far-off New Guinea for your edification and amusement!" The part about coming from New Guinea was a brand-new addition. Rab wasn't sure he liked it. He had no idea where that place was, but he foresaw some form of silly costume in his future.

A little old lady paid to see Rubberbones fall off a wall onto his head. He managed a nice bounce at the end of it, so she paid him to do it again and slipped him a sixpence as a tip. Rab noticed Peachey's eyes on the coin; he'd want half of it. Rab flipped it to Danny, who caught the silver piece and pocketed it smartish. Peachey grinned. "You're learning, my lad!"

And so the crowd rolled up, and threw things, and poked with sticks, and the pennies mounted up all morning.

The carriage pulled up before the big house on the square. Princess Purnah had no idea where they were. London was a mystery to her, and the pattern of roads was all a jumble. If she had been among the mountain peaks and deep ravines of her homeland, she could have retraced her journey easily. As it was, the carriage had picked up herself, Auntilucy and Lal Singh and brought them all here through a mysterious maze of cobbled streets. Dr. Watson and a policeman had followed behind. Glekk! All this trouble over this fiend-with-no-face, when she could have solved the problem with a nice bit of pointy metal and a cliff to toss the remains over!

As the carriage had passed through the prosperous streets and avenues, Purnah had watched from the window. Errand Boy might be out there, just a stone's throw away, if only she knew where. Not that she was going to throw any stones in London; Auntilucy had specifically told her not to.

The shining brass plate on the door bore the name "Drone-Tiffin." A haughty butler led them through the house to a drawing room. "The master will be with you shortly," he announced, giving Princess Purnah the sort of look you might give to somebody who is there to break the china and steal the silver. Lal Singh gave him a look in return, and the man retreated down a hallway.

Ten minutes later another man appeared, a wizened, elderly man with the kind of huge, old-fashioned side-whiskers, known as "dundrearies," that looked as if two dead squirrels had been stapled to his cheeks. He was squinting as he polished his glasses. He was very tall, but bent with the years, and Purnah thought he seemed a bit spidery. "Princess Purnah of Chiligrit, I presume! Your Royal Highness! Augustus Drone-Tiffin at your service! And you'd be Mrs. Butterscotch, then?"

"Butterworth," corrected Aunt Lucy.

"Ah, yes. You're the lady in charge of Her Majesty after the unfortunate incident at St. Grimelda's. As you probably know, there was a fire, and the princess must have run away in fear and got lost. We are very glad that you found her."

"Gorokkish! Toshh!" said Princess Purnah. That certainly wasn't what had happened at all. Princess Purnah had set the fire, had escaped by sliding down a rope and had not been lost at all. But what offended her was the notion that she had been afraid. "Chiligriti princess not knowing no fear," she pronounced.

"No, no, of course not," mumbled Mr. Drone-Tiffin. "Still, all right now, aren't we? Matter resolved satisfactorily."

Aunt Lucy pulled herself up to her full height and looked him straight in the eye. Actually, she looked him straight in the stomach, so she craned her neck upward.

"What exactly do you mean by that?" she asked.

"Come along, both of you. I mean, if you don't mind, Your Majesty. My study is on the right along the hall. There's somebody you'll be glad to see, no doubt."

Mr. Drone-Tiffin didn't seem to know what to make of Lal Singh, whom he thought should have been sipping a nice cup of tea in the servants' hall, so he ignored his existence. The Sikh followed silently and took up station outside the study door. Everyone else went in.

"Your Majesty, Mrs. Butternut, this is Mrs. Wackett from St. Grimelda's School for Young Ladies."

Princess Purnah gasped. Aunt Lucy gasped. These were gasps of surprise and horror—mostly horror.

The vast bulk of Mrs. Wackett nested on a sofa designed for three people; the sofa seemed ready to give up in tears and break. The huge woman's dark eyes flashed with the kind of malevolence that most people associate with the more dangerous sort of serpent. The headmistress of St. Grimelda's was as menacing as ever.

"Hello, Princess Purnah. Hello, Mrs. Butterworth. I do thank you for returning the girl to my, ah, care."

CHAPTER 29

The Belgian Birdman

The Belgian Birdman prepared for his flight with a few trial runs along the ground. He was a thin young man sporting a tight-fitting garment in the colors of his national flag, huge goggles and a set of wings. The wings were what interested Emmaline.

She walked across the squelchy grass, with Professor Bellbuckle bumbling along beside her, while Stanley explored each tree they came upon. The main display was to take place above the Thames, between London Bridge and the spectacular new Tower Bridge. The Birdman was going through his paces before he ascended in Mr. Pettipas's balloon and—he and everyone else hoped—flew above the river as young girls swooned in admiration and strong men threw their hats in the air in salute. Right now, he was running along in a semi-crouched position, the wings flat against his back, then making little leaps as he moved his shoulders and the wings opened.

As a pioneer of aeronautical science, Emmaline could be cool and dispassionate as she assessed the Birdman's efforts. He didn't look nearly as hopeless as she had expected or feared. The wings weren't silly little things, like pantomime fairy wings, that flutter pathetically as an aeronaut plunges to disaster. No, they were a proper size. She ran over the theory in her head (Emmaline could run over theories in her head). Two gentlemen called Henson and Stringfellow, in

her great-great-uncle's time, had calculated that a square foot of wing could support half a pound. So, an average man weighing ten stones, ten pounds (that's a hundred and fifty pounds) would require three hundred square feet of wing surface. Which was about thirty feet across by ten feet deep or, better, fifty feet across and six feet deep.

So, the wings appeared big enough to carry a man. The problem was the whole "flapping" aspect of the contraption. Emmaline was quite certain that this was an error. Perhaps a catastophic error. All her great-great-uncle's research had indicated that flying involved keeping the aerofoil (the technical term for the wing) at the correct angle to the wind so that the flyer moved forward and stayed up. There was a lot more to it than that, of course. But if you flapped the wings like a bird, you couldn't expect to maintain that angle at all; you'd be flopping them about, and there'd be no chance at all of staying aloft. It wasn't even as if you could propel yourself forward like a bird, because human arm muscles are very weak indeed compared with a bird's wings. A trained gymnast can support him or herself for a few seconds doing a chin-up, or swinging from rings; most people can't even do that.

Enough, said Emmaline to herself. Science lesson over. Let's talk to this Belgian Birdman.

Professor Bellbuckle was already doing just that.

"Monsieur De Groof! Ozymandias Bellbuckle at your service! Knew your uncle, twenty years ago. Right here in London. I was present at the, ah, unfortunate accident. We'd talked about the flying machine, and I'd made some suggestions about—ah, well, never mind. Water under the bridge. Talking about bridges, you'll be flying between Tower Bridge and London Bridge?"

Water under the bridge, indeed! thought Emmaline. The professor had put his foot in it. He might as well have said, "I changed the equipment so that it failed and your uncle fell to a horrible death." Of course, he might simply have suggested that painting a tiny Belgian flag on the wings would be a nice touch, but, knowing the professor, Emmaline thought that was unlikely.

Monsieur De Groof answered in a tone that suggested he hadn't noticed exactly what Professor Bellbuckle had said. "Ah! I 'ave read of you from my uncle's journals and letters. Of course! The famous *inventeur Americain* Bellbuckle! You and my uncle write the letters to one another, yes?"

"Many times, indeed! May I introduce my student to you? A most intelligent young lady. Emmaline Cayley, Monsieur De Groof. And vice versa."

"I am charming to meet you," said the aeronaut, bending to kiss Emmaline's hand. The fact that he was wearing huge goggles rather spoiled the chivalry of the action, as he smacked her wrist with his head. "And you are relative of famous Sir George Cayley, non?"

"Er, oui!" replied Emmaline. "And I am also interested in aviation myself."

"Ah, so sweet!" said the Belgian. "The beautiful flying, like the butterflies."

"Well," said Emmaline. "More the scientific aspects of aeronautics. Angles of attack, lift, practical applications of theory. That sort of thing."

"So darling!" replied Monsieur De Groof, reaching out to pat her on the head.

Emmaline seethed. Who was this—this *dolt*? This fool? But she was used to adults thinking that, as a girl, she should be interested in nothing more than pretty dresses and fripperies of that sort, so she didn't say anything. Instead, as De Groof and the professor walked off chattering, arm in arm, she went to look at the flying apparatus the young Belgian had put down.

"Miss Cayley, eh?" said a voice from behind her. Emmaline turned. It was Mr. Pettipas, the balloonist. Now that he wasn't being shot at or ordered around by Sherlock Holmes, he seemed more relaxed. "Did you enjoy our flight yesterday?"

"Aside from the shooting, and the almost crashing, and the blowing away without any sort of control, you mean?" she asked. But she smiled to show that she was joking. "I enjoyed it very much, actually. I am sorry about my friend Purnah. She does get rather, um, impulsive on occasion. Almost every occasion, in fact. She oughtn't to have cut the cable like that. We try to keep knives away from her, but it never works."

"Not your fault at all. I understand that you have an interest in aeronautics, eh?"

"I have experimented with gliders, yes. Just some basic aerofoils, really."

Mr. Pettipas hesitated for a moment. "Yesterday, when it

seemed that we were going to blow eastward and miss that boy by half a mile, you did something ..."

Emmaline tried to keep her face expressionless. "*Did* something?"

"Yes. You made the wind shift so that the balloon moved to the north, toward the boy."

"Mr. Pettipas, it was clearly very, um, opportune that the wind changed direction at that particular moment, but I am not a magician."

Pettipas smiled. "No, of course not. That'd be silly. It's just that ... well, as a balloonist, I know that my flight path—my destiny, even—is in the hands of the wind. If there were a way to control the direction of the flight, it would be ... fantastic, eh?"

Emmaline wanted to steer the conversation in another direction. Romany sorcery was not exactly the explanation that Mr. Pettipas was expecting, and if he was showing at least a polite respect for her interest in aviation, she was happy to encourage him. No mention of ancient Gypsy charms, though. Science wasn't ready for that, except perhaps the Bellbuckle sort of science.

"This contraption of Monsieur De Groof—it's forty feet from wingtip to wingtip. How are you going to get it aloft, Mr. Pettipas?" asked Emmaline.

"Aha! I wondered if you were going to ask that. The flying apparatus is strapped below the basket of the balloon, for release by means of a system of cords. Once they are let go, the flying machine is free to glide and, of course, to propel itself by Monsieur De Groof's wing action."

Emmaline looked anxiously at the balloonist. "Has he flown the device before today? I mean properly, not just flapping the wings while running around in the park?"

Pettipas looked puzzled. "I assume so. I only met the man today. Before that, he just sent me letters and telegrams. I mean, he must have, surely, eh?"

"I don't know. I read a little about his late uncle. Meaning no disrespect, the man seems to have been ambitious far beyond his abilities. It wasn't his fault that the machine came apart in midair, but it was quite rash to have tried the thing out for the first time four hundred feet over London. Of course, this Monsieur De Groof, the nephew, might be much more … er … careful in his approach."

Mr. Pettipas rubbed his chin with a worried expression. "I just hope you're right. I wouldn't want to be party to a man's death."

Emmaline thought that the balloonist was genuinely concerned and not just because he probably hadn't been paid yet. "I'm sure he knows what he's doing," she added. "Will he be strapped into the flyer all the time the balloon is getting into position?"

"No. He'll be in the basket with me. We may have to wait some time before the flight—the river needs to be clear of shipping. The bridge openings are carefully scheduled, you know—the authorities plan these things properly. So, rather than hang under the balloon for maybe an hour, Monsieur De Groof will climb over the side and strap himself in. There's more to the flying machine than just the wings. It has a tailpiece, based on how goldfish swim, operated by foot treadles, and a hinged portion of the wing for directing the path of the contraption, using strings that you tighten with your teeth. Monsieur De Groof's teeth, I mean. He's very excited about the whole thing, eh?"

Emmaline was not excited. Monsieur De Groof might be an insufferable dolt, but she did not want him to be a former insufferable dolt. The device—if Mr. Pettipas had described it correctly, and there was no reason not to believe him—was a deathtrap of the most outrageous kind. Strings that you pull with your teeth? Foot treadles to swish some sort of fin? Wings that you desperately try to flap as you dive toward the ground? Mr. Pettipas might as well toss the Belgian Birdman out of the basket with a hearty heave-ho, and save the trouble of strapping him in. He should probably go through the man's wallet beforehand, so as at least to cover his expenses for the trip.

That was unkind, Emmaline told herself. That last bit, anyway. The rest of it was all true. It was a shame, from a scientific viewpoint as well, because the wings—ignoring the stupid, flapping part—were nicely designed. The rest of it should probably be burned for everyone's safety.

As she thought about these things, Mr. Pettipas broke her concentration. "Miss Cayley, would you and your, ah, tutor care to accompany Monsieur De Groof and me in the balloon this afternoon? And your little dog, of course."

Emmaline looked across at the balloonist. "I would enjoy that very much, Mr. Pettipas."

Well, except for the part where the Birdman plunged to his doom in the watery depths below, it would be a fine afternoon out.

Princess Purnah stood with blazing eyes and fear in her stomach as Mrs. Wackett announced that she would be escorting the missing "gel" back to St. Grimelda's immediately. She was rising, the sofa squeaking as she moved her massive bulk, when Aunt Lucy spoke up.

"You kept this girl for three years, without providing her anything but cruel discipline and bad dinners. You never made any effort to teach her English—how was she supposed to understand the lessons that you made her attend? You just kept her there, like a prisoner, and accepted the school fees that the government sent you. And you call yourself a teacher! It's a scandal, that's what it is!"

"Glekk! Porok!" agreed Princess Purnah. She had always pretended that she couldn't speak a word of English when she was in the presence of her teachers, and the old habit

221

came back to her. She suddenly remembered that she could explain herself to Mrs. Wackett.

"Evil foulish witching-woman! Vilest of lizards! Not going with you, nohow nowhere! Much stabbings if you gets close-ish!"

"Oh, please, ladies," said Mr. Drone-Tiffin, smiling in an oily manner. "Let's not have any little disagreements to spoil our day."

Aunt Lucy smacked him with her handbag. This might have been an accident, or not. He fell back into his chair. Mrs. Wackett boomed, "Stop being silly and come with me, Purnah. We have clothes for you, so you won't need luggage or any of that nonsense. Just come along and we'll say no more. We can take a train in half an hour and be back at the school in time for evening chores and punishments."

Mr. Drone-Tiffin shook his head a little as if he wasn't certain his ears were working properly. "Er, I don't know that punishments are required," he began to say. Then he stopped and clamped his jaws together as Mrs. Wackett seemed to lurch toward him.

Purnah's expression was one of pure fury. "Not goings! Get back, snake-woman! Desist most nasty mouthings or I will have thee slain by a thousand cuts of daggers!"

"Do be quiet, gel," snapped Mrs. Wackett, taking a stride forward, arms outstretched toward Purnah. She pushed Mr. Drone-Tiffin aside with her bulk. The lanky bureaucrat stumbled into a bookcase, causing a vase to crash onto the floor beside him and a number of leather-bound volumes to drop onto his head, one after another.

Purnah stepped back toward the doorway. Mrs. Wackett loomed up before her. "It's no use being willful, you know. Things will only get worse for you if you resist."

The headmistress lunged forward like a cobra delivering the fatal bite. Aunt Lucy hurled herself in front of

Mrs. Wackett. "I said no! NO!" she shouted. There was a flurry of blows as her handbag whirled against the oncoming headmistress. Mrs. Wackett did not stop.

The door to the study opened silently. Princess Purnah dove into the hallway. The door closed as a tremendous hammering noise erupted on the other side. Lal Singh smiled as he gripped the handle, preventing the enraged headmistress from forcing her way out of the room. He whispered softly into Purnah's ear, "O Princess, run upstairs and hide in the nearest lavatory, and I shall say you have gone outside, and they will pursue you out of doors and will not find you."

The battering on the door continued, and Lal Singh had to put his shoulder to the wood to keep it from bursting open. Princess Purnah turned to run down the hall.

A tall figure stepped out into the corridor in front of her. "We meet again, Princess Purnah," whispered an icy voice. Purnah stared into the eyes of Miss Scantcommon, the gaunt, deathly pale woman known as "Matron." "I've a bone to pick with you, my gel!"

And, indeed, she did. The last time the princess had seen Miss Scantcommon, Purnah had launched fireworks at the matron, setting her clothes alight and sending her rolling down a flight of stairs. Most schools, even the more liberal ones where pupils are encouraged to "express themselves," don't allow that sort of thing.

Purnah panicked. There was a door to her left. She slipped inside the room in an instant. It was a parlor with soft, comfortable furniture and a smell of tea and crumpets, and two women partaking of the same, chatting on a settee in front of a large window.

Purnah leapt forward, crashing into the tea tray, and hurled herself over the settee. "Ayeeee!" she shrieked as tea and baked goods flew across the room and onto the terrified ladies. She was clawing at the window catch when Miss Scantcommon's voice screeched behind her.

"Do not even *think* of escaping through that window!"

Which, of course, is exactly what Princess Purnah was thinking. And exactly what she did.

Rubberbones knew that the whole "Amazing Rubber Boy" act was bound to come to an end. He had known instinctively that he could fall from high up onto a grassy patch without hurting himself, but not from the roof in Fournier Street onto the flagstones below. He knew that eventually somebody would come along and prove that, despite all claims to the contrary, he could be hurt.

It was late morning, and Peachey was loudly considering the prospects of sausage and mash from a stall he knew just down the row; succulent sausages, made with very little horsemeat, and potatoes that might have been bought today. Danny thought that sounded fine, and Banjo was just happy to be with them. He made little panting noises of enthusiasm; Rab thought that his chest probably wasn't as good as it used to be.

Then the biggest man any of them had ever seen appeared. He was nearly seven feet tall with a shaved head, a mustache like an angry hairbrush and muscles that bulged under a straining shirt. Even though it was a cold November day, the man wore no coat—only the bloody apron of the meat-cutter's trade.

"Benny the Butcher," said Peachey informatively. "Chops up beef at Smithfield Market. Dunno wot 'e's doing round 'ere at this time."

What he was doing was taking his pleasure, and his pleasure was to see the Rubber Boy put through his paces. A "sporting op-per-tunity," as the captain had described his ratting contests.

"Penny a throw, does it say?" the giant asked. "What if I supplies me own bricks?"

Peachey ought to have said "You must use our bricks," or something like that. Instead, he said, "A penny, either way." Which was a mistake.

Benny the Butcher picked up a loose flagstone from the pavement. It was the size of a door. Not a big door, but certainly not a half-brick, as specified on the notice that Peachey had set up. Not by a long shot.

"You can't use that!" shouted Danny. Banjo barked, quite fiercely for such an ancient dog. "'Ere! Not fair!"

spluttered Peachey, who saw his mistake too late.

Rab stood, trying to look "nonchalant." That was the word Miss Em would use—as if this were nothing at all to worry about. The small crowd that had been idly watching the Amazing Rubber Boy gasped and grew larger as people stepped over to see what was happening.

The giant meat-cutter reared back, the huge stone slab in his monstrous right hand and an expression of glee on his face.

"Not going to pay out on this one!" shouted Peachey, always the businessman.

"That's my brother!" shouted Danny in fear.

Banjo ambled forward to bite Benny the Butcher's ankle. But he was, as we've mentioned, very old.

Rab smiled and put his hands on his hips, and then everything went black.

Chapter 30

Windowsills and Eel Pie

Dropping from the window ledge onto a wet and muddy flowerbed, Purnah remembered what Lal Singh had said. Something about hiding upstairs until Mrs. Wackett and her cohort, Miss Scantcommon, had gone to search for her outside. It was too late to do this, since she was already outside, and even Purnah, whose planning skills were not the finest, recognized that ringing the doorbell to be let in so that she could hide in the upstairs lavatory was not going to work. *Zoot! K'ramba-gote!* She looked upward to see Miss Scantcommon waving a clenched fist as she began to mount the windowsill. Then the turbaned head of Lal Singh himself appeared, and Matron was hauled back into the room. A crash inside the house indicated that Mrs. Wackett had broken down a door (or a wall). Then there was a great deal of shouting. Some screaming, too. Glekk!

Princess Purnah took off running across the soggy lawn. Zogoth! This was a sign from the gods. She was running loose in London with no one to stop her or tell her where to stay or not to eat any more cream cakes. At the edge of the street was the cab they had arrived in. Behind it was a second cab, which had brought Doctirwatsun. He hadn't noticed her. But he must have heard the shouting because he leapt out of the carriage, hurried up to the ornate front door of the Drone-Tiffin house and rapped loudly on the knocker, demanding to be let in. Ha! Ha again!

She reached the first cab. "Taking me please to Beth-nell-grin. Right now, smartish if you wishings to live!"

The cabbie smiled that small smile of men whose living depends on the unreasonable demands of others, and the horse pulled away.

"Rab! Rab!" A distant voice echoed inside his head. Rubberbones awoke as a jolt of pain hammered through his brain. He didn't like that at all. It was the only brain he'd got, and he wanted to keep it in excellent condition.

"Wakey, wakey!" said Peachey. Rab recognized his cockney accent. "Rise and shine! Gerrup!"

"Urrghh!" explained Rab. "Me 'ead, me poor 'ead."

"Steady on," said Danny. "You had a nasty blow from a big bit o' stone."

"Where am I?" asked Rubberbones. It was a rule, as he knew from his penny dreadful novels, that a hero, regaining consciousness, should ask this question, phrased exactly so. The answer was always interesting: a dungeon beneath the cardinal's palace, or a lost city in the jungle, or—

"Mrs. Thomas's pie shop. We 'ad a bit o' dinner when

you wuz out like a light," said Peachey. "We didn't save you none, as you might not feel like eatin', an' anyway Banjo got your share."

"Oooggghh!" mumbled Rab. "No, don't feel like eating. We'd best get back and make some money. Me mam needs —"

Peachey gave him a thin smile. "The Amazin' Rubber Boy is retired for now, on account of 'arf East London saw 'im get pulverized by a large piece o' pavement throwed by Benny the Butcher. I doubt that the sportin' public is willing to invest in a rubber lad 'oo can't never get 'urt except wiv a ruddy great rock. I think that game got spoilt, rather." He scratched his pimply chin. "Anything else you can do wot's amazin'? I mean, worth a penny-a-punter sort of amazin'?"

Peachey probably assumed that Rab had already shown the breadth of his amazing abilities. It had been a good run, and the pennies had added up to nearly fifteen shillings, which was worth having, even divided up between partners. So he was taken aback when Rubberbones said, "I can fly, a bit. Just round the rooftops, really."

Peachey opened his mouth, but nothing came out, and while he was doing this, Banjo snapped up his remaining piece of eel pie.

———

The balloon was moored on London Bridge, which was briefly closed to traffic. Emmaline examined the flying machine, now rigged into position beneath the basket. The wings were spread wide, with a springy wooden rod holding them flat. The shoulder straps were set against a padded backpiece and were made of the brass-buckled canvas webbing that she'd seen in military equipment. Wooden struts connected to a tailpiece, which seemed sensible enough. What was not sensible, as far as she could tell, was the system of treadles for the pilot to operate while in flight; they appeared to have been taken from an industrial sewing machine and would tire out the aeronaut's legs without helping him to fly. Perhaps it was best to be so exhausted that you didn't have time to be terrified as you crashed into the ground. The strings that were supposed to be operated by the teeth were just plain silly. And the pulleys and clamps didn't make any sense, either.

Since the Birdman had to climb out and attach himself to the flyer while the balloon hovered several hundred feet up, there was a rope ladder and a safety harness to prevent embarrassment in case the aeronaut had a clumsy moment.

Emmaline thought about all the pictures she had seen of useless flying machines. Devices involving a sort of hamster wheel full of paddling geese. Inventions in which a man cranked a propeller with one hand, controlled the wings with another and kicked away with flippers on his feet. She had seen a man shown cycling with a windmill-like rotor over his head, and another pedaling to power an elegant craft with wings that could not have lifted a cat. Not that a cat would be foolish enough to volunteer. Although Stanley might. He was barking happily, lying in the basket.

Compared with those bizarre death traps, this was not all bad; but the bad bits were worrying enough.

"Stop it!" said Emmaline to herself. It was just that she was afraid for the Belgian Birdman. He might be a pompous windbag, but that wasn't normally punishable by death. There'd be nobody in the government if that were the case.

She turned around to see if she could catch Professor Bellbuckle's eye. He was engaged in a spirited conversation with Mr. Pettipas about the wisdom of propelling a balloon, possibly Mr. Pettipas's own balloon, with a battery of rockets fired in different directions to boost it forward. The balloonist appeared to dislike this concept. The eye that Emmaline did catch was that of Monsieur De Groof, the intrepid aviator of the moment.

He looked as worried as she was.

CHAPTER 31

The Amazin' Flyin' Boy

"Are you sure you know where you want to go, dear?" asked the cabbie. The exasperation in his voice grew as he drove down one street after another, his passenger repeating, "Not here. Movings along!" He'd been through Spitalfields, Shoreditch and most of Bethnal Green. Right now he was heading southward along Brick Lane, for the third time in half an hour.

"I knowing when I seeing. Glekk! You be obedient servant or get head stuck on spear point!"

The cabbie was a patient man, accustomed to the odd ways of difficult customers, but this was a bit much to put up with. Some schoolgirl who spoke the funniest English he'd ever heard making threats of the strangest kind. It wasn't right. And—a thought came to him—she was making a fool of him. She might not have any money to pay for this ridiculous jaunt around the East End.

"Got any money, miss?"

"Porok! Torok!"

"Yeah, but 'ave you got money to pay my fare?"

"Glekk!"

"Don't know any Glekk Street rahnd 'ere. 'Ave you or 'ave you not got the money for my fare?"

Inside the cab, Princess Purnah began to realize that not only was her plan of simply riding around the city until she spotted Rubberbones a complete failure, but the driver wanted something from her. What kind of servant demanded money of a princess? What sort of princess carried money? She certainly didn't.

"Not got no moneys, varlet!" That was what you called people like him, she thought; she'd seen the word in a story about Robin Hood, an outlaw in a forest, whom she would like to meet one day. "You be obeyings or death will still your tongue!"

The cab halted as the cabbie whistled to his horse. "All right. No more o' this monkey business. Out. Now!"

"I princess in mine own land. Has you facing death of a hundred slicings!"

"That's as may be. Now 'op out and be orf with you, afore I calls a copper."

A copper. That was one of the guards in blue costume. There had been one with Auntilucy and Lal Singh. He'd take her back to them before she could find Errand Boy. She didn't want that.

Princess Purnah slunk out of the hansom cab, giving the cabbie as foul a look as the one he had ready for her. She had decided not to stab him with her sharpened butter knife, however, because that would bring attention. She did not want attention. She could be cunning when she wanted to be. She'd get in another cab and go up and down the streets until she spotted the missing boy. London had a lot of streets, all full of people. There must be hundreds of people here. But she'd find him.

She raised her hand and another carriage came to a halt: a four-wheeler, well polished, with a fine team of four horses. It was, thought Purnah, much nicer than the vehicle she'd just got out of, with its single horse and rude servant. The door opened, and she climbed in, casting a final glare at the hansom as it pulled away. She stuck her tongue out at the driver.

"You seem displeased, Your Majesty," said a voice inside

the carriage. It was a deep, educated, male voice, quite unlike the cockney slang of the cabbie.

"Is rude man!" she explained, now putting her thumbs in her ears and waggling her fingers at the retreating figure of the rude driver. "Is disrespecting of my personage."

"I consider your personage to be most important. In fact, I have been waiting to gain possession of it."

A sudden chill ran through Princess Purnah as she turned to face the occupant of the carriage.

"Please sit down and make yourself comfortable. We are about to go on a long journey," said the man. He would have smiled at her—except that he had no face with which to smile.

"The Amazin' Flyin' Boy! 'Ere for the verrry first time! Astoundin' feats, available for viewing at most reasonable rates!"

Peachey was really laying it on. Danny looked worried. He'd spent a chunk of the morning's takings on balloons from the market vendor. Hydrogen-filled balloons weren't cheap, and Danny had a suspicion that they weren't safe, either. Danny was more careful than his brother about these things; then again, there were escaped lunatics more cautious than Rubberbones.

"Be all right, Rab?"

Rab nodded. There was no reason in the world why he couldn't fly, especially with a whole handful of balloons. They were better than kites because they rose of their own accord, without having to be set against the wind. Why, only yesterday, a very fine balloon had almost rescued him, and now he had about thirty of them. Not as big, mind you, as the one that he'd seen Miss Em and Princess Purnah in, but thirty was a lot more than one. If he had thought about it when he first saw the balloons last evening as he bought one for Danny, he might not have had to suffer the fate of the Amazing Rubber Boy earlier today.

Peachey had acquired a basket, too, from somewhere in the market. So Rab could sit in the basket—or, at least, lie across it—with the balloons tied to the handle. Then he'd have his hands and feet free to wiggle about. That was how Rubberbones made his old kite go one way or another, by flapping his arms and legs, like a swimmer … sort of. "Shall I give it a go, then, Peachey?" asked Rab. "You know, see if it works."

Peachey shook his head. "Nah. 'S not like the Rubber Boy game. That time, we could take the punters one by one. This time we needs to get an 'ole big crowd of 'em, waitin' for the big moment. Like a proper event. The more you gets waiting, the more comes, the more pennies in the kitty for us, yeah? Unnerstand?"

Rab understood. It was like a circus. You had to get the whole crowd alive with anticipation of something astounding. If he just floated around for a little while first, it would kill the big build-up. And you needed a big build-up. If you got dozens and dozens and hundreds of people at a penny each—

"Tuppence," said Peachey. "They'll pay tuppence. I'd ask for more, but they'd just 'ang back hoping to see the amazin' flyin' lad without paying nuffink at all. I know how their minds work."

So Rab and Danny and the ancient bull terrier waited with the balloons, holding them down until Peachey had done his ringmaster impression. "Roll up! Roll up! Ladeez an' gen'lmen! The most incredifyin' spectacle of the modern age! I present for your dee-lec-tation, all the way from Argentina in Africa—the Amazin' Flyin' Boy! For a modest fee of two pennies, you is privileged to witness the first London presentification of 'is aerial artistry! Roll up!"

It was Peachey who would decide when the crowd was

big enough. He would raise a thumb, and Rubberbones would throw himself onto the basket and wiggle and waggle as the balloons lifted him toward the sky. Clearly, a brilliant plan. It would have to be, since they hadn't practiced it at all.

An impressive crowd was indeed gathering. There were people shopping at the market, and a few of the traders themselves. There were people from the streets on either side, for Peachey's pronouncements had reached far; men and boys, women and girls, old and young. There were voices acclaiming the exciting new entertainment, and others dripping with the world-weary cynicism that comes from listening to thousands of liars over a lifetime in London. It was clearly "a good crowd" in that most had actually paid to be there, and there was no fighting, cat-calling or robbing the boy who took the tuppences. Peachey waved to Rab. There was room for a few more paying customers. "Anuvver five minutes, mate!" he called out. "Then we'll astahnd 'em, all right!"

Except that they didn't have five minutes at all. A boy in the crowd pointed at Rubberbones; another did so, too, and then a whole group of lads broke out of the gathered throng. Rab knew who they were right away.

"Danny, go and check on Peachey, would you?" he whispered. "I've got ter go *now*. Them's the blokes as is after me. I think they work for the Faceless Fiend. Just make sure Peachey hands you 'alf the money and give it to mam. I'm off now. Kiss me sisters for me, will you?"

Turning away, Rubberbones leaned forward into the basket, kicked off with his feet and felt the thirty balloons rise. There was a small jolt as Banjo launched himself on arthritic legs and landed next to his master in the wicker basket. The wind wafted underneath, and the whole thing climbed swiftly to the height of the rooflines. The sudden movement startled the crowd, which had been expecting an announcement that the festivities were about to start. A ragged cheer went up, and a few hats were thrown into the air in time-honored fashion. There was near jubilation on the part of some, a feeling that tuppence had been well spent. Rab waved with his left hand as he swiveled his body to steer the basket down Petticoat Lane, above the stalls and rooftops. The only people who seemed unhappy were the pursuers known to Rab as "them lads as is chasing me," but who called themselves the Baker Street Irregulars. They shook fists and cursed and told one another that Mr. "'Olmes" would not be happy about this.

"Message for Miss Cayley!" shouted the boy as he came to a panting halt at the spot where the balloon was moored. He had to scurry around a stout constable since the bridge was officially closed to traffic, pedestrians and gawkers in general.

Emmaline and Professor Bellbuckle were just about to climb into the basket. The Birdman was already aboard, looking serious and aeronautical. "I'm Miss Cayley," Emmaline replied.

"Said y'd gimme a penny," he announced.

Emmaline thought this was probably not true, but she handed over the coin anyway. The boy stood waiting. "Take a reply, miss?"

Emmaline opened the note. It was in Aunt Lucy's worst scrawl, which was almost unreadable. It said … "*Tinces Uunek hag nun awoy. Ioox oik fot der. Meet me aj j botel aj 6PM.*"

The boy looked at her expectantly.

"Um. Tell her I got the note, but I can't read it."

Professor Bellbuckle came over. "May I?" he said. Taking the paper, he read out the words, "Princess Purnah has run away. Look out for her. Meet me at the St. Cletus Hotel at 6 p.m."

Emmaline was aghast! Purnah had managed to slip away, despite her promise not to. She'd be somewhere in London, looking for Rubberbones, with the Faceless Fiend searching for her. This could not be good. Where would she have gone? Where was Rab if Sherlock Holmes's lads couldn't find him? And a Chiligriti princess in London was like a badger in a ballroom. She'd be completely out of her element. Just as long as she didn't … well, as long as she didn't do quite a lot of things. Uh-oh, as the professor might say.

"Uh-oh!" said the professor.

"No message back," said Emmaline to the urchin runner. "I wish I had given her one of my radiophonic communication devices," said Professor Bellbuckle. "That rascal of a durn-tootin' fiend took the only one I have off young Robert. I tried it again, but no luck at all. Still, I *do* have a telescope."

Emmaline opened her mouth. What did a telescope have to do with anything?

"If we are going up in this here balloon, might as well keep a lookout with the telescope."

"But, Professor, Purnah is a small girl and London is a huge city, and it isn't as if she is going to be climbing Nelson's Column or the dome of St. Paul's Cathedral. She'll be on the ground, with four million people and all the buildings in the way."

Professor Bellbuckle might have argued that there was every chance that Princess Purnah would climb Nelson's Column—if anyone was going to, who was more likely than she? But he didn't. He gritted his teeth and snorted a little bit. Then his eyes softened, and he looked at Emmaline.

"I have no doubt you are correct, my dear. But, as my friend Butch Cassidy said when I told him he was using way *too much* dynamite on that railroad safe, 'Do you have a better plan?' Do you?"

Emmaline was forced to admit that she had no plan at all.

"Well, then."

CHAPTER 32

Over London

The wind caught the bunched balloons, and the basket soared above the rooftops. Rab waved again, not to the crowd but to Danny. He was sure that his younger brother was looking. Then he spun around in an updraft and began wafting south-westward. For a moment, Rubberbones simply drifted with the wind, making only the slightest of gestures and, as he thought of them, "wiggles" to ensure he didn't crash into a chimney here or a tree there.

He gazed down at the crowded streets and narrow courts, and at the people below looking up at him in astonishment. Banjo barked happily. Rab had no plan except to evade the Fiend's boys. Besides, unless he felt like landing on someone's roof, there was nothing to do but keep flying.

Then, as he cleared one line of roofs and crossed a road, busy with carts and carriages, he spotted the finely polished coach-and-four that he had first seen days before in the lane outside Miss Aunt Lucy's house in Yorkshire.

"It couldn't be the same," he thought. "Probably belonged to some duke or lord or bishop. There must be loads of 'em in London. But surely not in Bethnal Green?"

Then again, it could be the person Rab wanted to avoid most in the world. So, naturally, he wiggled his legs and drifted in that direction. He had to find out what was going on.

They were several hundred feet above London Bridge. The river looked cold and gray. The wind blew gently from the northeast. And the Belgian Birdman, in his multicolored costume, goggles pulled low, chattered like an imbecile to himself.

"I cannot do it! I see now 'ow it is my uncle falls to 'iz death! I 'ave not tested the equipment adequately. It was all an illusion!"

"Get a grip on yourself!" snapped Professor Bellbuckle. "There are thousands of people lining the banks of the river and watching from windows, waiting to see you fly!"

This, apparently, was exactly the wrong thing to say. Monsieur De Groof began to blubber as well as babble.

"*Non! C'est pas possible!* I cannot do it. I 'ave never flown the machine before! *Het is onmogelijk*—it is impossible!"

Mr. Pettipas was indignant. "Good grief, De Groof! D'ye mean that you hired me for a fool's errand? All those people, and we are just going to say, 'Sorry, everyone, Birdman's lost his nerve, try again when he's feeling a bit happier, eh?"

Emmaline never knew quite why she said it, but she did. "If we can secure the wings straight, and forget about the strings and the pedaling nonsense, I'll have a go."

The Birdman looked pathetically grateful. Mr. Pettipas looked astounded, in a "Have you gone completely mad?" sort of way. If Professor Bellbuckle had been a responsible-guardian sort of grown-up, he'd have forbidden it immediately. But, of course, he said, "Why not? Why not, indeed?" Stanley barked his encouragement.

Emmaline was the sensible one. "Only if the glider is properly secure," she added. "And the wind shifts so that I float directly along the river. And"— she pointed at Monsieur De Groof— "I am not wearing that ridiculous costume. I have perfectly sensible clothes on and respectable undergarments. I am sure the people of Belgium will understand."

So the grown men helped Emmaline into the harness,

leaving in place the rod that held the wings flat and ignoring the flummery with the treadles and the strings. It was at least as good as the kite that she and Josie Pinner had rebuilt for her escape from St. Grimelda's.

"Just stay settled for a few minutes," said Mr. Pettipas. "There's a ship due to pass downriver just now, and they'll be raising the drawbridge on Tower Bridge. After that, we're, uh, fine."

"Am I supposed to land on Tower Bridge?" asked Emmaline, alarmed.

"No, that'd be a great stunt, but far too dangerous. Even for an experienced aviator. Not that there is such a thing." Pettipas cut his eyes in the direction of Monsieur De Groof, who was still babbling *en français* to himself. And in Flemish, too, because, as Emmaline knew, there are two languages spoken in Belgium, and you might as well babble in both. "No, you fly over the bridge, and you will be picked up by a boat just beyond," Pettipas explained. "Are you sure you want to do this? It seems, well"—the word he was looking for was either "insane" or "demented," thought Emmaline—"a bit dangerous, eh?"

Emmaline clutched the pendant that Madame ZaZa had given her. The ancient charm that allowed her to fly. Or, at least, was supposed to allow her to ask the winds to help her. It might all be mumbo-jumbo. But it had worked once before, hadn't it?

"I am sure I'll be fine," she said.

Princess Purnah fumbled for the handle to the door. But it had locked behind her. So she did what any sensible princess of the royal house of Chiligrit would do. She tried to stab her companion with her butter knife. Which would have worked perfectly, if he hadn't been expecting something of that sort. Glekk!

As Purnah flung herself at the Faceless Fiend, knife drawn and furious, the evil arch-villain laughed. "Do you think you can defeat me?" he demanded. The princess did not dignify this with an answer, but plunged the blade into the Fiend's ribs. It simply skidded off his chest.

"Chain mail," he explained. "Finest steel mail from the armorers of Circassia. I wear it under my clothes at all times." He lunged to grab Purnah by the arm. He was vastly bigger than the girl, although she was as nimble as a mountain goat. Suddenly the Fiend spotted the ring—the old silver ring that gave protection from bears—on her finger. He seemed to lose his balance, and he shivered uncontrollably. Purnah didn't understand what was going on, but she knew how to react. As the man threw himself at her, she twisted sideways and let him crash into the locked door. Ha! If he had had a nose, he'd have broken it. He recovered quickly, grunting like an enraged boar, and turned again. This time he flung himself forward like a charging panther. Purnah slipped again to her right, allowing the Fiend to catch her left arm with his shoulder. Porok! She snaked her arm upward to evade him and jabbed the knife under his ribs from behind. Once again, the butter knife made no impression. He jabbed backward with an elbow, striking Purnah in the stomach. Okk! That hurt! It winded her, too, and she knew that scrabbling about in a confined space was not going to work for long. She had no room to maneuver; if the Faceless Fiend got her in a corner, there would be no escape.

Purnah looked up desperately to see if there was a way out through the roof. None. The windows were thick glass, possibly bulletproof. The Faceless Fiend knew how a good carriage was built; he'd spent much of his career throwing bombs underneath the wheels of European nobility.

The sharpened butter knife seemed useless against this enemy, just a mere something you might find in a kitchen drawer.

The Fiend attempted a smile. Purnah was revolted to see the disgusting parody of a face contort its features.

"Oh, come, my dear. We can be … friends. I have a yacht moored at Greenwich, on the south bank of the river. It sails in one hour, precisely, and has an engine that will outpace anything the Royal Navy has on hand. We will be across the channel by morning, and thence by closed train to St. Petersburg. There are people who will be very gratified to meet the heiress to the vacant throne of Chiligrit. Such a small kingdom, yet so conveniently located."

The carriage bounced, very slightly, as the wheels hit a broken paving stone, and the door flapped open. It just popped open, quite suddenly, without sound or warning. One might think that shouldn't happen with an expensive coach, equipped with locks to prevent people from hopping out. The Faceless Fiend felt that way, having ordered the carriage built especially for nefarious schemes of this sort. But it was the door that the Fiend had smacked against a moment before, and he must have undone the catch as he collided with it. Princess Purnah dove for the opening, like an otter toward open water.

The Faceless Fiend dove, too, and caught her as she flailed for freedom beyond the swinging carriage door. The wheels were moving fast. Her head was outside the coach, but the arch-villain seized her legs and even her hardest kicking seemed to have no effect. She shrieked at the top of her voice, the ancient cry of a Chiligriti in distress: "Eeeeghkk!!! Tantarantu-tooty! Prrruurrk! Lemme goings you Big Nastee!"

A boy sweeping the road stepped aside in fear and consternation. An old lady waved a fist and looked around for a policeman. A man on a bicycle veered out of the way and muttered that he was going to write a letter to the *Daily Telegraph* about irresponsible coachmen.

And a boy floating in a basket overhead, with a bunch of balloons and an elderly bull terrier, drifted closer.

"This is completely insane," said Emmaline.

"What is?" asked Professor Bellbuckle, six feet above her in the basket.

"Launching somebody else's untested flying machine from a balloon hundreds of feet in the air. With thousands of people watching."

"I've done madder things," replied the professor.

Emmaline thought this was probably true.

It was a tremendous view of London, she had to admit. The wind was enough to blow away the city's famous fog. The sky was clear. The river, broad and deep, stretched out like a road before her, the embankments on either side jammed with crowds. A ship worked its way downriver. Directly ahead rose Tower Bridge, built in the Gothic style to look much older, with the famous Tower of London close by. The first was a marvel of modern engineering, just finished, while the other had been built more than eight hundred years before. She'd read about the bridge. It was designed with two towers, one on either side, not on the actual banks of the Thames, but some distance into the river itself. A suspended bridge ran between these great towers. The bridge was designed to split in the middle by raising each half, or "bascule," so ships with masts could pass through. Lots of ships still carried sails. With proper warning, the traffic on either side of the towers would halt to let the bascules elevate. She assumed that the bascules moved slowly, since they were massive things powered by huge steam engines. When they were raised, the gap between them was wide enough for any ship in the world to sail through.

There was an upper bridge for pedestrians, high above the river, between the towers. The whole thing looked marvelous. And frightening, too, if you had to fly over it or through it.

"What was I thinking?" said Emmaline to herself.

On either side of the riverbank, the buildings of London crowded in: the dome of St. Paul's, the Monument, which recalled the fire of 1666, the spires of churches and the roofs of the great merchants' houses.

"Holy mackerel!" shouted Professor Bellbuckle. "There's a boy flying beneath a bunch of balloons!"

Emmaline drew in her breath. "What was that, Professor?"

"I can see through the telescope that there's a boy—I'm sure it's a boy—just up, ah, that'd be north—of the Tower of London. Do you think it could be Robert?"

Emmaline was filled with impatient excitement. "Of course! Who else could it be?" Then she felt bad about snapping at the professor. He was a scientist. He had to allow for the possibility that there were dozens of boys above London, casually floating beneath balloons on a Sunday afternoon. "Tell me as soon as you are sure!"

"Always hard to tell one boy from another," said Professor Bellbuckle. "Mostly it depends on how much dirt they've got on 'em. But, yup, that's Robert. Always needs to comb his hair."

Stanley barked in agreement.

Emmaline waited while the American inventor scanned the distance. "He seems to be circling around something that's moving below. Cain't see what it is from here. I guess we'll see in a minute."

"If he's in trouble, we need to help him!" said Emmaline.

Mr. Pettipas called down. "Miss Cayley, wait until that ship passes through the drawbridge. I think the wind is shifting in your favor. Just a few minutes longer."

The wind was indeed changing. The glider was not really like a balloon, moving directly ahead of the wind, but more like a sailing vessel. Within limits, it could fly with the wind coming at it from an angle, although it would stall disastrously if it found itself facing directly into a headwind. At least, that was the theory.

"I can see him now!" cried the professor. "He's floating over a carriage and trying to—my goodness! It's that durned coach that pursued the Bellbuckle Steam Carriage, Mark II, down the lane from your aunt's house. It has to be! And there's somebody trying to climb out of the vehicle! I think it is—no, it cain't be—but I think it is … "

Of course, Emmaline knew who it was. And she knew that she couldn't wait another moment.

"I have to go *now*, Professor. Please loosen those straps for me and wish me *bon voyage*. I very much hope I shall see you again."

And then, with her heart in her mouth and her arms outstretched, Emmaline dove forward into the sky below.

———————

Rubberbones couldn't believe it. It was definitely the same carriage. Black horses. The driver in an elegant, old-fashioned coat. The decoration on the painted and polished coach. And there was hideous screaming coming from within. Gibberish cursing and ferocious yelling. He couldn't understand the words at all.

Well, of course not. It wasn't English. But some of it was. *Purnah!*

And then Princess Purnah's head suddenly thrust through into the open as the door came ajar. She was inside the Fiend's coach and in great danger.

Rubberbones kicked his feet out and moved toward the door. He wanted to drop down to reach Purnah, but the balloons did not permit him to descend. It wasn't like his old kite; balloons just wanted to go up and nowhere else. He fumbled at the knots and freed a handful of balloons,

letting them go in a rising display of drifting, colored orbs. In turn, the basket slipped closer to the earth. Not far enough to reach, though. Rab hovered above the carriage, stretching out as far as his arms would allow.

"Purnah! Stretch out and grab me 'and!" he shouted.

The princess gripped the edge of the door, hauling herself out of the carriage. Something was pulling her back. She was yelling, "Letting go of my most royal person, foulish thing! Thou wilt die in horrid agonies for this insult! Grokk!"

Her face contorted—was it rage? Was it pain? Rab couldn't tell. "Can you reach me?"

Purnah looked up for the first time. Her expression turned to a savage grin. "Ah, Errand Boy! Is come join in fightings! Excellent! Torok!" She kicked out behind her. Rab heard a muffled roar of outrage.

"You'll pay for that, missy!"

She grabbed the top of the door frame and stretched with her other hand. Rab could see her wriggling to pull her body upward. His fingertips were mere inches from hers. "Almost there, Yer Majesty!"

Princess Purnah smiled up at him. "You goodish servant!" she cried out. Then a much larger hand, massive and sinewy, appeared and wrenched her backward.

She wailed piteously as the Faceless Fiend—Rab could see a glimpse of where his face should be, but wasn't—hauled her without ceremony back inside the carriage. Banjo barked fiercely. He had taken an immediate dislike to the Fiend. Rab clenched his fist in anger. There was nothing he could do.

But there must be!

He hovered overhead as the carriage raced southward toward the river. Out of Brick Lane, down Leman Street and toward Tower Bridge.

Unless Rab could stop it.

CHAPTER 33

On Tower Bridge

"Villain! Throat-slitter! Accursed pig-dog-cattle!" cried Princess Purnah. She was not pleased at all. "I is ordering you to be throwed to crocodiles as soon as is convenients to all! Glekk!"

"Do be quiet," replied the Faceless Fiend, clutching the girl's wrists together in one mighty hand. He moved toward the flapping carriage door, and Purnah knew that he was going to pull it firmly shut. She'd be imprisoned inside with her brave Errand Boy floating above, helpless to rescue her.

Instead, the Faceless Fiend pulled a pistol from his pocket and fired upward through the open doorway.

"Noakkhh!" shrieked Purnah. Using the Fiend's huge hand against him, she pulled herself up by her elbows and swung her feet hard against his chest. Her weight was nothing compared to his, but she cannoned into him and knocked the man backward. The gunshot exploded, ripping through the roof of the carriage. "Stoppit!" she shouted. "Not you be shootings Errand Boy!" And she spat at the Faceless Fiend, which is considered very rude even among royalty in Chiligrit. He released her wrists, his lashless eyes ablaze with venom.

The Fiend raised his arm to deliver a backhand slap to the princess. Purnah raised her own arm, her silver ring of protection flashing in the watery sunlight. There was a sudden burst of bright light; an explosion went off. The horses were startled; the coachman swore; the carriage swung in its traces. The Faceless Fiend overbalanced and fell backward into the padded leather seat.

Purnah, recognizing magic when she saw it, leapt over the arch-criminal and into the door frame. With the grace of a mountain gazelle, she nimbly hooked her arms up and pulled herself onto the roof of the coach. Duzzah!

The coachman did not look round. He was trying to regain control of the maddened team of black horses, their coats flecked with foam. Tower Bridge was in sight, the vehicle aiming toward it at a canter. He was terrified, you could tell. Purnah could tell, anyway. And then she, too, was terrified. Because Rubberbones was on fire.

It is a shade under a mile from London Bridge to Tower Bridge. Emmaline was trying to calculate the angle of descent she would need to glide from nine hundred feet above the river to reach her objective. A mile is five thousand, two hundred and eighty feet, divided by nine hundred—no, wait, that's not how to calculate the angle

What Emmaline was really trying to do was to keep her mind off crashing. She had said a little prayer, or three. She had sung a verse of "O God, Our Help in Ages Past," but she kept getting the tune confused with "For Those in Peril on the Deep," which was about the dangers of water, and that, somehow, did not help at all.

She clutched her amulet from Madame ZaZa in her right hand, as both arms were stretched inside the harness of the glider. The craft bobbed in the wind, now breezing from the west. It did not soar, but it did not crash. It gained yards for every foot it lost in height. And it seemed to be going in the right direction.

Cold air struck her face. Emmaline was glad that she had worn a plain dress, a woollen jacket and the most sensible of sensible underwear. She had taken the Belgian Birdman's

goggles, which protected her eyes. Nevertheless, she was freezing. Her teeth chattered.

Ahead lay the bridge. A hulking cargo ship progressed slowly toward it, smoking from three stacks. The drawbridge was opening, very slowly, powered by massive steam engines in the south tower. She must be very careful of the bridge mechanism. She must be very careful of everything.

To the left of Tower Bridge, behind the Tower itself, came a sudden flash of light and a muffled noise.

Below her, the river looked very cold, indeed.

"Flippin' 'eck!" shouted Rubberbones because, despite the fact that he was almost engulfed in flames, his grandmother had taught him never to use profanity. He shouted very loudly, as the explosion had rendered him deaf.

The Faceless Fiend's bullet, aimed at the boy but jogged off-target by Princess Purnah's heroics, had exploded one of the balloons. Filled with hydrogen—there's a good reason why children's balloons should not be filled with hydrogen—the whole lot had gone up in a burst of exploding gas and a sheet of flame across the afternoon sky above Tower Hill. The flying boy remained in mid-air, just for a moment, as all heck broke loose around him. He was lucky not to have been incinerated on the spot.

"Eekky!" shouted Purnah from the roof of the carriage. "Ey-oop!" replied Rubberbones. Banjo added a small, elderly dog sort of comment, and the basket tipped them out with a jolt as burning rubber flew in all directions. The blast sent the stampeding horses into a frenzied gallop down the hill.

The boy and dog fell onto the coach roof as the carriage careened madly forward, splashing through puddles and terrorizing those who were fool enough to try and cross the street in front of it.

"That were lucky," said Rubberbones, grabbing a shiny brass railing. Only he would think that being on board a galloping carriage whose driver had lost control was "lucky." Another bullet ripped through the roof to his left.

"Stop that!" shouted Princess Purnah. "Otherwise you be hittings me, and then what you scheming plot worth? Heh? Hah!"

The entry to Tower Bridge was closed. A constable directed traffic away from the mouth of the bridge. The authorities were strict about people trying to drive across as the drawbridge was opening. As the fine, gleaming black coach with its fine, gleaming black horses raced down Tower Hill, the policeman raised his hand in warning.

The desperate coachman tried to turn the carriage to the right, along the embankment. But the horses did not respond and galloped straight ahead. The policeman waved his arm and blew his whistle. The horses raced on faster. The constable lost his nerve and flung himself aside. The coachman lost his nerve and threw himself off the seat into a crowd of milling pedestrians, which must've been nasty for everyone. The carriage launched itself onto the bridge, through the gates of the North Tower, which should have been closed, but the people in charge were occupied looking at something up-river; above the river, in fact. The vehicle crashed forward onto the main span of the bridge as the two bascules clanked slowly, unstoppably, upward.

Rab decided that perhaps he wasn't as lucky as he'd thought.

Purnah shouted, "Backwardsish! Turnabouts! Porok!" The Faceless Fiend had begun to haul himself up while Rab and Purnah stared at the leaping constable, the diving coachman and the stampeding horses. You could only look at so many things at once. Glekk!

Banjo could barely look at anything very well. His eyes were rheumy and dull, but his nose was still good, and he'd made the connection between the Faceless Fiend and the new smell that caught his nostrils. "Grrrr!" He indicated his feelings with bared teeth. Then, as the Fiend pulled himself up onto the roof, Banjo launched his arthritic body at the man's hand. His teeth, ratter's teeth, clamped down onto the fleshy part between thumb and fingers. "Aaargh!" cried the Fiend. "Arrghh!" He shook his hand, but Banjo would not let go. The Faceless Fiend was a powerful man. He flopped the ancient dog around, but still Banjo's teeth gripped the villain's meaty hand.

Purnah pulled out her butter knife once again. "Time for stabbings!" she announced.

Suddenly a thought flashed into Rab's mind. "No! No stabbings! We need the knife for something else."

———

The bridge was opening. Emmaline saw the motion distinctly. She was what—fifty, a hundred yards away? It was coming up fast. Once the bridge had opened, the cargo ship would pass through, and then close once again in time for the Belgian Birdman to fly over it to the applause of thousands of impressed Londoners. Of course, things already weren't going exactly as planned because Emmaline had taken the Birdman's place. She'd had no choice but to leap out from the balloon before the signal was given.

The first thing to worry about was the opening bridge. Emmaline had very limited control over the glider. All she could do was try to maintain some sort of balance by holding the wing at an angle where the air current kept it aloft and moving. So she might, quite regrettably, smash into the bridge and die horribly.

Secondly, there was the fact that her two friends were stranded helplessly on the roof of a driverless carriage, racing onto that very same opening drawbridge, the horses completely out of control. She heard a sound that might be shooting. If Rab wasn't actually on fire, there was certainly smoke and flame.

It could be worse, of course, thought Emmaline. The Faceless Fiend could be there, threatening their lives, even as the coach launched into space before its inevitable plunge into the river.

And then, he was.

CHAPTER 34

A Champion at Last

Princess Purnah knew nothing about horses, except that they made good stew. Chiligrit was not horse-riding country, being made up mostly of steep ravines and deep mountains. What she did know about was knives.

The terrified horses raced forward onto the hard surface of the bridge. As the bascules swung slowly upward, the horses' hooves slid on the steepening angle. As they began to slip, the team became even more frightened, snorting and whinnying in panic.

Purnah was as agile as a mountain goat, as she'd tell you, but the climb down across the driver's seat and onto the pole terrified her. It was a narrow wooden shaft extending forward between the pairs of horses, and not meant for balancing on. She stepped out on her left foot, balancing with the skill of a dancer as Rab held her right arm. "Is permitting to touch royal personage owings to deathly dangers!" She didn't even say "Glekk!" or "Porok!"

Rab's balance was less skilled. When you have a history of falling off things without being injured, you don't spend a lot of time carefully avoiding a fall. Right now, the boy was gripping the brass railing atop the coach with one hand, supporting Princess Purnah with the other, and stretching like a cat as he did so. He stared downward at the wheels thrumming madly beneath them. Terrified, he didn't want to look up. Behind him, he could hear Banjo snarling as he continued to bite the Fiend's hand, preventing the villain from moving toward them.

"You all right, Yer Majesty?"

"Akk! Cuttings is hard. Good leatherings, curse the craftermen!" She sawed at the tanned leather traces that secured the horses. "Grokk! That is one looss-ee!"

One of the lead horses leapt forward, eyes wide as it broke free of the carriage and galloped ahead. It cleared the gap between the two arms of Tower Bridge and raced off toward the South Bank. "Is more to cuttings!" shouted Purnah. "Is brakings off or ons?"

Rab knew that she meant the big brake on the driver's side, a long lever that put a clamp against the wheel. The driver had been struggling with it moments before he jumped. It wouldn't stop a team of stampeding horses, but it might slow them down. On the other hand, if it was off, the whole team and carriage might jump the gap by speed alone.

But that was just daft, as they said in Yorkshire. Surely, the coach could not leap the distance. They'd fall and drown, horses and all. He let go of the rail and reached for the brake.

"Curse you both!" cried the Faceless Fiend. "You have foiled me at last! I cannot abduct Your blasted Majesty without my coach and horses. I will not reach the ship before it sails!"

Rab swiveled his head. He was stretched between Purnah and the brake handle and even, though the wind cut through his jacket, sweat beaded his brow.

The Faceless Fiend had balanced himself on the roof. Banjo lay on his back, wriggling in pain where the Fiend had finally swatted him ruthlessly away. Gasping and whimpering, he seemed to be injured. Rab looked at the old dog who was faithful to the master he'd only known since yesterday.

"You rotten—" began Rubberbones. "You wicked—"

The Faceless Fiend laughed savagely. "Yes, I am." He raised his right arm. The pistol aimed at Rab's heart. "I expect I shall go straight to hell. I expect I shall not see you there, though. You are"—he paused—"a tiresomely good boy."

"Is almost done!" shouted Purnah from her precarious perch. "One more slicing!"

There was a sudden lurch as the remaining horses broke away from their traces and made their jump. Carried onward by its desperate momentum, the carriage tilted forward as the wheels clipped the edge of the drawbridge and toppled toward the chasm.

"Ayeehh!" shouted Purnah as she clawed herself up onto the driver's seat. One of her shoes, her new ballet shoes, fell and dropped into the Thames, perhaps a hundred feet below. Then, her blade did the same thing. "Aeeyyeeeh!" It was the only knife she had.

Rab helped pull Purnah up, his other hand still locked on the brake lever. He was braced for the revolver to shoot him.

The Faceless Fiend smiled once again—a terrifying display of mangled teeth in his grotesque head. "I am sorry to shoot you, Princess Purnah, but since I cannot take you, you must die." His finger tightened on the trigger. Rab could see his knuckles whiten as he raised the gun. "Who dies first, then? The Royal Heiress or the loyal servant?"

But Rab was not the only loyal servant. The Fiend might not have had a face, but he had a throat. A deep growl sounded, and a small, mostly white missile burst upward toward the villain. Yellowed fangs bit deep into the Fiend's neck, locking on the jugular, holding, snarling.

For fifteen years, Banjo had been a ratter. Never a champion, never a dog destined for a glass case and a paper caption beneath.

But, today, he had caught the biggest rat of them all.

The Faceless Fiend recoiled from the assault and slipped. His right arm went up, the finger jerking the trigger, and the shot pierced the autumn sky. His left arm flailed at Banjo, trying to claw the dog loose. As Banjo's teeth clamped down on his windpipe, the Fiend's eyes filled with horror. Purnah gasped. Rab goggled, rooted to the spot.

The ancient dog and the arch-villain were locked together as they fell, turning gracefully in the air. Then there was a splash, and the great river closed over them.

The carriage lurched again as the drawbridge made its inexorable sweep upward. Purnah lost her footing and slid across the varnished roof, her hand breaking free from the boy's grip. "Aeeyyee! Is all lost!" she screamed. Rab, impulsive as ever, threw himself toward the girl. He seized her arm and began his own slide toward the abyss and the cold, gray river below. His right arm flailed for a handhold, for anything that might stop his fall.

"Grab onto my feet," called out a voice above him. "Now!"

It was Emmaline. She had dipped under the upper walkway and was hovering, very slightly, above the half-raised bascule. It was a narrow gap, a frightening place for her to be. She prayed that the flyer would not stall and crash.

Rab reached upward and caught a foot. His hand closed around the ankle tightly. There was a jerk, and he felt himself pulled clear of the carriage roof. Beneath him, he felt the tug as Purnah's weight dragged his left arm almost out of its socket.

"Akki-ooh!" shouted Princess Purnah in relief.

"Cripes! Ey-oop!" shouted Rubberbones in surprise.

"Owwwww!" shouted Emmaline in pain. She had twisted that ankle days ago, had sprained it again dealing with the pterodactyl, and now had two people dangling from it as she flew. "Owwwwww!!!!"

Behind them, the carriage swayed once more, then tipped and fell from the bridge. There must have been a splash, but none of the youngsters listened for it.

There were now three children hanging from Monsieur De Groof's completely untested gliding device. The wing dipped dangerously and the craft sagged in the air. Emmaline knew that it was going to stall and crash.

She clutched at the Romany amulet. The tiny pendant that helped her to fly. The wind gusted gently below, lifting the wings. The machine levelled and glided slowly downward at a gentle oblique, like a toboggan on a winter slope.

Then they were all in the water.

CHAPTER 35

Arrests Are Made and Cakes Are Eaten

The boat was full of people who had come to see the Belgian Birdman. They seemed surprised that none of the three swimming youngsters were either Belgian or birdmen, but hauled them out of the water anyway.

"I say! That was ripping!" said the boy who pulled Emmaline out of the river. He was tremendously excited. "Can I have your autograph? That was the best show ever!"

Emmaline was exhausted, terrified and drenched to the skin. So, of course, she asked him his name and scribbled her own on the paper. "To Plum," she wrote. "Happy Landings."

"Excellent!" shouted a dripping Princess Purnah. "I is not dead at all!" Her hair hung in soaking ringlets, and she had a very wild expression on her face. "I wantings chocolate!"

Rubberbones, sitting with his head down, was inconsolable. He was soaked through, and the water running down his face mixed with his tears. "He were a good dog, that 'un. A real good dog."

Purnah went over and put her hand on Rab's head. "I is very sorry about the gallant pig what has sacrificed himself for ours safety."

"Dog," said Emmaline softly. "Dog, not pig."

"Oh. Me confusings two animals. Sorry. Trikk! Most gallant and heroish dog-not-pig. In my country we would—" Purnah couldn't think what they would do. Chiligrit was not a place where they put up statues or started scholarship funds in the names of heroes. "We probably make him a god. A lesser god, I 'specting."

Rubberbones snuffled some more.

The man at the helm steered the boat toward the North Bank where a group of people waited, waving anxiously. Aunt Lucy, Lal Singh, Dr. Watson and Mr. Sherlock Holmes.

"Hooray!" shouted Aunt Lucy. "All safe and sound!" She came forward to dry the wet adventurers. As she only had a handkerchief, this was merely a symbolic gesture. "There, there, children. I expect it's all over now. Or most of it, anyway."

Emmaline noticed that her aunt had a black eye. She suspected that she'd been quarreling with teachers again.

Mr. Holmes was excited. "Tremendous work! You have done this country—the Empire—the whole world, in fact—an enormous favor today! You have rid us of a master criminal second only to—well, never mind. You have helped us all. You were not supposed to be placed in this position, of course. None of you. There was supposed to be a large number of police officers under the command of Inspector Lestrade, but—oh, here he is!"

A black closed carriage pulled to a halt, and a dozen bobbies—Lestrade at the head of the group—piled out.

"Too late, Lestrade!" Mr. Holmes called out with evident satisfaction. "The fox has outrun your hounds. The villain we sought has just fallen into the river from a great height, thanks to these children, while you were ... what? Finishing your tea?"

Inspector Lestrade blushed, and Emmaline suspected that this might actually be true.

At the same time, a tattered band of urchins came running into view.

"That's 'im!" shouted the boy in front. "Only 'e weren't wet last time we saw 'im."

Rubberbones instinctively got up to run again. Emmaline asked him, "What's wrong, Robert?"

"It's them lads, Miss Em. They work for the Faceless Fiend. Them's 'is Minions, as well."

Sherlock Holmes laughed. "Do you mean, Master Burns, that you have been evading my Baker Street Irregulars for the past day and a half because you believed them to be agents of the late, unlamented Fiend?"

Rab's face turned red. "Er, um, yes, sir. I thought them was bad 'uns."

The first of the boys stepped forward to take Rab's hand and shake it. "My name's Wiggins, an' I've been after you since you come aht of the place on Fournier Street. You're a top-notch runner, you are. Not many's could give us the slip as you done. An' the trick wiv the balloons! T'riffic!"

Mr. Holmes sent one of his Irregulars with a message for "those gents and the small dog in the balloon still over London Bridge."

Aunt Lucy stepped forward to speak. "We really ought to get these youngsters into some dry clothes. Catch a chill, they will, out here in this cold wind!" Dr. Watson went off to summon cabs for them all. Emmaline noticed that her aunt's clothes were ripped as if she had been brawling.

"This Faceless Fiend, he's gone, is he?" asked Inspector Lestrade. "I mean, dead?"

"Fell in the Thames from nigh on a hundred feet,"

replied Mr. Holmes. "With a bull terrier's jaws clamped around his throat."

"Ah, so we won't be needing the handcuffs then!"

"I think not, Lestrade," said the famous detective, chuckling a little.

Suddenly, just as Dr. Watson returned with two large carriages in tow, a third cab appeared behind them, galloping across the cobblestones and almost crashing into a party of nuns. The driver looked scared, the horses nervous. The door burst open, almost off its hinges, and the vast bulk of Mrs. Wackett began to emerge like some monstrous creature breaking forth from its egg.

"You! Princess Purnah! I shall take you now!" she boomed.

Purnah recoiled and searched her clothing, hoping she could find yet another sharpened butter knife. Aunt Lucy pulled herself up to her full height of, well, hardly anything. Lal Singh smiled, which he did in most situations, and stepped forward as if to tackle the charging headmistress. He was taller, but Mrs. Wackett was much heavier and broader. In fact, she was so broad that she was having difficulty getting her body out of the cab. Emmaline noticed that she had a black eye to match Aunt Lucy's.

"Inspector Lestrade," said Sherlock Holmes. "You are in luck. That woman, who will claim to be an honest headmistress at a respectable girls' school, is in fact the Faceless Fiend's most dangerous ally, Countess Bloatova. I suggest that your twelve constables might just be able to handcuff her and remove her to a convenient cell for questioning. That way, your day will not have proven to be a complete failure."

Miss Scantcommon appeared from the other side of the cab, one arm in a sling.

"And that would be the villainous Olga the Cruel, wanted by every police force in Europe. Watch that one, especially!" Emmaline thought Mr. Holmes had a marvelous imagination and a convincing manner of telling the biggest of lies.

"Right!" said Lestrade, and within seconds both headmistress and matron were swamped by constables and placed under arrest, each arguing furiously with her captors.

"Into the cab, children," said Aunt Lucy. "It is wrong to tell untruths, you know." Then she giggled like a schoolgirl. "Quite wrong."

The parlor at the St. Cletus Hotel, already full of potted palms and stuffed furniture, was crowded. Emmaline had bathed—because the Thames was not at all clean—dried and dressed in the manner of a respectable girl of fourteen. Rab's new "old" clothes were in a laundry basket, and he was sporting items provided by the hotel. Even Princess Purnah wore a clean dress, which she disliked. However, since she had been provided with cakes in massive quantities—chocolate cake, lemon meringues, cream cakes of various sorts and iced buns—she was not complaining.

Professor Bellbuckle had arrived with Stanley and Mr. Pettipas, although the Belgian Birdman, utterly embarrassed, had taken the first train for Dover, where he could catch the ferry home. Stanley was given several cream cakes, which kept him quiet for a while, until he threw up and fell asleep on the rug. He'd had a lot of excitement, being in a balloon and everything.

"Well done, Miss Cayley!" said Mr. Pettipas. "A great day for aeronautical science!"

Aunt Lucy had done something with a piece of raw beef so that her eye was less swollen, and she had changed into a dress without rips. Lal Singh, as always, stood behind her. Mrs. Burns and her daughters sat on a sofa with Rab, astonished at the luxury of the room.

Inspector Lestrade was occupied in asking stern questions of the two alleged conspirators down at Scotland Yard. Since it was Sunday, there was no chance that the two would be able to prove that they were neither Russian secret agents nor international criminals before tomorrow. "You should never be wrongly accused at the weekend," said Mr. Holmes. "You can't get a lawyer or a judge until Monday morning. It's scandalous." He smiled broadly. Then he continued, "I have made some inquiries. The man we have come to call 'The Faceless Fiend,' also known as Number One, was definitely in contact with the Russian government in regard to kidnapping Princess Purnah as part of a plan to control the throne of Chiligrit. His Masked Minions were selected agents, chosen for their loyalty and ruthlessness, brought over from the continent when local hirelings failed to abduct the princess. Some of the Minions are in police custody, as you know. At least one is at large, possibly still in London—the fellow Miss Cayley struck with my book. Others, those known as Numbers Two and Three, are missing despite the fact that Number Three is alleged to have a broken arm and a broken leg. One would have thought that the police might be able to catch that one. The scheme was to keep the princess at the house in Spitalfields until she could be taken to a yacht moored on the river at Greenwich. Then, once the coast was clear, the vessel would sail for the continent, probably landing by secret arrangement at a fishing village or similar. From thence, she was to be taken by private train across Europe to Russia. It was a devilish scheme, well devised by cunning men. Once in Russia, the princess would never be allowed to leave. Some lackey of the Czar would become Mir of Chiligrit, and the country would be full of Russian soldiers within the year."

"Porok!" declared Purnah. "I forbids Roozhian invadings! Freeeeeedom!!!"

"So, is that the end of that?" asked Aunt Lucy. "The Faceless Fiend? The Masked Minions? That odd little man from the India Office? The unpleasant school?"

"The Faceless Fiend and his underlings? I believe so. I suspect that the heroic dog Banjo has taken that villain to a watery grave. The Masked Minions were mere henchmen, although of a particularly disciplined variety; henchmen don't show initiative of their own, they merely … hench. The India Office and the school in question— I don't know, but, surely, if Mr. Tiffin-Drone saw what Mrs. Wackett was like in person, he wouldn't—"

"Books fell on his head," said Aunt Lucy. "During the fisticuffs in his study. He was knocked unconscious."

"Hmm," said Mr. Holmes. "Perhaps we should assume the worst."

There was a knock at the door. A uniformed footman came in and whispered to Mr. Holmes. "Send 'em in!" said the detective.

A cockney lad, one of the Irregulars, sauntered in. Danny and Peachey followed. Rubberbones jumped up and hugged his brother. "Danny!"

"I heard about Banjo. I am sorry, Rab. Peachey and I … we brought yer money."

Peachey held up a jingling bag, once used, as the faded letters indicated, for "Simpson's Finest Oats—Accept No Other." "Two pounds, nine and fourpence, at tuppence a time, which is a lot o' punters to see the Amazin' Flyin' Boy. We did deduct the price of an eel pie, divided atween us on the grounds of us bein' 'ungry. An' bus fare. The rest is yours."

Rab looked at the London lad in amazement. He had assumed that Peachey would simply disappear into the crowd with all the takings. "'Alf is for you," he said.

"Nah," Peachey shook his head. "You got a mum and all them sisters ter look after. Give it to them. I 'ad a few decent meals off your astoundin' and most remarkable talents, and that'll do me. Still, if you do ever want to go the rounds of the London music 'alls, look me up as yer manager and agent. Everyone knows Peachey around Bef'nel Green."

Emmaline offered him a plate of iced buns, and he took three to be going along with. Danny stayed and took two, because one wasn't enough, and iced buns did not come his way every day. Any day at all, really. Princess Purnah, who felt that all the cakes in London belonged to her by right, smiled at Danny as if to say it was permitted with no "punishings" or "beheadings" because he was Errand Boy's brother.

Mr. Holmes spoke once again. "I imagine there may be some form of reward for today's work. Foiling the enemies of England, saving an important ally of the Queen, that sort of thing."

"I is ally of the Queen?" asked Purnah. She had cream all over her chin and cheeks.

"In a manner of speaking. I don't imagine she wants you running amok at Buckingham Palace with a sharp knife or anything. But she doesn't want you to be kidnapped. The Queen—or, at least, the Queen's Government—sees you as an honored guest."

"Which is why the government thinks she ought to be placed with Mrs. Wackett?!" spat Aunt Lucy. This was a very sore point for her.

"Givings reward to Errand Boy for his mums and sisters and nice Danny-lad, here!" suggested Princess Purnah.

"Yes!" Emmaline exclaimed. Stanley barked in agreement

"Lawdy, that's a fine idea," said Professor Bellbuckle, who had been silently drawing plans for a submarine on the white linen tablecloth.

Mrs. Burns gasped and her girls shrieked with joy. Rab and Danny looked at each other with delight.

"I shall see what I can do to arrange that," said Sherlock Holmes. "But for now, Mrs. Butterworth, you might consider taking your, er, family on a holiday for a few weeks. That way, if the India Office still thinks Princess Purnah ought to go back to that school, Princess Purnah won't be available, will she? And, in the meantime, those of us who have the ear of important people may be able to change the official position."

"We running aways?" asked Princess Purnah.

"Well, not quite running—" interjected Dr. Watson.

"Yes," said Aunt Lucy firmly. "We are running away."

CHAPTER 36

Running Away from Home

Emmaline had always thought of "running away" in the childlike manner of putting your few belongings inside a bundle tied onto a long stick, hoisting it over your shoulder and walking off down a country lane. You'd go toward London, or the next village, or your distant-but-affectionate relatives, who would take you in and treat you as their own. Running away with three grown-ups, three young people, a scrappy sort of dog and half a houseful of luggage was a much more complicated activity. Especially as one of the adults was a mad scientist who couldn't decide which of his half-finished inventions he most needed to take with him. (Previously, the decision had always been made for him by stern policemen, or angry landlords, or the fact that his home had burned down, taking all his scientific discoveries with it.)

They had taken the train back to the house in Lower Owlthwaite. All the way home there had been long discussions as to where the "holiday" should be taken. Aunt Lucy said that since it was growing colder by the day, she'd enjoy a trip to somewhere warm. Rab wanted to spend time with his family, whom he had seen ever so briefly, but he didn't say so; besides, the Old Nichol really was a dingy, nasty place. What he wanted to do was to get his family out of there, not go and live there himself.

Princess Purnah was quite clear. She wanted to reconquer her homeland. They must march into Chiligrit and throw out the usurpers. She could make a flag out of an old bedspread. It was true that she did not have an army, but she had her friends. With the professor's rockets, Stan-lee's fierce barkings, Lal Singh's mightiness, Errand Boy's rubbery bones, Emmaline's flying machines and Auntilucy's poisonous cooking, her enemies must flee before her. Glekk! Porok!

Aunt Lucy did not appreciate this last bit.

"I don't appreciate that last bit, Princess Purnah," she said severely.

"Is true, all sames," replied Purnah. "Groakkh!" She crossed her eyes and pretended to die horribly.

Emmaline wanted to go somewhere she could work on her aeronautical discoveries. Perhaps they could visit Professor Chanute, whose book she had flung so effectively. She believed that he was in Chicago, in the United States. But Professor Bellbuckle warned her that it was a cold city in wintertime.

"We could go to see my hometown, Savannah," he suggested. "It's pretty warm there, even in the winter months. I've got my kinfolk there, and we could go out on the river, or walk through the squares, or—"

"Don't they pay you to stay away, Ozymandias, dear?" asked Aunt Lucy. "Aren't I correct in saying that?"

The professor lapsed into silence.

So they wrote down suggestions as to where they wanted to go, three ideas for each of them, on pieces of paper and put them in Rab's hat. Princess Purnah wrote "Chiligrit" on all of hers, spelled wrongly (but differently) in each case. Rab put down three places he'd only heard of: "Africa," "Antarctica" and "Birmingham." The others kept theirs secret, although Emmaline did spot that the professor had put down his hometown, no matter what his family thought about it.

Lal Singh made no suggestions. Sometimes he liked to pretend that he really was just a servant. So it was he that drew one single piece of paper from the hat.

"That is most interesting." He smiled and tucked it away within the folds of his tunic.

———

The boy known as Plum wandered along the riverbank, now empty of spectators. The crowds had gone home, and it was a raw, windy night. He had Latin to translate for the morning, but instead he wandered alone alongside London's great river. He was a solitary boy who wrote stories rather than playing games with other children. As he pulled his scarf up, the boy heard a snuffle from the water's edge. He peered through his wet spectacles, then, smiling, stepped carefully toward the sound. "Here, boy!" he called out. "Come to me!"

A bedraggled dog waddled toward him, slowly, as if very old. Plum picked up the dog, wrapping him in his scarf, and walked toward home.